THE TRUE HISTORY OF THE

An Abaddon Books™ Publication
www.abaddonbooks.com
abaddon@rebellion.co.uk

First published in 2018 by Abaddon Books™,
Rebellion Publishing Limited, Riverside House,
Osney Mead, Oxford, OX2 0ES, UK.

10 9 8 7 6 5 4 3 2 1

Creative Director and CEO: Jason Kingsley
Chief Technical Officer: Chris Kingsley
Head of Books and Comics Publishing: Ben Smith
Editors: David Thomas Moore and Michael Rowley
Marketing and PR: Remy Njambi
Design: Sam Gretton, Oz Osborne and Maz Smith
Cover: Rebellion Developments Ltd

Characters created by Gordon Rennie.

ISBN: 978-1-78108-610-0

Printed in Denmark

THE TRUE HISTORY OF THE

STRANGE BRIGADE

CASSANDRA KHAW • GAIE SEBOLD • TAURIQ MOOSA
GUY ADAMS • JONATHAN L. HOWARD
MIMI MONDAL • JOSEPH GUTHRIE • PATRICK LOFGREN
EDITED BY DAVID THOMAS MOORE

ABADDON
BOOKS

CONTENTS

INTRODUCTION

THE "TRUE" HISTORY of the Strange Brigade? The *absolute* truth? Now there's a tricky one.

There's not much of a paper trail, you see.

We've never really *fit* into the system in a neat way. We don't like to make ourselves too visible. I'm sure you understand.

We don't fall under any particular ministry, for starters. We've ties to both the Foreign Office and Home Office, as you'd expect, but we don't *entirely* come under either purview. We're military, of a sorts—or at least, we have a fair number of soldiers and the like—but you won't find the Strange Brigade on any military organisation chart.

For that matter, you won't find the "Strange Brigade" on *any* paperwork; it's more of a nickname.

We've people, here and there. There's a team quietly beavering away in the Government Code and Cypher School in the Broadway Building, for instance, across from St. James Park Underground. But it's not really a headquarters, per se; more of an outpost in the broader efforts of the agency.

Maybe further afield, then?

Webster Hall's a handsomely appointed house in Buckinghamshire; it's small for a stately home, but pretty and of some historical interest (part of the building was an abbey in the sixteenth century, and I gather Disraeli stayed there once). Meetings of the Brigade's leadership take place there from time to time: Sir Henry convened them before Lady Imelda, and Sir Henry's father Arthur before him, and Arthur's aunt Margaret before *that*. The Websters have a long history with the Brigade.

But it's rather out of the way. Hardly the beating heart of the organisation.

The Lyons Corner House on Oxford Street is a quiet retreat—a tearoom, really; not even a gentlemen's club—where London's better-off can take their leisure in peace. Lady Webster spends a good part of her time there, and it's where most of the Brigade's day-to-day concerns are discussed and addressed.

But here, frankly, you'll find no paperwork *at all*. That's rather the point of them meeting here.

Some sort of archive, then.

Take a walk down Fetter Lane, in that odd neutral ground in the City between the bankers, the lawyers and the presses, and you'll find, if you're looking for it, a rather drab building, fading out of sight amidst all the monumental architecture. It backs onto the Public Record Office on Chancery Lane, and since boxes and files come and go most days, people tend to assume it's some sort of annexe, a department within the grand enterprise that is the soul of British bureaucracy (indeed, a modest, verdigrised plate on the masonry declares it the *Department of Antiquities*).

Perhaps you'll find something here, assuming the archivist has any patience for you. She's not known for it.

Oh, nothing about the actual *Brigade*, no. As I say, we prefer not to leave a trail. Formed under Victoria, I've heard, although I've suspicions it goes back further that.

But you might learn a little about our *people*...

AND WAS JERUSALEM BUILDED HERE?

CASSANDRA KHAW

"Burn it."

In the pale, poor light of the dormitory, old Mrs. Phillips' face was all jutting angles, lines that went nowhere. She frowned at Gracie, a wrinkled hand outstretched, like she was offering salvation in the seat of her palm.

"You want to know what *I* think you should be doing?" said Mrs. Phillips—widowed and forgotten and fierce—without particular rancour. "I think you should find yourself a few cans of paraffin, a good match, and something to eat as you stand on a hill, watching all of this burn to a bad dream. You heard me, Gracie Braithwaite. Burn it. Burn it *all* down."

* * *

"A JOB, MISTER?" GRACIE raked a cool eye over the new arrival, a frown stitching her brows together.

He was tall, elegantly dressed, every inch the London bourgeoisie. His collar and his cuffs were precisely creased, but his stare was something else. Gracie knew that look. She'd seen it in the cellars of her brothers' favourite pubs, crocodilian and stuporous, the look of an animal who knew good things came to those who wait. The man pressed the pink tip of his tongue between his teeth and cocked a wider smile.

"A job," he repeated smoothly, and Gracie had to stifle another spasm of loathing, bite down on the impulse to kick the man in his shins and take off. Manchester churned behind them, incurious; the smell of smoke coiled in the air. "A job at the greatest show on earth."

"You sure don't look like P.T. Barnum to me, sir."

That surprised him. "Sorry?"

Gracie stood up straighter, jaw set. Her father'd once despaired of that chin of hers; too much like his, not enough like his wife's. But after Gracie added a back alley's worth of scars and a broken nose to her face, he gave up his grumblings, along with any hopes his daughter would tame at a man's command. "Sucker every minute. That's what he said."

"No. No, he didn't." The stranger's face pulled into a frown.

"What?"

"Barnum never said that." And a chill fed itself up Gracie's spine, a slither of unease, slow and dangerous. "He was, first and foremost, a businessman, you understand. While his clientele tolerated a certain amount of impertinence, they were customers and the customer is someone you never insult."

His expression ripened with a savage, sudden glee, and the man, who was built like a razor, like a wire stretched out, leaned down to whisper into Gracie's ear. "You can have that for free, Miss Braithwaite. Everything that follows will cost you."

He reeked of French cologne and incense. Not the kind that swung from Catholic thuribles, vapours rising thick as the dream of the New World, but a fainter smell, softer and sweeter, woody and weird and foreign. Still, the blend wasn't quite enough to hide something worse, something closer to the bone. A stink that reminded Gracie of cows in summer, hoof-deep in their own manure, flies spiralling around their horns. A burning, animal odour, which sang to something older than common sense.

Run, it said. *Run far.*

"Mate"—Gracie fanned the air in front of her nose before she pinched the bridge—"you *stink*."

"Do I?" For a moment, the man's eyes burned a colour she'd never seen, a gold so bright it hurt a little to look upon its light. He bared his teeth at Gracie and she scowled in reply, even as he stood straighter, silhouette blocking out the noonday glare. His eyes, hazel again, sparkled with glee. "I suspect, my girl, it is not my fault but yours. Do your brothers wear cologne? Does your father bathe?"

"*Excuse me—*"

"No, no. That's unkind of me. I beg your forgiveness.

I'm sure he does, but I suppose the question needs to be asked. How often? A week? Twice? Do you ration your soap, my girl? Is it rationed for you?"

The words poured like oil, sleek and suffocating, and if it wasn't for the conversational lilt to his baritone, Gracie might have punched him then. Instead, she swallowed and listened, habit usurping reason. After all, she'd seen this scene play out ten thousand times before: her father with his head bent, sheepish, his boots scuffed, two buttons missing; a man at the door, enviously rotund, cravat at his throat and a hat on his head, badge and balding pate gleaming in the sun.

It was like a stage performance, a show at the Old Vic, with its players, its beats, its pauses all lined up, waiting to go. And Gracie knew the role her family played in this production: they were the blue-collar extras, hanging on the lip of a command. When people above their station spoke, the Braithwaites listened. Defiance belonged to men and women without hungry mouths to fill.

Still, Gracie couldn't help but itch beneath her collar, sweat pearling on her chin. She gritted her teeth. "That's our problem, not yours. If you don't mind, I'd be leaving."

A purr this time, baritone smoothing to velvet. He encircled her shoulder with an arm before she could speak, smiling prettily the whole while. "Miss Braithwaite, we've known your family for years and years. Would you really walk away from a job with me and mine? What with everything that's going on with your daddy? Poor Mrs. Braithwaite, too, already fat with your eighth little brother? Do you think she could afford your pride?"

"She wouldn't want me to whore myself in London. I know that much." She shrugged his arm loose, glaring. "Why don't you—"

"Fourteen pounds, eleven and eight. A week."

The sum stole the air from Gracie's lungs, and she sank down into herself, fingers splayed over her sternum. What had her mother said—everyone has a price? It was a devil's dowry, enough to buy ten Gracie Braithwaites and all of her brothers. The man had to know this. He *did* know this, Gracie decided, walking her gaze over his pencil smile. There was something unpractised about the expression, like he was teaching himself the trick of it as they conversed.

"Twat."

"Ah, child, what would your mother say about that mouth of yours?"

"She'd say she raised a girl who knew when someone was trying to be a wanker, that's what she'd say. I'm still not going to spread my legs for your diseased, plague-riddled—"

"*Miss Braithwaite.*" It was a whisper, no louder than that. No threat, no venom, nothing but faint disappointment, but it felt like Gracie had cannonballed into a gulch choked with ice. He clicked his teeth in that London way, shook his head.

Gracie did not apologize. She had enough dignity for that.

"You will not be whoring yourself for my company. In fact, I feel compelled to say that you are the *last* thing my fellows would hope to bed. I do not know about your brothers, your uncles; I suppose they find dirt attractive. But those I call my peers? No, ma'am. They prefer their women nubile, lithe, skin as pale as ice nailed to bone. We like them big-breasted too, if you'd excuse my language. Pregnant with milk, if we happen to be lucky. A skinny, cat-boned thing like you? No, no. That's not at all for us, my girl."

"What do you *want* with me? You could get a whole mining facility to turn their backs on their mothers for that amount."

"Yes, but would they be as discreet?" He chuckled. What was his name again? She had to know his name. There was no way that she didn't. Yet Gracie couldn't put two syllables together, two sounds to evoke an image of them exchanging courtesies like normal people. They'd been talking for so long. Surely, he'd allowed a name. Her spine writhed in place. "We *need* you, Gracie Braithwaite. We've waited and watched, and then waited longer. We spent decades waiting for you to come into your own. And now that you have, no one will do but you."

Gracie thought of wine and whiskey, cheap booze smuggled from Ireland, blazing like a lie. She'd just been a little bit too young when she swigged from her brother's bottle the first time, and they'd laughed like foxes as she coughed through that first mouthful of smoke. The man's company reminded her of the fugue from that first evening, how its edges had blurred, had become crowded with nightmare possibilities. She swallowed.

"What would I have to do?"

Piously the man—the marionette in the three-piece

suit—clasped his palms together, as though in prayer. Even Gracie, an atheist from the marrow out, found the gesture profane. "An honest woman's work, of course. Miss Gracie Braithwaite, sweet summer girl of ours, I'd pay you a king's ransom if you'd bend the quick brilliance of your ladylike fingers to your gender's god-given task. We'd like you to *sew* for us, beautiful child. Plain and simple. Needle and thread. Body and soul. Say yes, baby girl, and we'll make it worth everyone's while."

GRACIE SAID YES, of course.

There was no universe where she would not have.

THE FACTORY BELCHED columns of salty black smoke, ash fountaining in clouds so dense that they couldn't disperse into the overcast afternoon, but instead lingered in the air and in the skins of the women milling within the compound. Gracie wondered how the oldest of them might look, if there were grandmothers on staff with eyes and teeth and hair the colour of burnt soup bones.

Gracie shuddered and spat the charred taste of the air from her mouth, discomfited by the sudden image of an old woman in silhouette, silently knitting her shadow into a mountain of shirts. There was something inherently *wrong* about the idea, something so fundamentally unholy about the notion that Gracie couldn't help but cross herself, a guilty prayer mumbled beneath her breath.

Somewhere ahead, someone began to sing in a high

sweet voice, a mournful ballad about one highwayman or another, and the bargain he made for a shipwrecked love. Something about scrimshaws and stitchings of silver, a noose of hide that someone'd braided from the skin he'd pared from his own calf.

"Into Hell's mouth," Gracie sighed. She plodded onwards.

Rain began to fall, a cold soup that smelled to Gracie of London. She had lost two brothers to the city, was midway into losing the third: the youngest of them, straw-haired and sullen, with a mouth like a sculptor's despair. It felt like treason to say so, but Gracie wasn't sure he would survive the capital.

Still, there was hope. Assuming the money the man—

—what *was* his *name*? Why couldn't Grace remember? They'd both signed the contract; she'd watched as he wrote on the yellowed paper, his penmanship beautiful as heartbreak—

—had promised did not vanish like faerie gold, Gracie'd have an excuse and a half to keep the boy home. He would no doubt complain, but he'd thank her one day, when he was old and loved and still innocent of grief.

Swallowed by her musings, Gracie took no notice of how the singing slowed at her approach, and how the women's eyes—not one of them was any colour but linen and soot—grew wide as the doors to the factory opened, and how they cringed as a straight-backed girl, hair the hue of menstrual tissue, descended the steps.

"Grace Dominique Braithwaite." Her smile was bright as the coming of Christ, was red as his wounds. "We've been waiting for *you*."

* * *

MISS VELVET DID not walk; she *prowled*.

Her gait was long and certain, and shared more with the wolf's long-legged lope than a lady's mincing tread. It stood in contrast with her wardrobe. The impractical jodphurs, the high equestrian boots, oiled and fur-trimmed. Miss Velvet's corset made Gracie wince, as did her cropped ruby jacket, buttoned beneath high breasts. Someone else must have chosen the pieces; Gracie couldn't imagine Miss Velvet deciding on this florid arrangement herself. Yet the woman bore her ensemble without complaint, even a kind of truculent dignity, enviable in its cut-glass precision.

"—been around for at least fifty years now. We've seen entire families come and go, marry into money, forget that they ever were a part of our humble household. But we understand that is the working-class dream. No foul, no harm." Despite her carriage, Miss Velvet's voice was soft and sweetly breathless, an ingenue's lilt, absent of coquetry. "Sometimes, they come back. Introduce their children to us for apprenticeships."

"Do you get many boys—?"

"No. No, no, no. Never male children. Girls, Miss Braithwaite, are more intuitive, more malleable, more—" Miss Velvet fluttered a gloved hand. "More worthy of attention, I think. There's a power to be found in knowing that you are always second best, always a little bit weaker than the rest of the world. I'm sure you know what I mean."

Gracie, who grew up with seven loyal brothers, who

could throw a right hook faster than a man could lie, did not. But she thought it might be impertinent to say. "If you say so, miss."

"Mm. We'll get along perfectly. Anyway. Where was I? Yes, the factory's practically an institution, a shining beacon in Lancashire's fiefdom of poorly ventilated, poorly regulated factories. *Our* girls have weekends. There are benefits too, possibilities for advancement, and if you make the mistake of becoming gravid with child, we can accommodate for that too. Especially if the spawn is male."

Gracie narrowed her eyes. She'd expected grime in the factory's corners, penumbral hallways half-lit by bare bulbs, rotting beams and whimpering from behind closed doors. Not this industrial austerity. No music, no sound but for the clack of careful footsteps, nothing but the machinery's humming gospel, which seemed to seep through the bones to sing in her marrow. "Th—the spawn?"

"Son," Miss Velvet said, with a million-dollar smile, gaze lidded. "We acknowledge the difficulty in raising sons. So rambunctious, so *loud*. If you were to have the ill fortune of giving birth to a boy, we'd do everything we can to streamline your existence, to make it easier to attend to your duties. Rest assured that your son would be loved, provided for like he was our own."

A pale girl, hair bound in an off-white scarf, trotted by the pair.

"You don't have to worry about that. I don't have any plans for—"

"Excellent, excellent. Miss Braithwaite, we'll get along just perfectly. Have I said that already? Because I feel the need to do so. It is a thing that humans do not do enough. Appreciate each other. Appreciate themselves."

There it was again. *Humans*, not people. *Spawn*, not son. The tiniest aberrations in word choice. Gracie decided she wouldn't be half-surprised if this was merely a reflection of cosmopolitan fashion; this calving of one's self from the unwashed proletariat. She could see it being funny for these people, even satisfying, to act as an entomologist might. Certainly, London acted like it was a world of its own, a perfumed paradise, separate from its rural relatives.

Why not its reluctant exports?

Still—

"Glad to hear—well, glad to hear that you had to share that, Miss Velvet. But d'you mind awfully if we talked about the *practicalities* of my position here? I'd hate to be a waste of a good salary."

"Yes, of course." Miss Velvet, much to Gracie's bewilderment, was beginning to *purr*. There was something else, Gracie thought. Something to the way Miss Velvet chewed on her words, as though there were extra syllables seeded in every sentence, colloquialisms of mandibular motion that only the rarefied understood. "Of course, of course. But that's hardly my area of expertise. You'll want Mrs. Phillips for that. She is the caretaker, the kindly mother of your particular division. Everything you need to know, you'll hear from here."

They took another turn, then a second, a third, before at last Miss Velvet walked Gracie up a spiral stairwell, two storeys past identical-looking floors, every last corridor lit exactly the same way. The effect was dizzying.

"Careful, Miss Braithwaite." The girl's voice, warm against her ear. A smell of leather and tannic acids, skin curing beneath a blistering blue sky; the stink of guts beneath that burning animal scent, a coppery aftertaste. "You've only just arrived. We have so very far to go."

Gracie swallowed. "I hear you."

"Good." Miss Velvet grinned and said no more.

The two marched on in silence. Down the throat of a passage that appeared no different from the others, its walls scalloped with thick wooden doors. Miss Velvet halted at the end of the hall, narrow frame haloed by grey light. She turned—two sharp taps of her heel against the brick floor—and dove into a bow, a hand to her frilled collar, the other arm outstretched.

"Your dormitory."

Feeling like something was expected of her, some reciprocal ritual, Gracie bobbed an anxious curtsey, eliciting a cool trill of laughter.

"We'll have so much fun, Miss Braithwaite. I look forward to the days to come." And with that, Miss Velvet took her leave.

THE DORMITORY WAS plain: a single wide window stretched across a wall, the glass so dirty that the world outside smeared into shadows; cots with scant bedding; several small cabinets; laundry lines drooping under fresh-washed undergarments, water bleeding from their hems into shallow pools. Everywhere, there were women, milling under the steepled ceiling, and a damp musty odour, as though of hounds come slinking from the rain.

"Hello?" Gracie said, setting her father's one good suitcase, crammed with all the hand-me-downs that would fit, onto the floor.

A silence curled around the room. Linen and soot, Gracie thought, not for the first time. They were all the colour of linen and soot, nothing in between. Would she look like that one day too? While Gracie worried at the idea, an old woman rose from her chair. When she spoke, it was with a faint Bristolian brogue.

"Another one." The woman laid down her knitting needles, shooed away a cat that had taken residence between her ankles, a burly black tom with pound coins for eyes, one ear long chewed down to a withered stump. "What'd he promise you?"

"Benefits, a pension plan, and opportunities to purchase the family plot in the next five years," Gracie declared promptly, pleased by her own informative alacrity. Emboldened, she continued, bantering the terminology of landlords, not entirely certain whether the context fit, but she figured it wouldn't be a problem, not if she spoke with enough wit. "It's a seller's market these days, you know? Rents picking up. Even if it's a bit of an investment now, value will appreciate."

"No doubt," said the old woman, still unnamed. Her hair hung in unkept ringlets; someone'd thought to braid them at some point, but she'd since allowed the plait to fallow, the tips uncoiling into a grey mess. Despite her age, she stood unstooped, her posture almost mocking in its straight-shouldered geometry. There had to be at least fifty years between Gracie and her counterpart, and she wore all of it like honours from the King. "At least you've sold your soul for practical reasons."

"I think," Gracie said, "I take some offence at that."

The woman smiled. "I'm sure you do. The name's Mrs. Phillips, poppet. I suggest you take some time to think long and hard about what your goals are in life. Whether you'd rather be the lone wolf, full of vim and vinegar, or the one who survives to the end of this story."

Anger spasmed in Gracie, instinctive. She'd not come here to be mocked; and more than that, she tired of riddles, of meanings slithering between mealy-mouthed platitudes. All that unspoken truth, odorous and seasoned with a winking malevolent delight. Everyone who wasn't poor Gracie Braithwaite knew the score. But Gracie kept her bile down, kept her mouth shut.

Then, after a time:

"I'm here to work."

Mrs. Philips regarded her with a cold, pale eye. Linen and soot, Gracie thought, looking the old woman over from head to toe.

"Good."

IT WASN'T DIFFICULT work.

Gracie had expected much worse. More back-breaking labour, the kind that loosened one's ligaments, undid the cords that tethered bone to muscle, rubbed tendon against calcium until the body was reduced to mere wires and will. Work that'd make old age nothing but a decade of whimpers.

But her chores weren't anything like that. Oh, they weren't *easy*, per se. The hours were endless. Gracie woke before dawn, went to sleep with the nightjars. Meals were regular but tasteless: porridge leavened with strands of some unidentifiable meat, chopped carrots, occasional bits of onion, celery and other vegetables, all cooked to mush.

In between, Gracie developed an almanac of new scars as she basted, sewed, stitched, unseamed a thousand lengths of good leather, each sheet more beautiful and delicate than the last. Lambskin, Gracie told herself. Maybe slink, uterine-soft. From time to time, her drudgery diversified to more taxing endeavours: kitchen chores and the movement of crates and sacks, every container innocuously branded with symbols that made no sense to anyone but Miss Velvet, who cooed over every fresh arrival.

The oddness of having but one ostensible administrator was not lost on Gracie. She spent the first week attempting to oust plain-clothed overseers, conspirators among the other women, but none revealed themselves. It was Miss Velvet and no other, not even the man who had officiated over Gracie's employment.

Occasionally, there'd be visitors, convoys of festively dressed gentry, all smiling, every one of them euphorically pleased with the very act of breathing. They spoke with the cadence of the opulent but conducted themselves like children, seething with questions that made no sense. One, a round-faced woman attired in violet, asked for Gracie's tailor, praising their avant-garde aesthetics. Miss Velvet had led her quickly away. "Rich people," she'd giggled.

Gracie eventually surrendered her investigations, focused instead on surviving to the end of each week, where a decadent Sunday roast inevitably waited. Potatoes crisped in duck fat, thumb-thick slabs of roast beef, Yorkshire puddings, mountains of roasted carrots, sweet corn, enough gravy to drown every one of Gracie's fears.

"Who the hell were those people? On Wednesday? Bit of a weird bunch, don't you think?" Gracie moved her peas around her plate, glancing over a shoulder.

"Customers."

"They don't look like the sort who'd shop here."

"They're still customers," Mrs. Phillips said placidly, jaw tightening. "Not for us to discuss their tastes."

"Speaking of tastes, what *are* we making, anyway?"

Mrs. Phillips didn't miss a beat. "Attire."

"Well, obviously." Gracie sucked on the pad of her thumb. She had sliced the meat open on something in the latest shipment of leathers: a jag of ivory, the shape and size of an infant's toenail. "But what kind of attire? Don't you think it's strange that we're working on sleeves and flaps, pant legs but no trousers, panels for jackets that we've never seen?"

"No." Mrs. Phillips sipped at her pea soup. "And if I were you, poppet, I'd stop asking questions I don't want the answers to."

Ah, Gracie thought. There it was. Tacit acknowledgement of the truths that she hungered for, and the insinuation that Mrs. Phillips knew them all. Now, all Gracie had to do was crowbar the answers from the old woman's chest and everything would be as she wanted.

"That's up to me, isn't it?"

"No."

"Freedom of choice and all that. The young are allowed to make their own mistakes. Everybody chooses how they live their lives and all—"

Anger kindled in Mrs. Phillips' lined features, eyes thinning. She put down her spoon, curled her palm, as though begging for some relief from Gracie's relentless audacity, and then sighed, a long, wounded noise. Somewhere, someone was singing again, that song about highwaymen and the bargains the desperate make.

"Don't you have a father, Gracie Braithwaite? A mother? Seven brothers who love you more than life itself? And a little newborn sibling, who'll grow up to think you're the sun and the moon itself?"

"Yeah, but I don't see why—"

"Let it go, Gracie."

"Let *what* go?" A third voice intruded, appallingly jubilant. Before Gracie could register how Miss Velvet had come so close unnoticed, the administrator pirouetted into view, a hand clapping down on Gracie's shoulders. The woman smiled, lips a bright pink today, the hue of raw beef.

"Her belief that she might one day marry above a station, find a good London man—"

Gracie's lips curled. If she married, it'd be to a man like her father, someone who knew the calendar of the soil and the migrations of the earthworms, who could not only coax a horse to drink but would lay its head upon his lap in perfect trust. The very thought of wedding a pansified dandy, palms soft as a newborn's, both horrified and repulsed her. She said nothing about the matter, however.

"—that might forgive her rough tongue and love the fact she can carry a calf in each arm." Mrs. Phillips rose, clasped a withered hand around Miss Velvet's wrist. The administrator smiled, all small white teeth.

"We are so close now, Mrs. Phillips. I remember when you were afraid to touch me." Today, Miss Velvet wore white like a bride might; with stirrings of lace and seed-pearls galore, a little fascinator shaped like a tiara atop her crimson hair.

"I was afraid of a lot of things once. But then, Mr. Phillips—God rest his poor soul—had the poor taste to die, and now the only thing I have left is hate."

Gracie went still. The air cooked with the tension from the two women, one small and quick and grinning, the other so ancient that her flesh had lost all elasticity, furrowed and canyoned wherever it'd been brushed. *Hate.* Mrs. Phillips had said 'hate,' and Gracie would bet all the souls of her brothers that she meant it exactly.

But for all the rich loathing in Mrs. Phillips' voice, Miss Velvet seemed unabashed. Indeed, if anything, it excited an unctuous pleasure in her. Miss Velvet peeled from Gracie's shoulders, oiled up to Mrs. Phillips, gloved fingers walking a path around the old woman's left clavicle. "Your hate is such a beautiful thing. If I could parcel it in silk, wrap it up in a box, I'd make a gift of it to sweet Saint Peter. Do you ever wonder, Mrs. Phillips, what dead men sing when no one's around?"

"Whatever they like you to sing, poppet." Granite would have been more pliant at that moment, less cold.

"Yes. Yes, you're right." The problem with Miss Velvet's smile, Gracie decided, wasn't that it looked like it had palsied into place, or was pinned there with fish-hooks slotted through her cheeks. The problem was her *teeth*. There were too many of them, and they were all the wrong shape, molars rather than incisors and bicuspids, no fangs in sight. Bovine dentition, small enough to stud an infant mouth. How had Gracie not noticed?

"But in the meantime..." And suddenly there Miss Velvet was again, fingers kneading Gracie's shoulders, the heels of her palms jammed into the slope of her scapulas. With a snarl, the young Braithwaite attempted to extricate herself, but it was too late. Miss Velvet's grip could have manacled a stallion. "I've something to show you, Miss Braithwaite."

WHAT GRACIE BRAITHWAITE would remember most of that day, when the nightmares had dulled to routine and she, at last, had a private room that did not reek of mould, would be the smell. The wretched animal stink; warm grease, fresh skins only beginning to cure; a rind of sweat overlaying it all.

And the darkness, red-tinged and seething with strange shapes.

She'd remember that as well.

"These are—"

"Products," Miss Velvet said gaily. "But I suspect the word that you might have been looking for was 'people.'"

There was no mistaking the upside-down silhouettes for anything else: men and women and children, pared of entrails and extraneous hairs, pomaded coifs holding still even as the bodies stuttered along the production line. From where Gracie stood, she could, from time to time, see the fine sutures in their skin. She thought she recognized her own handiwork. Nausea welled within her.

"Oh."

The wan light gleamed in Miss Velvet's small teeth. "Yes. You see now."

"You can't do this," Gracie said, because there needed to be words in her mouth, and she needed to say something, or she'd begin to scream. "This isn't right. This is—this… These are people."

"*Were*." A disdainful flap of the overseer's hand. "And I would hesitate to call them people, really. They were, as the French might put it, the bourgeois. I think? It doesn't matter. These *donors*—yes, I like that word more—were all part of the great British Empire, a fiefdom built on telling other countries they aren't quite clever enough to live without our supervision."

As Miss Velvet spoke, the promenade of corpses continued to tick forward. Masked figures, bellies obscured by mottled blue aprons, inspected each cadaver in turn. Those still pregnant with viscera were scooped clean, the fetid remnants chucked into enormous kegs. Looms clacked and chattered in the shadows. *Custom suits*,

Gracie decided detachedly. "There are *children* here."

"Who'd grow up to be well-fed, well-read, well-intentioned, but ultimately only interested in people that look and act and smell like them." Miss Velvet twitched a shoulder. "Despite what the church would have you think, Hell has no love for the haughty. In fact, you might argue that it is our business to rehabilitate the proud, or at least make them think about what they've done."

Once, when they were much younger, Gracie and her brothers had argued the economics of morality, whether Lucifer was truly a reprobate, or if he'd been maligned— was instead the assiduous concierge of a prison with no exit policy. Once, they'd debated the phenotype of demons, their disposition, and how an encounter might take place. They'd agreed there would be fire. But Miss Velvet was only smiles, and somehow, that was worse.

Gracie swallowed. "That isn't up to—"

"No, it absolutely is up to us. We are Hell and its myriad subsidiaries. Our purpose, the very reason we were massaged into shape, given intellect and wit to distract ourselves between working hours, was to sift between the dross of your souls, and determine who merits an eternity singing praises to Heaven, and who"—Miss Velvet's eyes flicked to a point behind Gracie's shoulder, smile blissful—"*doesn't.*"

A scream, as though choreographed.

"By the way," Miss Velvet resumed, a finger angled to the floor. "I suppose this is as good a time as any to note that you have no say in this matter. None whatsoever. No matter what you might think, you are the lowest of the low in this food chain."

"So, you're threatening me, then?" Gracie squared her stance, fists balling at her sides. Violence, with its bruising poetry, its choir of split bones and cracked bones, she understood.

"No. No, you understand me." Miss Velvet wagged that elegant finger, an eye winking shut. "There are no threats here. You cannot threaten someone who has neither authority nor ability to reciprocate in kind. To *threaten* someone, you must be, in some way, afraid that the other party might be able to do you harm. You're a lamb, Miss Braithwaite. You are a hircine fetus, expunged from the womb and given a meagre talent in conversation. You are nothing. Therefore, you cannot *be* threatened, because you are not *worth* threatening, and I am tired of this discourse. Ask me something more interesting."

"Something more interesting? Okay, fine. Why the hell is all this, then?" Gracie demanded, feeling like more was needed of her, a response more profound than slack-jawed observation, than the scream worming at the base of her throat. "Are you planning an invasion or something?"

"That knowledge," Miss Velvet said, smacking her lips, "is what they call 'above your pay grade.' I like you, Miss Braithwaite. I genuinely do. I really like you. But there are things we can't talk about. One of them is that. But we can discuss an adjunct purpose. The skin suits, you see, facilitate tourism."

"*What?*"

"Well, I suppose 'tourism' isn't necessarily accurate. The word suggests pleasure and pleasure alone, which is certainly not true. Most of our clientele are here on work trips, I suppose. Half-work, half-pleasure. I really don't know how you humans categorize these things. But that is the nature of our arrangements. The skinsuits are multi-purpose, and also modular, I'm proud to say."

Miss Velvet blinked. Sideways, as a cat might; the membrane that closed over her cornea was heavy, mottled and ridged in a way that strained against the socket. Gracie winced reflexively, before deciding there was no need. Though it had not been explicitly stated, it was clear: Miss Velvet was one of them.

"Are we next? Once we get too old, do we join them?" Confronted with an uncertain end, Gracie lost her capacity for all emotions but one: defiance. Fortunately, it was tempered by an inherited sense of practicality. The lie most often told by the rich is that the working class is uneducated, but the truth is substantially more complex: Gracie had no knowledge of Socrates, no grip on Chinese medieval philosophy, and little understanding of the spice trade, but she knew when to speak—and more importantly, when not to.

Bodies were being boxed into crates; first ironed and then folded along the joints, then folded again, into neat halves and quarters, and finally swathed in paper and stashed away. "No. Yes. Perhaps. Who knows? The world is such an interesting place. But more likely than not, the answer's no. We've found that there is no point in dressing ourselves as plebians. No one pays attention to people like you, I'm afraid. To be blunt: we prefer to inhabit people who matter."

People who matter. Gracie's gorge rose.

"I'd also like to suggest that you don't contact the authorities. For one, your story will sound ludicrous. For another, there's at least a forty-nine-percent chance you might encounter one of ours, and imagine what kind of words they might say about your treasonous behaviour? In case I hadn't made it clear before, let me say it again: you do not matter at all, Miss Braithwaite. So, be a good girl and do what your family has always done."

"And what's that?"

"Serve."

"You really expect me to keep working here?" Indoctrination only went so far, Gracie thought ruefully, itching to do more than prattle. "You think I'm going to do what you say, now that you've shown me the terrors of Hell?"

"Quite frankly, Miss Braithwaite? Yes. No, wait; that's not right. Let me rephrase, Miss Braithwaite. I don't expect you to keep working here in the holistic sense of the word. I expect you to wake up tomorrow, give your privates a quick scrub, and then come down here to perform quality-assurance. I wasn't lying when I said you have deft hands."

"Well, I won't. You can kill me. I'm not afraid. Come on, then, give me the worst that you've got. I'll make sure you never forget—"

"Ah, this is the part I love the most. Where the mouse tries to negotiate, and the cat bobs its head and waits until its dinner arrives at the correct time. Miss Braithwaite, let me tell you something: you will say 'yes' in the end. You will say 'yes,' because it is not a question about you. Because as brave as you are, as faithful to the romantic idea that one may die for their beliefs and be lauded by those they leave behind, you are also a woman who loves her family."

Miss Velvet, so much taller than Gracie remembered, stalked closer. Her tongue still lolled from her smile, florid and obscene. The muscle stroked a route up Gracie's trembling cheek, even as Miss Velvet leaned down to say:

"Would you give them up, Miss Braithwaite? Would you condemn your mother to an uneasy birth? Would you let eight brothers nurse on her teats, empty her like a waterskin? And when your father kills himself in despair, would you let those sweet brothers of yours, driven by desperation, whore your poor mother out? And the newborn! I suppose there's a market for orifices that young. Why, I should think—"

"Enough!"

"I won't lie, Miss Braithwaite. I am enjoying this so much. After all, I am a demon; and demons, by nature, have a predilection for despair. Sadism is embedded into our molecular code, or—oh, don't mind me." Miss Velvet withdrew, expression nearly carnal, her delight as blasphemous as anything else in the mill. "I make no apologies for my lusts. I do, however, wish to extend my appreciation. Rarely have I tasted hopelessness so sweet."

Miss Velvet's tongue, unremarkable save for its excessive length, laved across her teeth, before it started to metronome, like the tail of a skinned cat. "Yes, you start here tomorrow."

* * *

GRACIE CRIED THAT night for the first time in as long as she could remember, while Mrs. Phillips' cat kept watch, and the women in her dormitory tiptoed and murmured, faces slanted away, the soft rustling of their dresses like whispering ghosts. At some point that evening, Mrs. Phillips came to sit beside Gracie's shuddering body. She spoke no platitudes over the girl, knowing they'd be neither needed nor welcomed.

The reason for this was obvious to anyone who had at least an ear, an eye, or some rudimentary ability to decipher human emotion. Gracie was not weeping because she was afraid—or even because she was heartbroken by the horrors of the world—but because she was *angry*.

And she cried because sobbing was less suspect than screaming, than fists beating themselves to shrapnel. When she was done, hours after the last candle-wick had been pinched by scarred fingers, Gracie sat up.

"Burn it," said Mrs. Phillips.

AS IT TURNED out, the fire was the easiest part. Two brothers who'd worked both ends of construction, two brothers who made their money in war; you pick things up from siblings like that. No, the problem wasn't rigging the factory to detonate, or even disguising her endeavours, but something that Gracie hadn't expected.

"WHAT DO YOU mean, you don't want to leave?" Gracie tried not to shout but already, she was catastrophising, listing opportunities for failure, body clenched in anticipation for the moment the door would erupt, disgorging monsters. "You have to go."

"Go? Where?" demanded a rail-thin woman—Abigail, Agatha, some name that made Gracie think of radio plays, her accent effortlessly metropolitan—as she wrung her hands, mouth tapering into a frown. "Where d'you want us to go? Back *there*? Back to our husbands? Our in-laws? You don't understand at all, Braithwaite. It's easy for you."

Gracie crossed the space between them in three long strides, fingers digging into the woman's blouse. With one fluid move, Gracie heaved the woman up, pinned her against the wall, bared her teeth, even as she fought down the urge to bludgeon sense into her adversary. Yet despite the manhandling, the other woman held Gracie's gaze without apprehension, a coolness that further antagonized her.

"They're *demon*s."

"There are worse things out there."

"You tell them, Agatha," someone shouted across the dormitory. "You think Miss Velvet is bad? I don't. She's a saint. She saved me from a murdering husband. If it weren't for Miss Velvet, I'd be dying in that hospital."

"There are institutions out there." Gracie dropped the woman, swearing beneath her breath. None of this was how it was supposed to go. Over the last week, the factory had all but piled its secrets at Gracie's feet, seeming to exult in her horror, Miss Velvet most of all. Yet it was neither the entrails nor the work that had Gracie so traumatised, for all that they chafed against her moral compass. She had been raised with farmers, and knew that everything came back to blood.

It was the other women. It was their slope-shouldered exhaustion, their ennui, the way they donned their white masks without complaint, and the way they shambled back to the dormitories hours later, businesslike in their ablutions, no trace of repulsion, no tears. They were *alright* with this, with being accomplice to the post-production efforts of standardised slaughter, with purling skin and gut into new bodies, homes for the estimable damned.

"There are places to get help." Gracie kept going, even though hope was pouring between the slats of her fingers. "You have family—"

"Sometimes, family's the *problem*," Agatha snapped, quick as a crime, adjusting her wimple. The mask came on next: white, with no ornamentation at all, only pinholes for eyes.

"I—" Gracie dropped her hands. "Fine. Forget the rest. How can you all sleep at night? All of you. You know what they've done. I don't understand how you can stomach this—this—"

"Far as I can see, the only thing they're doing is taking from the rich and giving pensions to the poor." Agatha shrugged a thin shoulder, securing the mask in place. Her voice clattered against the thick leather, hollowed of anything recognizable. "You're young, Braithwaite. One day, you won't be; and when that time comes—well." A sharp inhalation. "You'll see why it matters that the demons give receipts."

At that, the women began to file out of the dormitory,

some adorned with masks, others not, until all that remained was Mrs. Phillips, her cat, and Gracie, her chin drooping.

"I think there's something you need to understand, poppet." Mrs. Phillips—it was her turn at the canteen that day—tied an apron around her waist, pulled a hair net into place. "You're not going to save us."

"Then *what's the damn point?*"

"The point is everyone else. The point is shutting down this operation. The point is cutting a hole into these cock-nosed bastards, because who knows, maybe the sepsis will do them in this time. We're too far gone, poppet. If there's anyone still worth saving, they'll know to leave on their own. But the rest of us, well, it won't be bad." The smile faltered, nonetheless, and not for the first time, Gracie found herself wondering exactly how old Mrs. Phillips was, how old any of the other women were.

"You'll burn."

"We're just linen and scrap these days." At Gracie's startled expression, the old woman laughed, a bark of pale noise. "Don't look so surprised. You'd never wondered? Why we're all the same colours, why none of us ever goes home? The demons take from the rich. But they bleed the rest of us, too. It's just a question of degree, Gracie. It always is."

THEY HELPED HER board up the factory. Gracie didn't expect that either. The women filed out of their dormitories, silent as guilt, their skin ashen and their eyes pale in the moonlight. They looked like the dead to Gracie, who said nothing to them in return as they worked in tandem, applying nail and plywood to the doors.

The staccato beat of their hammers was barely audible, however. Inside, their employers were throwing a gala, celebrating some deal or another, and the clink of champagne glasses was loud enough to carry into the black-soaked night. Music played, a discordant wailing straight from hell, a bastardization of Mozart and some Irish jig, a little bit of a funerary jingle. Shadows flickered in the windows, bodies spinning in a caricature of waltz.

When the women were done with their labour, they filed back inside through the one door that Gracie kept free. The latter followed behind.

Inside, the factory smelled of dried semen and skin, leather steeping in vinegar, and something like old eggs. What little light existed left the edges of the shadows red-rimmed, flame-haloed. Gracie moved slow, fingers gliding over the walls. She'd left kegs in every room, tripwires too; it'd only take a spark.

A door that Gracie had never seen opened inches from her face, and light cut the darkness into a rectangle. She held her breath. Waited until a silhouette staggered into view, head lolling forward. Gracie could see the stitching along its spine, the needlework exquisite, so fine that you might miss it if you didn't look where to look. The figure stretched and the skin pulled taut along its forearms, straining over too many bones, too many angles.

It took Grace a moment to make her decision. These things weren't even human. She repeated the words to herself as she carried the figure into the darkness, a hand at its throat, a hammer in her fingers. *Not even human*, she told herself again as the skull concaved into brains.

No ONE BUT a cat stood with Gracie Braithwaite on the gentle hill that night, after she'd bolted the doors of the factory and lit the fuse. The air had smelled of salt and textile and skins curling in the heat. *Linen and soot*, Gracie thought to herself, crouching to stroke the tom's lean spine. Linen and salt and fat, crisping in an inferno. Gracie, although she did not know it then, would never eat meat cooked on a grill again. Nothing that carried with it the taste of charcoal.

She stood and bit down on a green apple. Mrs. Phillips had made her promise.

"Are you Gracie Braithwaite?"

Gracie looked over her shoulder, tensing, watching as a silhouette loomed closer. The voice was male, its pronunciation crisp in that way that made her instantly distrust its owner. "Depends on who's asking."

"Sergeant Colin Jurgens."

"That means absolutely nothing to me."

The newcomer marched closer. He had a soldier's poise, a soldier's walk. Gracie could hear the rattle of a sabre in its scabbard. Old-fashioned, Gracie thought wryly, turning to face whatever was coming next. The man didn't look like anything that she'd expected. Smaller, slim at the shoulders, with long hair messily restrained in a ponytail. Older, too, than Gracie had expected, and stranger still, more incandescently alive than she thought possible. She'd become accustomed to thinking of soldiers as tired men, chewed down by time, morassed by the things they'd seen.

But this stranger fairly *bounced* with glee.

"Quite right," he said. To Gracie's confused horror, he began waggling his eyebrows. "That's because I represent an entirely unknown organization."

"If you're here because of the fire, I—" Gracie paused, halfway towards articulating something brusque, before she shrugged, hands jammed into the pockets of her overalls. She glared. "Sodding hell. I'm tired. I don't care. You from the station? The halls of Hell? Whatever. Do what you will. I'm done. I did my share."

"Do what—" The man spluttered. It took Gracie a moment to realize that he was, much to her chagrin, laughing at her. "Ma'am. Ma'am, you mistake me. I'm not here for anything of the sort."

"You're not a demon, then?"

Colin pulled at his moustache, looking so positively aggrieved at the suggestion that Gracie almost laughed. He shook his head. His uniform was unlike anything that Gracie had seen and briefly, giddily, she wondered if he might be an envoy from Heaven, sent to congratulate her on her actions.

"Absolutely not." Probably not, Gracie decided; that hangdog look was nothing celestial. "We *fight* demons, in the Strange Brigade."

"Sorry, I think I might have misheard." Gracie took another bite from her apple. The cat circled her ankles again before padding over to Colin, tail coiled questioningly. The soldier promptly went down on one knee, patted him without embarrassment. "Did you say the Strange Brigade?"

"Yes." Something in the burning factory split in half, gave way, came crashing down into the blaze. "The Strange Brigade. Actually, officially, we operate under the much less interesting moniker of the Department of Antiquities. Politicians; I'm sure you understand."

"No. No, I don't."

A flush crawled over his bridge of his nose, settled along his gaunt cheeks. "Hrm. Yes, quite. That'd make sense. Sorry. That was rather presumptuous of me. Age, you understand. Age has its privileges, also its problems."

"You're still not making any sense." Gracie ventured closer, feeling out of her depth. "What are you talking about?"

"The Strange Brigade, my girl, is the British Empire's first and last defence against supernatural threats that would, uhm, threaten the Crown. We are proud, we are few. We have faced man-eating lions. We have confronted mummies, vampires, no small number of hellions, and even pruned a garden overrun with carnivorous roses."

"Right." Gracie frowned. "And what's this got to do with me? Don't tell me. You want me to join with you, then?"

"Spot on!"

"I see." Gracie breathed in. "The position. Does it come with benefits? I expect a posthumous pension plan that extends to all my family members, including any and all adjunct relatives, such as in-laws and cousins."

And Colin laughed, brassy and rich, a sound like a future coming together. "My girl, I can already tell we'll get along famously."

RIPPLES IN A POLLUTED POOL
JONATHAN L. HOWARD

THE CAPTAIN WAS nearly at the end of his support shift, and was considering which bistro he should visit to slake his thirst and assuage his appetite when the corporal attending the observation point called, softly yet urgently: "Sir! He's on the move!"

"What?" Captain Francis Fairburne made first to the table to take up the field glasses before joining Corporal Winters at the more powerful tripod-mounted binoculars. The observation point was in an apartment in the third floor of a block in Marseille's *2e arrondisement*, not far from the docks. It was easy enough to see the blue of the Mediterranean from here, and the Frioul archipelago a couple of miles out to sea. The view, however, was not the reason the British Secret Service Bureau had posted them there.

There were four of them: a captain and a sergeant seconded from the Naptonshire Regiment, and two corporals from the Royal Signals. They were surveilling an apartment some two hundred yards away across a small square, where an agent of the SSB was supposed to be in possession of some documents that the SSB's German counterparts—the *Abwehr*—had very unkindly taken from a British courier, and which the agent had rather more gently taken back from them.

There was good reason to believe the *Abwehr* had not taken this reversal in good humour, and were scouring Marseille to abscond with them once more. Obeying his orders, the agent (codenamed "Malvolio" by a bored clerk somewhere in the Admiralty) had gone to ground in an assigned safehouse. There he was to wait until contacted. That was Fairburne's job, but it was his orders to make sure that the safehouse had not been compromised; a couple of days' surveillance should answer that one way or the other.

Reports indicated that, after a frantic few hours, the *Abwehr* abruptly halted their investigations, suggesting either that they had given up—unlikely—or that they had found some useful intelligence and were acting on it more quietly. Yet in the first thirty-six hours of observation, nothing untoward had been noted. It would have been useful if *Abwehr* agents were as thunderingly unsubtle as their *Gestapo* counterparts and wandered around in black hats and leather overcoats, but they were not. In all likelihood they were using local assets—Frenchmen with Nazi sympathies, born and bred in the city. All the SSB team could do was look for unusual activity and familiar faces. So far, nothing.

Another commanding officer might simply have assigned each of the NCOs under his command an eight-hour shift and wandered in and out as he liked, but Fairburne was a great believer in leading from the front. He had assigned three eight hour shifts, yes; but as each man came off observation, he stayed awake and rested for the next shift, to be there to take over for necessary breaks and provide a second pair of eyes and a second opinion. This pattern meant Fairburne took on the same duties as the others and, if it didn't make them like him exactly, at least they respected him for it.

Fairburne was not, in truth, an easy man to like. He came from a military family that regarded him as a paragon of their blood. A pure soldier, he was dedicated to the crown, to his country, and to his regiment, although not necessarily in that order. His soldiering in the field was *sans pareil*, to an extent that even worried his superior offices. Every man, when confronted with the decision to take a life in battle, may hesitate for a heartbeat before committing to the deed; that is what it is to be human. Fairburne never had, and likely never would. He would squeeze a trigger as soon as think it when an enemy stood framed in his sights. His colonel had commented once that Fairburne had "the coldest eyes in the Empire," not altogether in admiration.

This, then, was Captain Francis Fairburne; "Frank" to his friends, of which there were vanishingly few.

Fairburne stood in the shadows by the sun-bleached

curtains and looked out into the street. He spotted Malvolio instantly, already halfway across the street and heading towards the waterfront. More worryingly, he saw the soft brown leather briefcase the man held firmly under his arm and strongly suspected he knew what was within.

"What the blazes is the fool playing at?" Fairburne ran to the door. "Whistle up Control on the radio set. Tell them what's happened and that I'm going after Malvolio. Await instructions."

He hardly heard the corporal's confirmation of his orders. He was already out on the stairwell landing, shrugging into the slightly grubby pale brown jacket that was part of the disguise and checking the soiled red 'kerchief at his throat was in order. At least he already had a tan and so passed easily amongst the locals; the corporals had both come freshly assigned from Britain and were as pale as cave fish.

He was hardly aware of the descent down the flights of stairs, only how long it took and how far Malvolio might have got in that time. Fortunately, the *2e arrondisement* was not unused to seeing dock workers running late for their shifts, and—as the clock struck two—no one gave Fairburne more than a sympathetic glance as he sprinted across the road and down the path he had seen Malvolio take. After a minute or so, he saw the figure with the brown briefcase ahead of him on the other side of the street; he slowed his stride so as not to attract more attention than need be. That said, Malvolio was employing little in the way of tradecraft, barely bothering to look around him for signs of pursuit or performing any of the tricks that agents are taught to keep themselves alive in the sometimes brutal game of spies.

He was just walking.

It was the damndest thing Fairburne had ever seen. One would think he was taking a packet of top secret documents out for a stroll because they had grown fractious, like a bored dog.

Malvolio took a sudden turn into an alleyway, and Fairburne crossed the road quickly to get closer while unobserved, not that Malvolio seemed at the top of his game that afternoon. Fairburne leaned on the corner, lighting a cigarette, and took a sideways glance down the alleyway. There went Malvolio, off to the left into what looked to be a tenement of the Victorian period, or whatever it pleased the French to call the Victorian period. The building was a big, ugly block, walls stained black, windows broken by the stones of ill-bred children, and looked like it was well overdue for demolition. Evidently the local authorities agreed: it was surrounded by a battered wooden fence upon which hung *Entrée interdite!* signs. Fairburne saw Malvolio shift a loose plank aside and enter. Not a stroll, then.

He tossed the barely smoked cigarette aside and followed, loosening the Webley Mk 1* he wore in a concealed holster at the back of his belt as he did so; a model specially customised for the SSB with a shorter barrel and a smaller grip, to aid concealment. He had a strong feeling things were about to turn very nasty, and he had no desire to get into a fight that didn't involve him returning fire.

He slid aside the loose planks much more quietly than Malvolio had managed, and moved cautiously towards the isolated building beyond. He was used to the sense of heightened reality combat or the threat of imminent combat could instil in a man, but the curious sense of isolation behind that wooden wall, the utterly cloudless blue sky, the black slab of a building with the empty eyes of its windows looking down upon him, engendered a sensation he did not often feel. Fairburne realised he was afraid.

Not at the growing likelihood of violence, but at the sense that matters were not quite right, and that there was something occurring that he did not understand. He feared no man nor beast, but Fairburne had a healthy respect for the unknown. The unknown drew men into darkness and sucked their bones dry. He had experienced some matters during tours of Africa and India that were not easily explained by parochial English education. Almost unaware of his actions, he slowly drew the revolver.

There were few places Malvolio could have gone, and Fairburne went to the most obvious first; an archway leading into the tenement's courtyard. Even before he reached it, he could hear voices in conversation, speaking French. He knew the language well enough to discern accents, and was slightly baffled by what he gleaned from Malvolio's interlocutor. He'd only ever heard one person speak like that before, and he'd been Belgian. Malvolio's contact was a Belgian? Curiouser and curiouser.

Fairburne eased his head around the corner of the archway a couple of inches; just far enough to get the lay of the land without exposing himself to fire—or, he hoped, even being spotted at all. There was Malvolio, and a small man in a grey suit and a very neat homburg. He did not seem at all at home in the wonderland of debris and building refuse the locals had enthusiastically dumped in the courtyard before the fences went up. If he had to guess, Fairburne would have said the man looked like a minor governmental functionary. He certainly wasn't a player; he was nearly in a flop sweat, dabbing repeatedly at his brow with a large white handkerchief while Malvolio explained what was in the files he was handing over.

Fairburne had previously lived in blissful ignorance of the papers' contents, but now as he listened to Malvolio's description, he suddenly understood why both the Germans and the Belgians were keen to have them. He briefly wondered if the SSB was perhaps playing a deep game, and the papers were a feint, placed to misdirect. No matter; he was here to recover them and he did not intend to fail.

Fairburne considered his options: he could march in and take the briefcase at gunpoint, or he could let the exchange take place and then relieve the worried-looking Belgian subsequently. The latter seemed a much better idea to him, not least because he did not trust that courtyard. All those empty windows might conceal a small army of Belgian intelligence agents.

It struck Fairburne that he had no idea what the Belgian security or intelligence arms were called. He wondered if even the average Belgian knew.

At last an exchange was performed, with Malvolio

showing the Belgian the papers within the briefcase before handing the whole thing over, and the Belgian handing Malvolio an envelope doubtless stuffed with bank notes or negotiable bonds, or something else of the sort. The Belgian passed the envelope over very abruptly, as if glad to be rid of it. He seemed to regard this business as unseemly and likely to besmirch his dignity. He was certainly right about that, if Fairburne had any say in the matter.

Then matters went west in an unexpected way. Malvolio and the Belgian were startled by a man emerging from one of the doorways onto the courtyard. His accent was rough and local, but the pistol in his hand was a P.08, an expensive piece of artillery for a street thug. So this was why the *Abwehr* had seemed to lose interest in matters so suddenly; they had already learned that this exchange was to take place and very sensibly reasoned it was the ideal moment to take back their spoils. Fairburne braced himself in preparation for a meeting that was surely about to turn bloody.

The *Abwehr* agent—definitely a local French fascist recruited to the role—seemed very pleased with himself, as well he might. Fairburne scanned what windows of the courtyard he could make out from his vantage point; the *Abwehr* man would hardly have exposed himself like that unless he had at least one partner lurking at a window. He could see no one. Time to shift priorities.

Previously, the plan had simply to deprive the Belgian of the documents when he was alone, and deal with Malvolio later. With a couple of Nazi agents in play, however, he would have to become more involved, and sooner. His only real tactical advantage was surprise, which he would preserve until the last possible moment. His primary objective must remain recovering the documents, but to do that, he had to deal with at least four men. Of those, the *Abwehr* agents would cheerfully shoot him on sight and consider it part of their job, so they must be dealt with first. Malvolio was an unknown quantity; yes, he had betrayed his country, but would he kill a fellow Briton to cover up that betrayal? Quite possibly, given that treason was a capital crime, so Fairburne would have to keep an eye on him, but with any luck Malvolio wasn't an immediate threat. The Belgian was plainly not cut out for this line of work and had emitted a strange terrified squeak at the appearance of the *Abwehr* man. Fairburne suspected he would present of the least trouble of the four.

Targets prioritised, Fairburne moved to deal with his foes.

Going through the archway would simply serve himself up to the enemy on a plate, so he went back to find one of the many shattered windows at the ground floor level. He didn't have far to go. He clambered through the frameless window into the dark corridor beyond.

Now he had to make a few assumptions. Firstly, that the *Abwehr* men would have nothing larger than handguns. That meant they would want to keep range to a minimum. It was also likely that they would be needed in the courtyard at some point, and probably rather urgently. All in all, he doubted they would go above the first floor. Fairburne found a staircase, climbed the first flight, and started hunting.

It did not take extraordinary tracking skills to find indications of the German agent (singular, to judge from the evidence). He'd climbed through the self-same window as Fairburne had—most likely due to its lack of jagged glass—then climbed up the stairs and gone left, looking for an apartment with a commanding view of the courtyard. Judging by the disturbed gravel and plaster dust with which the corridor floor was strewn, he had found it in the corner apartment. Being careful where he placed his feet, Fairburne went to beard him in his lair.

The door of the apartment was lying across the floor, and Fairburne stepped cautiously around it, his pistol up and ready. There was the *Abwehr* man, crouched by the far window. His weapon was something else again from his partner's; a Mauser C-96 with an attached butt, converting the pistol into a sort of short-barrelled carbine. Another German weapon; whoever was handling these men for the *Abwehr* did not especially care if anyone guessed their allegiance.

He was still formulating a plan to deal with the man as he silently advanced across the room. Capturing him would be useful, if he could only—

The floor creaked sonorously beneath his step, and the Nazi agent looked back at him. He stood no chance; the Mauser was pointed away, and both his posture and the bulk of the weapon slowed him. Fairburne, nerveless in such circumstances, shot the man twice in the chest, took a long step to ensure no possibility of a miss, and shot the collapsing man once through the brain.

There went the element of surprise, but as it had taken half the *Abwehr* contingent with it, he was content. Holstering the Webley, he took the Mauser from the dead man's hands and stepped up to the window. He had worked through the situation in his mind based on what the other Nazi agent was likely thinking—that his colleague had fired accidentally or was just generally trigger-happy. The possibility of other agents in the equation would occur to him shortly, though, so Fairburne didn't waste time. He shouldered the Mauser and opened fire on the *Abwehr* man in the courtyard.

Malvolio and the Belgian were as startled by the change in circumstances as their persecutor. He already had the briefcase in his hand and was backing away from them when the shots rang out. Now it was all happening at once. He looked up as the first round whined off the courtyard floor. Fairburne shifted his aim accordingly as the Belgian shouted an imprecation to an unhelpful God and ran. Malvolio drew his own gun.

That was a surprise; Fairburne would have expected the *Abwehr* agent to have searched him as a known British agent. It also worried him, since he had no idea where Malvolio's real loyalties lay; it was a small relief when Malvolio aimed it at the *Abwehr* agent's back, and...

...and didn't fire. His brow creased as if a terrible thought had happened upon him, and then he steadied his aim as if steeling himself to squeeze the trigger. Again, he did not. The *Abwehr* agent looked back, saw the gun in Malvolio's hand and, without a moment's hesitation, shot him. Malvolio staggered back, his pistol falling to the floor, then followed it down a moment later.

The Nazi returned his attention to the window just in

time for Fairburne to shoot him three times in the chest. He collapsed beside Malvolio.

Fairburne gauged the drop and leapt down from the window, then ran to where the two stricken men lay.

The Nazi agent was plainly dead, which hardly surprised Fairburne. Malvolio, however, still breathed; the bullet had been a snapshot and not well placed. But the man was losing blood rapidly. Fairburne could see his death had only been deferred.

"Why?" he asked, not unsympathetically. A man's death is no small matter and he didn't care to badger someone standing at that last threshold. "Why did you take the documents?"

Malvolio's gaze slid onto him and past him, his eyes becoming unfocused. It was already too late to expect any cogency from him. All Fairburne could do was sit by Malvolio that he might not die alone. Fairburne was not a sentimentalist, but there is a rough sanctity in the moment of passing, and he would not begrudge a fellow creature his vigil in that time, freely given and fully felt.

Malvolio's breath was rasping, becoming irregular as his body lost the knack of living, stumbling its way to an untidy quietude. He convulsed briefly, his head juddering back and forth, his jaw rattling like a castanet. All that was human was passing from him, leaving only the failing machine. A spray of blood erupted from his mouth and splashed onto the concrete, and Fairburne was surprised to see it was watery, with pieces of grey meat caught in it. He was minded of a spray of cerebral matter. But how? Malvolio had been shot once in the chest.

Malvolio hacked a single violent cough, half rolling onto his side, and then ceased to move altogether. His jaw sagged open, and a thin rivulet of diluted blood ran from the corner of his mouth to pool on the concrete. Fairburne was about to rise when something else fell from the dead man's mouth, splashing into the growing red puddle. It made him think of a shard of bone, and for a moment he tried to rationalise it as coming from the dead man's skull. Unlikely, but then he had seen some very curious wounds over the years.

The thought vanished from his mind the next moment, because now he saw the strange thing—bone-white, yes, but with a faint silvery patina to it, like a thin layer of mother-of-pearl—had legs. Like a ghost crab in form, but too many legs. Too many legs by half. It unfurled them and tried to find a footing in the bloody filth, fully alive and possessed of a wilfulness that Fairburne found atavistically intolerable. Without another thought, he stood up and stamped the creature flat, grinding it into extinction beneath his sole with a shuddering satisfaction.

When he searched Malvolio's body, he found a small glass jar in his pocket, its stopper sealed with wax. Inside the jar was another of the crablike creatures, plainly alive although the jar had no ventilation holes.

When he later searched Malvolio's apartment, he discovered a box containing nine more identical jars, each home to another of the twelve-legged creatures. They scratched at the glass, eager to be out. It was a warm day, but Fairburne felt a coldness travel across his neck and shoulders as he looked at them, and as they tried to reach him.

*   *   *

"GOOD WORK," WAS the general consensus of Fairburne's superiors. A fishing boat crewed by Royal Navy sailors in mufti had extracted him and his team the same evening, along with a steamer trunk containing the unfortunate Malvolio. The two *Abwehr* men would be found in the dock in the morning, victims of some criminal vendetta as far as the local police were concerned. Fairburne carried a suitcase containing the recovered documents and anything incriminating from Malvolio's apartment. The box containing the jars was inside another box, which Fairburne sealed tightly with wax and string. He kept thinking of how the creature had flexed and moved, seeming very at home in a dead man's blood.

Good work indeed. He had recovered the documents, seen off two enemy agents, and humiliated the Belgians, all while exposing a traitor. The latter perplexed his superiors; Malvolio had never been regarded as anything but reliable and resourceful. There were no indications whatsoever in his background of the usual reasons a man might try treason. Why he suddenly decided to sell the Belgians documents dealing with British covert activities in Uganda, up to and including sorties across the border into the Belgian Congo to destabilise the place, baffled all. The money he had been paid was a decent sum, but not substantial, and Malvolio had far more than that in the bank anyway. It seemed an unlikely motive.

Fairburne, however, had a theory, and included it in his report.

As to the creatures, Fairburne did not mention in his report that one had emerged from Malvolio's mouth—some things are beyond easy credibility. He handed the corpse over to the medical officer with a mention that an investigation of the mouth might prove interesting based on the blood that poured forth, and he handed over the creatures to his commanding officer, a major nominally of the Guards but now a spook handler for Military Intelligence.

The major's reaction was interesting to Fairburne; he had frowned thunderously at the sight of one of the vile little beasts scrabbling around in its jar, and instantly made a note. That meant it was being kicked upstairs. Fairburne was relieved; it was somebody else's problem.

His relief, in the event, proved premature.

A day later, the medical officer—a Dr. Goole, a name whose comic possibilities had evaded no one—sought out Fairburne in the mess, looking serious. He took Fairburne to one side.

"What in blazes did you *do* to him, Fairburne?"

"Do?"

"There is a *dreadful* wound through the man's soft palate. Was that your doing?"

"He was shot."

"Good Lord, man, I know he was *shot*. I drew the bullet myself; a .38, or more likely a 9mm, is what killed him. But somebody dug through this man's mouth into his brain. As to his brain, well…" He signalled a white-jacketed waiter to bring him a drink and remained silent until it had arrived. After the waiter had gone, he said, "There are lesions on the frontal lobes. Small things, and I doubt they were sufficient to cause a change in the behaviour of the deceased, but I've never seen the like. They're in a neat pattern, very nearly circular, half on the left lobe, half on the right. Nature is rarely that tidy in these matters. They were caused artificially."

"Have they anything to do with..." Fairburne signalled vaguely but evocatively at his own mouth.

"No. Or, at least, not directly. But the track of damage from the soft palate goes along the underside of the brain and stops right at the lesions."

Fairburne took up his whisky and soda for a moment to give him time to think. Beyond the open door he could see the blue sky and the light fracturing from the waters of the Strait of Gibraltar. He was suddenly and unpleasantly reminded of Marseille. "Write it up and send it to me, old man. I'll pass it on to the interested parties."

Goole grimaced. "I hardly know what I'm going to write."

"You're not alone in that, I assure you. One thing; you said multiple lesions. How many?"

"Twelve," said Goole. "As regular as the numbers on a clock."

USUALLY, THE GEARS grind slowly in a governmental bureaucracy. It was therefore a shock when, a mere eight days after Marseille had been kicked up the ladder to the faceless paper-wallahs of Whitehall, Captain Fairburne found himself in receipt of a small bundle of files brought directly from London by personal courier, a taciturn young man in a linen suit with, noted Fairburne, a shoulder holster and pistol beneath the jacket. Definitely not common issue to civil servants. Hardly had the man left with assorted signed receipts when Fairburne's CO swept in with a sheet of paper in his hand and an expression of purest astonishment on his face.

"Fairburne! What's all this? You've been reassigned!"

Fairburne eyed the files he'd just signed for with deepening suspicion. "I have, sir? Where to?"

The major frowned at him, his astonishment diminishing not a whit. "You mean you didn't request it?"

"I did not, sir. It's as big a surprise to me as it is to you."

The major consulted the piece of paper. "Says here you're removed from my command and seconded to a special investigations group. DA-01." He looked at Fairburne as if he was party to a conspiracy intended to make a fool of him. "Never heard of it."

"For what it's worth, sir, neither have I. What do they do?"

The major examined his printed orders again, but it apparently imparted no great wisdom to him. He sighed, folded the sheet and put it in his pocket. "Something to do with antiquities? Never had you down as an antiques sort of fella, Fairburne."

Now Fairburne suspected that he was the butt of a joke. "I don't know a Ming vase from a spittoon, sir. There must be some mistake."

"I'll query it, but until confirmation or otherwise comes through, orders are to be obeyed. I can't assign you to anything until this matter's cleared up. It looks like you're in the antiques trade in the interim."

After the major had left, Fairburne turned his attention to the files. They were bound with a sealed ribbon marked *TOP SECRET—Capt.F.Fairburne EYES ONLY*, a designation he did not find reassuring or flattering. Cutting the ribbon with his pocketknife, he examined the individual files briefly to get their measure. It was a curious mix: two case files and a folder containing an unfamiliar cypher and its associated codebook, along with his orders from the mysterious 'DA-01' group. The mystery was only deepened by the brevity and specificity of the orders; he was to examine the files and then communicate his report to the group, suitably encyphered.

Now convinced that his orders had been issued in error—who would ask a field agent to do analyst work?— he opened the first case file and started reading.

An hour later, he called for coffee, and told them to leave the pot.

Five hours later, he sent a coded report to London.

THE LYONS CORNER House on Oxford Street, hard by the junction with Tottenham Court Road, was generally accepted to see intrigue every day, albeit of the more mundane sort: illicit meetings between married people who were not married to one another, the occasional planning of a felony, the *very* occasional planning of murder. What was less well-known was that it was also the preferred venue for meetings upon whose outcomes rested the survival of Britain and, with increasing frequency, that of the world.

One such meeting was taking place now. A man in a nondescript building near St. James Park had studied an incoming decrypted message, frowned, put on his bowler, and caught the Tube for Tottenham Court Road Station with dispatch. He had found his superior ensconced in her habitual place in the corner of the most genteel of the tearooms within Corner House, sipping Darjeeling and making notes in a precise hand in a pocketbook. One might have thought her a dowager duchess making notes about her favourite charities—but one would have been quite wrong.

"Why, Mr. Busby," she said, smiling as a nippy brought him to her table, "an unexpected pleasure." As soon as the waitress left, her smile disappeared. "What brings you here?" she asked quietly as he seated himself.

"A message from our new friend in Gibraltar, Lady Webster," said Busby, and passed over the decrypt. She read it quickly, her clinical eye quickly extracting the salient details, the smile returning somewhat. "Your analysis?" she asked finally.

"I think it's very promising, my lady," said Busby. He waved away the returning nippy with her open order pad. "He's got to the nub of it in record time, spotted the commonality in all the cases."

Lady Webster nodded. "One had hopes after the Marseille business. Always pleasant to be proved right. I agree with his view that Malvolio's treachery was intended to destabilise the African situation, probably as a distraction. Ah, and his recommendations. A man after my own heart."

"His wanting to go to India himself?" Busby raised an elegant eyebrow. "You approve?"

"Our Captain Fairburne is a man of action and wishes to see the matter through. That is exactly the sort of man we need. Release the necessary monies and authorities, Mr. Busby. I want him there as soon as is possible."

"Is that wise? It may well be more dangerous than we think."

Lady Webster tested the outside of the teapot with the backs of her fingers, then refilled her cup. "If he fails, then we shall know that for a certainty. But, I have faith in Fairburne. He's a thoughtful killer; a rare enough breed, and ideal for us. Send him on his way, and we shall see what he stirs up."

CURIOUSER AND YET curiouser. Fairburne's report and request to go to India were both accepted and acted upon within eight hours of receipt.

"What is going on, Fairburne?" demanded his former CO when he was summoned to the office. "I've been ordered to provide you with full tropical kit, and have you ready to depart at 0600. I'm told they're sending a ship for you. A *ship!*" He looked around the room in disbelief as if he might find an explanation written on a wall or a lampshade.

"Once again, sir, I have no idea. Things seem to be hotting up, whatever is going on."

This turned out to be a sad understatement, when the ship arrived the following morning. All eyes were on the Atlantic approach into the strait, and so the deep thrumming from the morning sky in the darkness of the west took everyone by surprise. Fairburne's batman, terribly underused since his officer had been called into the spying game, was the first to spot it.

"Bloody hell, sir," he said, and pointed. "They've only gone and sent an airship for you!"

And so they had. Fairburne, who prided himself on staying abreast of technical matters both civilian and military, was disconcerted to realise the design of the dirigible was entirely unknown to him. How could anyone have built an experimental airship—a huge undertaking—without him even hearing a whisper?

Fairburne's perplexity deepened on boarding. The crew were not entirely military, nor even entirely British. He noted a senior black officer—Kenyan, from his accent— and the navigator seemed to be a native Canadian of some sort. He also recognised the taciturn man in the linen suit who had brought him the files, now in the uniform of a petty officer.

As the airship left Gibraltar heading east, no one aboard seemed keen to speak to Fairburne. For his part, the silence suited him; he had much to think on.

APART FROM A slight deviation to avoid flying over Italy, the airship travelled as straight as anything can, favouring open sea, or nations in thrall to Britannia, or that lacked the wherewithal to challenge a high-flying vessel. Greece, Turkey, Persia, and Afghanistan passed beneath the silver grey hull, and they arrived over the Aravalli mountain range in Rajputana before the end of the third day. Fairburne had advised swiftness in his report, but he had never anticipated anything like this.

He was put down by rope ladder in the lee of a mountainside witnessed only by goats, instructed as to the direction of the local railhead, wished luck in a perfunctory sort of manner, and then left to his own devices as the airship turned ponderously to the west. Picking up his kitbag and wishing he had been allowed his batman, Fairburne started walking.

At least the walk was downhill, and no more than three or four miles. As he walked, he took in the landscape. The mountain tops were arid and brown, devoid of ice, but the slopes and valleys below them were green and filled with dense tree growth—he spotted mahua, kaim, and even jhinjeri—while above him a lone shikra circled, looking for prey.

Presently he arrived at the railhead, finding it deserted but for an ageing but plainly well-maintained Austin 12, parked in the shade of the platform shelter. That it had been necessary to drive onto the platform seemed not to concern the driver at all. He was sitting sideways in the driver's seat, feet on the running board, reading a battered novel. He looked up when he saw Fairburne coming, got out, tossed the novel back onto the seat, and walked towards him, smiling broadly. In truth, he was faintly terrifying—6'2" if he was an inch, with a full beard and hands that looked powerful enough to crush a coconut. At the same time, there was an air of good humour about him, from the base of his boots to the top of his turban, that reassured Fairburne.

"It's been a long trek from Sariska," said Fairburne.

"The rains would have made it worse," replied the man.

"True, but the rains are in God's hands."

"That must be very uncomfortable for Him." He saw Fairburne's expression and sighed. "*Yet the season will surely turn.*"

"Your English is excellent."

The man frowned. "Are we still speaking in code phrases? If so, nobody told me about that one." Fairburne laughed, and the man smiled again. He bowed slightly and put out a hand. "I am Jagmeet Singh Janda. I hope you are Captain Fairburne, or I shall probably have to kill you."

Fairburne shook his hand. "That won't be necessary." He lowered his voice. "You're acting for the SSB?"

Janda looked at him with mild distaste. "No, captain, my orders come from DA-01, as do yours. I was asked to come here and observe until they could find an executive agent to deal with matters at first hand." He nodded at Fairburne. "And that is you."

"Observe?" Now it was Fairburne's turn to frown. "How long have you been here?"

"Three months. The lie I was told to tell the villagers and the garrison was that I am a humble driver who has had to leave Chittorgarh for a little while, due to a 'misunderstanding'. They are happy to have me here; they use my poor Austin as a beast of burden, and never ask where I get my petrol from." He leaned forward and said in a confidential tone, "They are mainly Jains here. Good people. I like them. Although"—he nodded at the station wall where the *Jain Prateek Chihna* had been carefully painted, an open hand below a swastika—"they are very unhappy with that European fellow with the little moustache defaming their symbol."

"I can't say I blame them. But, look here, Janda, I've only just been assigned. Are you telling me that DA-01 have been aware of possible trouble at Fort Chippenham for *three months?*"

"Oh, no," Janda said, shaking his head, "much longer than that. It has only recently become an operational concern, however. Alas, captain, I have little to report. The occupants of the fort keep themselves very much to themselves. This may be the policy of the current commander."

"Colonel Aspern." Fairburne had assiduously memorised the files he had been given.

"Indeed, although... he has done a strange thing. You know of the high regard in which the Jains hold their holy people? Well, the colonel has decided to put the local *sadhu* under arrest."

"Really? Has he said why?"

"The story changes. At first it was because the sadhu was inciting insurrection, wanting to bring down the Empire, being rude about the King, and other such nonsense. The village was astonished! Their sadhu? Never! And... the story changed. Now he's being held in protective custody because mysterious Mussulmans want him dead. Why? And where from? It makes less sense than the first story, but it does not paint the sadhu as an evildoer, and it did placate some."

"But still a lie?"

Janda nodded sagely. "Oh, yes."

*   *   *

THE DRIVE TO the fort was filled with conversation, some useful, some less so. Fairburne found himself sitting on Janda's book, and picked it up to examine it.

"Rudyard Kipling?"

Janda nodded. "An officer left it in my car when I was delivering him from the station."

"What do you think?"

There was a pause. "Could be worse," said Janda finally.

After twenty minutes, Fort Chippenham hove into view on the mountain slope. Like many British garrisons, its design was an uneasy combination of the militarily practical and the economically viable. Nor was it a Victorian building, like many of its brethren. Chippenham had been built just before the Great War as a base for mountain patrols, in an attempt to control the intermittent banditry in the area. As such it was not a massive fortress, for shrugging off artillery, but a checkpoint to control entry and exit, and keep the occupants safe from rifle bullets. Indeed, despite the title, it was quite small.

Janda halted the car and said, "Fort Chippenham. It is... underwhelming, but I like the name. Listen: Chip. En. Ham. Chippenham. Chippenham." He nodded to the valley. "The village is just beyond the curve in the road. I shall deliver you to the fort and then go on."

"What is that?" Fairburne asked, pointing to a bungalow some hundred yards from the fort, partially obscured by an ill-kept garden with far too many magnolias.

"For visiting types, captain. Empty all the time I have been in here. If they put you in it, beware of snakes."

FAIRBURNE'S PAPERS WERE checked with almost insulting care by the sentries on the gate before he was permitted entry. Even then, he wasn't even offered refreshment after his journey—a fictional trip aboard a chartered train had been manufactured to explain his arrival—but ushered directly into the presence of Colonel Aspern.

Aspern was well known to Fairburne by dint of his file, and by what there was to read between the lines. Aspern was a veteran of the Great War, during which as a junior officer he had advocated the virtues of rapid movement and flexible logistics, and championed tank warfare. This early vigour, however, had become depleted by the 'twenties. He developed a reputation as something of a martinet. Fairburne had seen it happen to others, and entirely expected to be grilled by an embittered man sent to fritter away the end of his career guarding some distant corner of empire.

The colonel was a man of good figure in his late forties, and he rose to meet Fairburne with a smile, a not overly rigorous salute, and a firm handshake. "You've rather caught us on the hop, captain," he said, examining Fairburne's orders. "We were expecting no new personnel at least until after the rain season." He looked up from his reading. "The Naptons? Aren't you all supposed to be in Egypt?"

"There's a possibility we may be replacing you in a year

or so, sir. As I was in Chittorgarh on personal business anyway, my colonel asked me to make the trip here to get a measure of the place. Lay of the land, and so forth."

"I see. Not a great deal to take in, to be frank. You seem a capable officer, Fairburne. I doubt it will occupy you for very long."

"As you say, sir. The next train is in a week. With your leave, I should like to be aboard it."

As he spoke, he looked at the walls of the colonel's office and noted empty nails and dark patches, where things had hung until fairly recently. Shield shapes and circles, some of them ill-defined around the edges.

"By all means. Sergeant Major Dickens and I will be happy to speak to you about any operational matters, the locals, quirks of the establishment, and so forth."

And so concluded the interview.

FAIRBURNE WAS ASSIGNED, somewhat to his chagrin and certainly over his polite protests, the ugly little bungalow in the fort's shadow.

"The fort has never been attacked, sir," said Beddoes, the batman assigned to him. "If it is, it's only a quick trot and we'll be safe within the walls."

Fairburne was looking disconsolately at the rope-operated fan on the veranda, swinging gently in the cool breeze that seemed to run constantly down the hillside. It was scarcely warm enough to warrant a punkah wallah, but Beddoes constituted his entire staff. No locals were employed. From what Janda had told him, they had quietly withdrawn their labour when the sadhu was arrested, and not purely in protest.

"They are simple village folk," he had told Fairburne during the drive, "but they are not fools. There has been... how might I say it? A change in the air."

The atmosphere. The villagers avoided the fort because it made them uneasy. Fairburne could sympathise. Nothing about the place seemed quite pukka to him.

Sergeant Major Dickens was a case in point. Fresh from his interview with the colonel, Fairburne found Dickens overseeing drill in the fort's courtyard and watched until the exercises were complete. In Fairburne's experience, troops on the edges of the Empire were generally either over-drilled to the point of automata, or altogether slovenly. This exercise, however, was unique in his experience. The sergeant never shouted, yet the men responded perfectly, and without the mechanical motions of soldiers who would prefer death to another 'present arms.'

After the men had fallen out, Dickens came over to meet Fairburne. "Captain Fairburne," he said, "sah!" He snapped a salute, which Fairburne returned. The ensuing conversation was banal in the extreme, touching on Fairburne's story about a handover, but the sergeant major spent the time quickly working through the fort's eccentricities and assorted details that would be useful to the officers of a new regiment as and when it took over the site.

Fairburne made plentiful mental notes of such minutiae, but the larger part of his attention was upon the vexed question of how he had known who Fairburne was, when he had only just introduced himself to the colonel. It was possible, he supposed, that one of the sentries at the gate had told him.

Yes, that must be it.

On the second day, Fairburne made the acquaintance of a Lieutenant Oswald, a relatively new addition to the fort's complement and apparently the former owner of Janda's Kipling novel. Oswald was the sort of bland young creature that had been washing into the British Army as 'the thing to do' since Victoria's time, and were blithely under the impression that the Great War had changed nothing. They could not see the cracks forming as the Empire began its inevitable decay. Certainly his chatter was as light and amusing as it was devoid of content, right up to the moment when, walking, they passed out of view of the nearest soldier.

"There's something very *rum* going on in Fort Chippenham, sir," he said, suddenly very serious.

"Rum? In what sense?"

"Oh, come now. I'm a freshly minted product of Sandhurst, I know, but we're terrifically military, my clan. I know how soldiers act and"—he looked around, lowering his voice still further—"*this* shower just about take the biscuit, wouldn't you say?"

"It's not unknown for soldiers on a long deployment to adopt—"

"Oh, rot, sir. All due respect, I hasten to add, but we've got a sergeant major who barely raises his voice. He *smiles* at the troops. It's unnatural. All the non-commissioned ranks are as thick as thieves; sergeants and corporals and privates all awfully chummy. You're not telling me that's normal, are you? It's like something from the Book of Revelation."

Fairburne stopped walking. "Are you suggesting that there's been a failure in military discipline here, lieutenant?"

"No! That's the worrisome thing. Discipline is as tight as a drum, but it *never has to be enforced*. The glasshouse is gathering dust. Well, apart from the cell they've got that guru-wallah in. This garrison functions *perfectly*. But it *should* be a shambles."

"Perhaps they respect the colonel?"

"Oh, yes, the colonel." Fairburne had plainly touched on another concern. "I was terrified when I was posted here. The old man has a fierce reputation, you know. Eats a subaltern for breakfast every day, they said. But you've met him; he's a dear! No goose need fear booing from that quarter. And"—again the quick look around—"see here..."

He led Fairburne to a door further along the corridor, looked around, and opened it. "Look at this lot."

The room was being used for a store, apparently of the colonel's belongings. Most notable by far, however, was a huge collection of hunting trophies from across Asia, Africa, and Europe. Rhino, tiger, wildebeest; even an Indian elephant foot. For Fairburne, they confirmed the suspicion the voids on the colonel's office walls had put in his mind. Oswald drew the door shut, and said significantly, "The old man's a famous hunter, yet all of a sudden he can't bear the sight of his trophies. He's sworn off hunting." He leaned forward and said in low tones of horror, "He's gone *vegetarian*..."

FAIRBURNE MENTALLY PENCILLED in Oswald as an ally, although not a very effective one. He had obliquely mentioned the men who had travelled through the fort and whose behaviours had subsequently changed, but the visits all predated Oswald's time there. Still, it now seemed undeniable that the fort was the seat of the curious changes and, perhaps, where the strange crab-like creatures originated. He was at pains to cook his own meals in his bungalow, to do so from canned supplies, and to thoroughly boil every drop of water that passed his lips. It made his diet unrelentingly dull, but he was mindful that large creatures can grow from infinitesimal larvae; if the men of the fort were being infected that way, at least he might defend himself.

It was, admittedly, unlikely. The village over the rise had been there long before the fort, yet the villagers demonstrably had not 'changed' in the way that the Britons had. He had walked over that way himself to speak with Janda, and the villagers—initially reluctant—had then seemed to accept him, and with visible relief. It seemed they had grown sensitive to the mannerisms of 'the changed,' and Fairburne was not exhibiting them. His Hindi was weak, and his grasp of the regional dialect non-existent, so he was grateful for Janda's magisterial presence as a translator. They could tell him little that Janda hadn't already relayed, however; relations with the garrison had been distant and not entirely amicable until the sadhu had gone to act as an emissary for the village in an argument over water rights. About a week after that, the sadhu was arrested, "for his own safety." Members of the village council had been permitted to visit him briefly, and he had seemed perfectly happy in his cell, saying that he was being well treated and speaking to the colonel frequently. He assured them that he was free to leave if he so desired, so they should not worry, but considered it more fruitful if he stayed where he was for the moment. Relieved if confused, they had left him there.

Fairburne returned to his bungalow to find Beddoes laying out his mess uniform. "Colonel's regards, sir," he said. "You're invited to dinner in the senior officers' mess at twenty hundred hours."

"I see." Fairburne regarded the scarlet shell jacket with disfavour; a necessary evil in regimental etiquette. "And will it be a vegetarian meal?"

"I would think so, sir," said Beddoes, examining the dress trousers with an eye to a quick pressing. "Eating the flesh of our fellow animals is barbaric."

He quite failed to notice Fairburne's expression.

VERY AWARE OF how absurd he must appear in mess dress against the rugged Indian hillside, Fairburne made his way from the bungalow to the fort, giving and receiving curt salutes to the men on the gate. He was en route to the senior officers' mess—formulating a lie about the state of his digestion to avoid eating anything—when he was mildly surprised to see Lieutenant Oswald leaning out of a door and frantically signalling to him, like a supporting character in a West End farce. Checking he himself was unobserved, Fairburne went to see what Oswald had found for him.

"In here, sir!" whispered the lieutenant in a *sotto voce* so pronounced he might as well have just spoken aloud. "You have to see this!"

It might make Fairburne a minute or two late for dinner, but it might, perhaps, be worth it. Inwardly willing Oswald not to be wasting his time, he went quickly to the room and went in.

It seemed to be an office, possibly Oswald's own, but all the furniture had been pushed up against the wall. As Fairburne looked around for what might be so important, the door closed behind him, and his heart sank.

"Sorry, old bean." Oswald sounded truly sincere. He was leaning against the door. On either side of it stood a corporal and a sergeant. "But this really is for the best. You'll see."

The NCOs rushed him. Fairburne dodged the corporal and landed a straight right on the sergeant's jaw, knocking him back. "You'll face court martial for this!" he barked at Oswald. "All of you will!" The corporal reversed his course and grabbed Fairburne around the chest from behind. The two men struggled as the sergeant cleared his head and came to join in again.

"Don't be like that, sir," said Oswald. A note of

concern was evident in his voice. "Violence really is unnecessary. Frankly, it's abhorrent to us, and it won't change anything, you know. Better just to accept it."

Fairburne didn't fancy his chances against the two burly men, but he intended to go down fighting, *violence is unnecessary* be damned. He elbowed the corporal hard enough to drive the air from his lungs, and broke the bear hug just in time to be bowled over by the sergeant's bull rush. Fairburne found himself flat on his back. He struggled, but the sergeant held onto him like grim death, and a moment later the corporal was there too. Fairburne was down again, this time for good, his arms pinned against the office floor.

"I can't say that I blame you, sir," said Oswald, his regret apparent. "I can't lie; I fought like a cat when they did it to me. But, believe you me, it was all wasted effort. This is all to *help* you."

He went to the desk and opened a drawer; Fairburne watched with rising horror as Oswald took out a small glass jar. Something pale moved within it.

"Bit unpleasant, I grant you," said the lieutenant, holding up the jar to examine the crablike creature within. He tapped at the glass with his fingernail, and it scuttled around inside. "But no worse than eating an oyster. Well, not much like that, actually. There's some blood, and it hurts a bit... hurts quite a lot at first, but then it's all done, and bingo! You're a new chap! Better than the old chap, mark you." He nodded at the NCOs. "Get his mouth open, would you, lads?"

One hand clamped onto Fairburne's lower jaw and

another onto his forehead. He fought hard, but—a fraction of an inch at a time—his mouth was forced open. He stared helplessly as Oswald found a place to crouch by him and broke the seal on the jar. The creature seemed almost frantic to be out. Fairburne wrenched his face aside, futilely—the men's grip was still solid—but managed to squirm his left arm out from beneath the corporal as he did.

"You are going to feel very silly you made all this fuss in a few minutes, let me tell you," said Oswald. "Now just hold still and take your medicine. *What are—?*"

Fairburne had just used his freed left arm to drag Oswald's service revolver from its holster. The bark of the shot, so close to them both, was stunning in its ferocity, but the jar and creature alike vanished in a fountain of powdered glass and unnatural ichor.

The NCOs released Fairburne instantly, and he had the curious sense that they did so not out of fear of the pistol, but in reaction to the creature's fate. Certainly Oswald clutched at his head as if suddenly prey to a violent migraine. "Oh! Why do you keep doing that?"

Fairburne scrambled to his feet, seized Oswald by the shirt front and dragged him upright before planting the gun's still-warm muzzle between his eyes. "What do you mean, '*keep* doing that'? Doing what?" Oswald only looked at him with vague awareness. "Killing those creatures? Is that what you mean? How could you know that?"

Oswald said nothing, and Fairburne smiled. "You *know* where we're going next, don't you?"

* * *

IT HAD ALWAYS been his plan to pay a visit, sooner or later. In a fort riddled with anomalies, it had stood out right from the first. The fort's cell block was designed to double as a last redoubt in case attackers somehow breached the outer walls; Fairburne kicked Oswald away, slammed the heavy door in his face, and bolted it in the reasonable expectation that it would give him at least a few minutes' grace. Entirely unsurprised to find no guard on duty, he took up a lantern from the rack by the door and the bunch of keys from the hook, and descended into the gloom of the cells built beneath ground level.

He found the sadhu sitting cross-legged on a bunk in an unlocked cell at the end of the row on the right hand side. He was bearded and long haired, his whiskers as white as the loose robe he wore. It was open at the chest, and Fairburne noted his flesh was soft and rounded. He had seen monks such as him before, and they tended towards boniness. This one did not seem unusually well fed, and the lack of visible ribs was one more thing to trouble him.

Fairburne drew the cell door shut and locked it, then stepped back and regarded the man. "You were no doubt expecting me," he said.

The sadhu said nothing, but only watched Fairburne keenly, a slight smile on his lips. Fairburne sighed. "Don't pretend that you can't understand me. You understand English as well as I do. Perhaps better."

"You are very perspicacious, captain," said the sadhu. "An unusually open mind for your race."

"I work with facts, and I go where they take me, no matter how unpalatable. When you say *race*, do you mean *white*, *English*"—he leaned against the wall opposite the cell—"or do you mean *human*?"

"*English*, to be specific. The English want everything in its place, and a place for everything. They do not deal so very effectively with anything that falls outside the norm."

Fairburne found himself thinking of DA-01 and its airship. "You may be selling us short on that last point."

He heard a clatter as someone tested the door to the cell block, then the thud of a kick against it. It seemed to make little headway against the heavy door, and Fairburne was grateful for the thoroughness of the fort's architects.

"They will get in, captain. You are only delaying the inevitable."

"Perhaps." His brow furrowed. "I recognise that voice. Sergeant Murdoch, isn't it?"

"I like the burr of it," said the sadhu. He spoke again, and his voice shifted, becoming very Home Counties in the process. "Perhaps you'd prefer this, old bean?"

"Oswald. Poor bloody Oswald. When did you take him?"

"He was snooping around. He'd have joined us sooner or later, anyway."

"Not by choice."

"Only I joined by choice, but change is always painful, and really, old man, it's all for the better. Once all humanity is joined as a single great mind, nothing will be beyond us; and so much will be left behind. Bigotry and prejudice are impossible when every man, woman, and child shares every thought and experience."

"And what of the individual?"

"Overrated," said the sadhu in the voice of Colonel Aspern. "Really, Fairburne, you only cherish individualism because it's all you've ever known. Don't be such a dry stick. All art, all science, all *thought* in a single mind, a whole world of Renaissance men and women."

"Sounds utterly stultifying. History is built on the backs of great men, and you'll have rather a shortage of them."

"It is built on the backs of the nameless, and 'great men' take the credit. That will be a thing of the past. *All* shall be great. All shall be humble. All shall be equal."

"Some more equal than others, I notice. Your vegetarianism leaked to the others, but I bet you don't have any sudden desire to tuck into roast beef."

The thuds against the door were getting louder and more rhythmic. The corridor beyond was deliberately designed to be too narrow to allow a battering ram, but it was still only a matter of time, and Fairburne was running out of it. He regarded the revolver in his hand; he would have to bring matters to a head soon, but first, there was something that he needed to know.

"The creatures... those obscene little twelve-legged things. Where did they come from?"

"You would not understand."

"A wise man once told me that I'm very perspicacious. Try me."

"Colonel Aspern wished to divert the river to supply the garrison, did you know that?" Hearing Aspern spoken of in his own voice was disconcerting, but Fairburne ignored the unpleasantness of it and listened. "The village would have to move, but that did not concern him. The villagers were just dirty peasants. Why should an English colonel worry about their welfare in their own country? They came to me, but I had no wisdom to impart, no advice that might turn aside men with guns and explosives. Perhaps I allowed hatred into my heart. I do not know. I meditated at length and then, one night, my mind went somewhere it never had before. A space between moments. There are no words to describe the truth of it, in English or Hindi. The creatures live there, along with many other things far less pleasant or friendly."

"Friendly?" Fairburne couldn't keep the contempt from his voice.

"They are"—his voice became Cole's, the garrison's medical officer—"symbiotic creatures. Beneficent parasites. We give them warmth, security, and nutrients, and they give us unity. Every mind joined. Why cannot you see the glorious future they offer?"

"Perhaps I don't want a crab in my head."

"And yet the British never tire of speaking of how they are beneficent parasites in the lands they claim for Empire. The difference is that *we* are not lying."

Fairburne started to answer, but something prevented him. The banging at the door, perhaps; too little time to think of an answer.

"You're the core of all this." He levelled his pistol at the sadhu. "I dislike killing an unarmed man, but in a sense"—he glanced at the cell block door, where the men were becoming frantic—"you're not, are you?"

The sadhu only smiled. "You don't even know my name."

"Whatever it was, I don't think you deserve it anymore."

"Then perhaps I need a new one." When he spoke again, it was as a chorus of voices, Aspern, Oswald, Beddoes, Dickens and every other man in the fort. It roared, dark and crackling, so filled with humanity as to be inhuman: **"I am Legion."**

Fairburne fired. He was an excellent shot, the light was good enough, and the range was short. The bullet took the sadhu in the forehead, aimed to kill the creature in his skull along with the human brain behind it. The man rocked back on the bunk, his legs splaying out, his head hitting the wall, his mouth falling open. After a moment, he smiled. Fairburne could only stare as he started to laugh in the voice of dozens. Beyond the cell block door, the laughter was taken up, echoing insanely.

Fairburne took a sharp breath to pull himself together. His options had suddenly become very limited. He had trusted the gun to do what was necessary and now... Four bullets. These were his options. Three for the sadhu, and the last... Well, no creature would ever nestle inside *his* skull while he still had a live round in is gun.

He fired again, this time to the left of the sadhu's brow. Another solid hit that seemed to break the man's skull. His face distorted, planes shifting erratically beneath the skin, but the smile only grew more sinister.

Fairburne fired a third time, and the sadhu's face collapsed, like crockery in a cloth bag. Fairburne stepped up the cell bars, and fired his fourth bullet. The sadhu's head split open.

The pale, silvery shells of the creatures glistened slickly

in the yellow light of the lantern as they tumbled from the man's destroyed flesh. There were dozens of them, *hundreds*, spilling across his torso as the split extended and widened across his jaw, tearing down the side of his neck and across his chest. The man ceased to be a man, reduced to a paper mannequin stuffed with the loathsome alien life that now poured from him in a torrent. They fell to the floor in an abhorrent flood, scrambling to their thousands of feet, and swept in a tide across the concrete floor towards him.

Fairburne had his solitary last bullet, which clearly wasn't going to be nearly enough. But—somehow—he still had his wits, *and* he had a lantern. Without hesitation, he dashed it to the ground, leaping back as the liberated paraffin slicked across the floor to meet the oncoming horde, a pale flame travelling along its back. The creatures paused at the first touch of the liquid, and scurried back as the fire arrived in its wake. Behind them, the flesh casing of their colony unravelled and slumped across the bunk.

Fairburne ran to gather more lanterns—three of them, four—and found the can of spirit with which they were charged. He threw it all into the spreading fire at the end of the corridor, feeding it with sticks of furniture from the guard post and bedding from the other cells until the paint blistered and the cell bars glowed. He bore it as long as he could, the heat and the smoke, before unbarring the main door and stumbling out into a corridor full of unconscious soldiers.

*   *   *

JANDA HAD GONE to the bungalow to speak to Fairburne, and there found an unconscious Beddoes. After making him comfortable, Janda made his way to the fort to seek medical assistance, only to find the sentries also comatose. No fool he, Janda helped himself to one of the sentries' rifles and made his way inside, discovering what seemed to be the whole of the garrison in a stupor as he went. Scenting smoke, he followed his nose and finally happened upon Captain Fairburne trying to waken Lieutenant Oswald.

"What has happened here, Captain Fairburne?" he said as he rushed to help.

Fairburne glanced warily at him. "If I told you, you'd have me thrown into the madhouse."

Janda snorted, unimpressed. "'There are more things in heaven and earth,' captain, 'than are dreamt of in your philosophy.' An Englishman wrote that, yet was there ever such a race as the English for ignoring that truth?"

He helped Fairburne carry Oswald to the sick bay, where they put him on a bed.

"The sadhu's dead," said Fairburne. "To be frank, I think he's been dead a while."

With great reluctance, but because he felt he ought, he told Janda of his experiences. His tale was helped by Janda plainly already knowing many elements of it, including—vitally—the captured creatures in the jars. This eased Fairburne greatly; it was good to be of one accord. As he finished, Oswald stirred and sat up abruptly.

"Oh, my giddy aunt. Oh, what—?" He lay back down and groaned. "They've gone."

"You're free now, Oswald," said Fairburne. "I destroyed the colony."

"Free." Oswald sighed. "I'd never felt freer in my life. More part of *something* greater than myself in every respect." He closed his eyes. "Oh, God. You haven't freed any of us, sir. You've put us back into lifetime solitary, confined to our own skulls. Would it have been so awful to let it continue? All of Earth, every human soul sympathetic to every other one. No hatred, no war, no cruelty. Just think on it."

"At the cost of individuality."

"No. We were still ourselves. Just... better." He looked up. "How can I make you understand? Tell me this, why do you do what you do? Why do you defend the Empire?"

Fairburne frowned, not liking the question at all. "Because I'm a patriot."

"My country, right or wrong?"

"If you like."

Oswald laughed, a small, bitter sound, full of ash and longing. "And yet you speak of individuality."

ALL THE MEN recovered—physically, at least. In the ensuing weeks, six of them committed suicide. Fairburne preferred to think it was because of what the sadhu had given them. The unpalatable alternative was that it was because of what Fairburne had *taken* from them. Post mortems showed nothing attached, nor any damage to the pre-frontal lobes, but for twelve tiny, inconsequential scars.

Fairburne's assignment to DA-01 became permanent; he

learned the code referred to a department with the wilfully anodyne name of the "Department of Antiquities." He also learned that the civil service mandarins that knew of it referred to it smirkingly as "The Strange Brigade." He could understand why.

On his return to London, Fairburne asked to see the captured creatures. He was shown the jars. All unopened, all sealed. All empty. It seemed the creatures had returned to "the space between moments." He wondered if they would stay there. After all, now they knew the way.

"More things in heaven and earth," Janda had said, and such things were the meat and drink of the Brigade, such as it was. *So be it*, thought Fairburne.

A new set of orders arrived at his desk. He opened them with neither enthusiasm nor trepidation.

Iraq.

THE PROFESSOR'S DILEMMA
TAURIQ MOOSA

PROFESSOR DE QUINCEY rarely allowed others to use his first name, but here was a man who had a right to. A man he begrudgingly respected and hated, loved and loathed, standing here in De Quincey's office in Queen's College as if it belonged not to De Quincey but to the old man himself. The towering figure sniffed at De Quincey's drafts for the professor's newest book on the reigns of Khentkawes I, Nefertiti and Cleopatra.

"Archimedes—you really believe Khentkawes was a pharaoh in her own right?" The old man spun so his back was to De Quincey, and from some invisible pocket withdrew a pipe De Quincey had hated since childhood. Immediately, De Quincey opened his desk drawer, retrieving a clean ashtray, then opened a window.

Clearing his throat, De Quincey said: "Please."

The old man squinted his eyes at the book spines, biting down hard on the pipe stem, muttering to himself. He jumped, after a few moments, and turned. "What? It's a controversial position. We debated this with Cambridge…"

"No, the ashtray. Please use the ashtray." De Quincey twisted his mouth and nodded at the ashtray he'd placed on a table beside the visitor's couch. He stood, waiting for the other man to respond.

"Hm, well. I've barely started, you know." The old man began fishing for his matches.

De Quincey extended his arms. "Well, I'm not going to be interrogated on the book, when the publishers…"

"No, I mean, I've not begun smoking." The old man smiled without looking up. His perfectly round glasses enlarged his grey eyes, and his receding hair enlarged his forehead, while wisps of a beard poked out from his thick coat collar.

"Yes, well…" De Quincey cleared his throat. "Do you want to sit, or do you plan on staring down the spine of my entire library?"

"This?" barked the old man. "*This* is your entire library?"

"No, of course not." De Quincey breathed out slowly. "Now, to what do I owe this… visit? I have a class in ten minutes."

"Ah, the students never cared if I was late. They found it charming." The elder professor smiled, still not meeting the younger man's eyes. Without looking, he struck a match with one hand. The flame went to the pipe and seemed to disappear at once. Smoke and the sour smell of Southern Leaf filled the tiny office, as De Quincey tried not to breathe.

De Quincey's orderly office held only two seats: one behind his desk and one larger couch for visitors. Both were custom made from leather De Quincey had chosen years before. Small lanterns burned in the corners, as winter chill stirred the leaves of his one arrowhead vine. Snows, some said, would come early this year.

De Quincey sat behind his desk, scratched his chin and tapped the armrest with one finger. The other man could not be rushed for explanation.

"I hear you're taking another trip." The old man finally looked at De Quincey, smoke clouding his face. "Who will you be digging up this time?"

De Quincey pinched the bridge of his nose and sighed. "Iddin-Dagan."

"Dagan!" squawked the older man, followed by a cough. The smoke briefly cleared. "You're going after Sumeria, again? Are you chasing Langdon's delusions, or your own?"

"I am chasing no delusions!" De Quincey stood and shot to nearby smaller cabinet, ripping it open, grabbing fistfuls of paper and slamming them down on his main desk. "I have funding, support, approval." He nearly added *all the things you never gave me*. "I am going."

The old man leaned back, nodding.

De Quincey's flat hand trembled slightly on the completely blank pages he had withdrawn from the desk.

"To class? I wasn't finished—"

"*On the trip*. I'm going on the trip."

"Very well." The old man rose and the smoke trailed after him, as if he were a dragon prowling through his lair. His teeth clenched tightly around the pipe, until he pulled it out and pointed it at De Quincey. "I know about your fool's errand and your refusal to see the world as I do. You think this"—he spread his arms and gestured at the room—"is it." His leathery, callused hands knocked De Quincey's table. "You think what you can see and touch is all there is to the world."

"Enough. I will not entertain your foolish beliefs." De Quincey had no need to raise his voice; he'd said it a thousand times before.

"You think I would leave it all behind because of 'foolish beliefs'!" The pipe's stem was now jutting at De Quincey's face. The smell was nauseating. "You think I would toss away my life's work, what I'd built from nothing..."

He fell into silence, shaking his head and turning.

"I am going," De Quincey repeated, slowly scooping the papers back into the drawer. "I always go. I simply do not agree with you. I *cannot*. We are meant to be men of science, yet you enter my office with..."

"*My* office!" roared the old man. His turned on his heel quickly, his thick cloak billowing out. He stood by the desk. "This was *my*... office."

"*Was*... yes," De Quincey said, fighting back a smile. "Like Dagan, you're the past. However, unlike Dagan, I have no interest in your views." The old man drew away, his face unchanging. "You gave up what you built because of your beliefs in... *more*." De Quincey nearly spat the word.

"There is more, son. There *is*." The old man sucked on his pipe and turned.

"*She's not coming back*." The words were harsher than De Quincey intended, shocking even him. He couldn't see the old man's face. With one more puff of smoke, the old man walked away, disappearing into the gloom.

THE HOUSE GROANED in the night. Mist swirled in the courtyard. A long-unused fountain dripped dead leaves, while a tree creaked and hacked the moonlight with its bare branches. The gate tapped closed, then opened, but not loud enough to disturb anyone—it was located far away from the house itself, and too distant from any street. If you were to walk through the gate, to the front door, your feet would knock stones and twigs, leaves would enter your socks—not that the grounds were unattended, but more that the wind had a particular fondness for dumping its contents around the grounds. With the moon behind it, the house was barely lit, its white walls gleaming dully. All the windows were dark except for one light on the first floor.

The old man wrote furiously, a single oil lamp burning on the corner of the table. He was muttering to himself, occasionally having to steady the inkpot to keep from spilling.

On the floor, other pages were scattered and heaped, filled with writing on both sides—sometimes even in the margins. Some contained symbols and words long forgotten to the world, whether through mere passage of time or deliberate efforts of those who knew their power.

The scratching of the pen filled his ears. He needed to finish his task: the boy must know, must believe, must *see* what is at stake. Scratching, forever scratching, cutting at the world presented to him because he refused to think *this was it*. Science was once a map on which the old man would navigate the world, dipping his hands in its waters to know more. Now it had become a shroud, hiding what lay beneath, hiding a greater truth. He needed to scratch through it. There was more.

Science could be a bridge, too. He was too steeped in the discipline to discard it. Had they not extended lives and cured ailments through science? What was death but another ailment deserving scientific scrutiny? And would not the ancient world have found all sorts of ways, with their various forms of genius, to combat the greatest sickness of all? He could not believe that societies that could create pyramids and chart the entire world had not found or stumbled into domains those too narrow-minded would think were "supernatural." These ancient ones who put divinity alongside physics, gods alongside geography, were not so trapped by conceptual divisions. The problems of the gods were the problems solved by science.

He wanted that to happen again. He needed it to.

He found fear rather than reason from his colleagues. Or so he wanted to believe. Needed to believe.

Scratching. Scratching.

He stopped, hearing a voice. And the voice, new but familiar, began whispering...

* * *

DE QUINCEY CLEARED the chalk board. Students were slowly leaving the lecture hall, clutching their books. He scratched his chin, feeling the stubble growing, looking at the problem before him. On it, he had written *Nefertiti* and drawn a long line to *Dagan*. He had been trying to convince his class that, contrary to what many of his esteemed colleagues believed, Nefertiti had been a ruler in her own right. Her husband, Akhenaten, had died; but De Quincey firmly believed that she was, in herself, a highly accomplished, capable leader.

De Quincey was not some radical activist—he had little time for politics. Yet he was accused of being a radical, in proposing that any woman of the ancient world had ever had power rivalling a man's.

He heard a throat clear behind him. "Professor De Quincey?"

He turned to face a large bearded man, with jowls that would make a bulldog jealous. His coat was white with snow. He removed his hat to reveal curly grey hair, and a thick moustache bristled beneath a large nose, atop which sat perfectly round glasses.

"Yes?" De Quincey put down the chalk, automatically put on his Smile for Strangers, and dusted his hands.

"Good afternoon, professor. I hope I'm not interrupting some, er, some kind of formula?" Even from a distance, De Quincey couldn't help stare at the man's large hands, now gesturing at the board behind him.

"Ah, don't worry. The point of writing it down is so you don't forget it." He stepped from behind the large lecture desk. "Sorry, but who did you…"

"My manners. I'm Inspector Warren." The two men shook hands fiercely. "I'm sorry to meet you under these circumstances, but I figured it would be better to come and ask you the questions myself."

De Quincey's brain moved through the man's position to questions. "I'm... I'm sorry. Questions about...?"

Warren blinked at him. "Your father, sir. His... disappearance?"

De Quincey frowned. "I saw my father only last week."

Warren licked his lips and cleared his throat. "My apologies, sir. But... I'm sorry, has no one informed you? This... I—"

"My father is very old, Inspector, and known for his vanishing acts. I'm surprised his nurse didn't tell you."

"She's dead, sir."

De Quincey felt the world slip beneath him. He took several sharp breaths and grabbed the side of a desk. The lights in the lecture theatre seemed, suddenly, only to extend the gloom, instead of creating the comfort he was so used to. He felt a slow, creeping shiver.

"...of the crime, though no money was missing." De Quincey realised Warren was talking, or rather reading. The man had not yet noticed De Quincey's sudden discomfort. "So we—Oh, my, professor, are you quite well? I'm sorry for this news."

"No, please, continue. You say Sarah is dead?"

"I'm afraid so, sir. I'm afraid this doesn't appear to be a burglary gone wrong, as I indicated. The body was... well. I suppose it'll be in the news, anyway: It was vicious. Very vicious. We've seen that kind of viciousness before and we suspect... well, there may be a pattern, were it not for the fact that your father is missing."

"Do you think he...?"

"I'm afraid I can't say much, sir. We are concerned for his whereabouts, naturally. Right now we mainly just want him for questioning. I'm afraid I can't go into much more than that."

De Quincey tried to breathe.

"Alright, let's go through this... slowly." De Quincey looked around. "I have a half an hour until my next class. Please won't you come to my office."

After showing him through the dusty halls, dodging students and other faculty members, the two men arrived at De Quincey's office. He tried to shove tea at the inspector, providing an opportunity to do something with his hands.

"I apologise again for being the one to bring this to your attention, professor." The other man took the cup in his hands, leaning back in the old couch, making the leather squeak. De Quincey waved his hands.

"Please. It is not your fault it happened. I... I just find it strange I wasn't informed earlier. A week, you say?"

"Yes." The detective sipped the tea and De Quincey realised he had not asked about milk or sugar. Too late now, and the other man didn't pass comment. He looked back at De Quincey through steamed glasses. "Though, forgive me for saying, I had heard you and your father were not on speaking terms." De Quincey didn't know whether to interpret this as accusation or not—or indeed whether the observation was of a criminal or familial nature. He had never been the best son.

"He and I never quite saw... eye to eye." De Quincey walked to his desk, sitting down and nursing his tea.

"Even though you took over his old position? My father would be ecstatic if I'd stayed at the factory..."

"It was never *his* position," snapped De Quincey. "Plenty of great professors came before him and many came after." The other man touched his mouth and looked down. De Quincey closed his eyes, focusing on breathing. "What I mean is... today, my father would not be caught dead near an institution that so dedicated itself to science."

The sound of pen scratching filled the room, and for once, it was not De Quincey.

"I have to ask... what does this have to do with my father's disappearance?"

"As I'm sure a man of your intelligence knows," Warren said, pointing at him with a pen, "knowing more about an individual helps you locate them. After all, isn't that how you managed to uncover..." Warren flipped through another little book De Quincey hadn't noticed before. "Ur?"

"Ur was an ancient city, not a person," De Quincey said, clasping his hands together. "And, no, I didn't *discover* it. I found artefacts there, true, but Ur is not mine."

"The point is," Warren said, shrugging, "information helps discovery, whether it's ancient cities or elderly academics."

"Very well." De Quincey sighed. "What else can I help you with? And who exactly is looking for my father, while you are questioning me in his old office?"

"I'm not the only person assigned to this case, professor. Given the brutal murder's pattern to... other cases you may have seen in the news, it is of high significance to the higher ups." Even De Quincey's unconscious provocation withered before Warren's focus. He was nothing if not persistent, a quality De Quincey had tried to foster in his own students and colleagues.

After finding out about De Quincey's whereabouts and more information on his father, the inspector finally stood up, thanked him and left, muttering apologies for the inconvenience and sympathies for his father's disappearance. De Quincey remained seated after the other man had left. He stared out at his empty office. On the other wall hung a ragged map of a part of Egypt De Quincey knew well, from old expeditions. This map, a copy of a copy of a copy, from a time long passed. Writing, in a jagged script something like cuneiform, coiled around the corners, though mostly lost where the cloth had tattered. His father had put it there; as a boy, he would often enter the old man's office and find him staring at it.

De Quincey squinted. He stood up slowly, making his way toward it. Something was off about this giant unfurled map—a map that had haunted him since he'd entered this office years ago, as its new occupant. He had never been able to remove it, for reasons he had not fully understood. But today something... itched. Like noticing the hour hand had moved on a clock.

He put his face close to the glass. In the corner of the map, ink and writing. De Quincey leaned in close, his breath steaming the glass. His eyes widened as he recognised his father's terrible handwriting:

Find me.

H*E GOT TO* his father's house.

De Quincey looked up at the quiet, empty family house. His mother gone, his father missing. He couldn't tell how long the police had remained and investigated, but he wanted to return. It was to be his house: his mother had left it in her will to him. While his father had been raised in wealth and lost it to habits and vices, his mother—with her dark skin and unspoken history—had created wealth from ashes in a world that made barriers of her race and gender.

He unlocked the front door, entering the cold, dark house. He immediately felt the damp. How long had the house been left in this state?

He closed the door behind him and locked it. His mother had been almost obsessive about security, locking windows and doors, keeping blinds shut. The house was patrolled, and there was never even once an attempt at a break-in, but still he would find her peering intently through the blinds at night. It was only now that he thought maybe she'd not been afraid of burglars.

He lit a candle and began walking through the halls of childhood. The lounge area, with a fireplace that remembered only the ghost of flames; chairs covered in dust; a carpet that had not been straightened for some time. He tried to find lamps to light but saw only their skeletons, knocked to the ground. His mother never entered this room—this was the domain of his father, for entertaining guests. No, his mother dwelt elsewhere, making a life for the family.

He walked to the large doors on the other side of the floor. One of the ornately carved handles had fallen off, rolled into the darkness and never been put back. How long had it been since someone had been here? He turned the other handle, pushing at the wood, hearing its groan. Light poured into the next room with difficulty, struggling against spider-webs, overturned tables, books, lamps, clothes, maps, globes. It stumbled over statues and busts, stubbed its toe on a bookshelf and eventually dived into a dusty corner. He entered and slowly waved away the webs, raising his candle high to look at his mother's study.

Here. This was where she had crafted her legacy: the invisible woman creating a business empire, her great many ships traversing the world, staffed by the most skilled of workers.

A brown woman was not an entirely uncommon sight in England these days, but a brown woman who was not only married but seemed to rule over a white man was. Of course, his father had been the face of any business aspirations, and spoke on behalf of the hidden empire that grew in this study; but it was not his empire, but that of the woman rarely seen, with the hint of an accent no one could identify. De Quincey poked at the dust on the desk, wondering just how it had begun. How could a woman in this time achieve so much, yet still be regarded so little?

And now she was gone, lost after one of her many

voyages. An entire ship full of people, vanished to the sea, joining a long chorus of forgotten expeditions, swallowed by the tides of history.

Her legacy still floated to the top of his mind, however. Someone with so little, achieving so much.

This was central to his book on the woman-kings of Egypt, which his publishers did not like at all. Those who spend their lives digging into the past find themselves first compelled, not by knowledge of the world, but of themselves.

A sudden sound behind him made him turn. He squinted but could make little out in the gloom. "Hello?"

No one replied. He walked further, back down into the main hallway. It came again, this time from upstairs.

"Father?" He ascended the staircase, his light swinging across rotten portraits and old photographs. He avoided one broken stair that for decades they could never fix, due to 'foundations' and 'rot' and other terms that had a builder shrugging. Now he was on the first floor, curtain billowing, shadows stretching.

His father's bedroom. That was the source. His footfalls pounded like a heartbeat as he made his way forward. He opened the door and saw nothing, for a moment; then a shadow by his father's table. A shrouded figure started, scattering papers. Whoever it was, they had no lantern.

"Stop! Who are you? This is private property!" The figure froze, and De Quincey felt cold. He looked around and saw that parts of the room were wreathed in… fog? That wasn't possible. His breath misted in front of him. He reached his hand out and saw cold begin to take it.

He looked up, then, and the figure was gone. Only moonlight streamed in, covering his father's desk.

"Hello!"

He was sure there had been someone there. He walked to the desk. His father's large chair was slightly crooked—that's what it must've been. From a certain angle, a certain viewpoint, it had… what? Caused the room to get cold? The fog was gone; his breath no longer misted. It was the dark, and this room, and the memories. His confusion.

His father's messy desk had been this way since he had grown up. He wasn't sure how a man so disorganised had managed to obtain the respect and standing of a professor. His father had never been particularly talented at remembering names and dates; he was undisciplined; yet his proficiency with words, his ability to be amicable with every person of any background, race or gender, seemed to tide him through everything.

But looking at the desk now, it was not the messiness of a troubled intellect, but a frightened, desperate, lonely man.

Gone was the large, looping script he always knew, giving way to a hasty, crabbed scrawl. Letters and numbers and strange symbols seemed to dot every inch of a page. Different colours, different pens—and, it appeared, different hands? But why? He scooped up the papers, wondering why the police had not obtained them.

He took the steps downstairs two at a time. He stepped through the door and closed it.

* * *

SHADOWS FLOWED THROUGH London's gaslit streets, as horse-drawn carts echoed their way down cobbled roads. Mist swirled around the few people still outside on Fetter Lane at this hour, casting each in an effervescent cage. A figure moved purposefully down these streets, barely acknowledging others. It turned into a grimy building— one of the few well-lit on the street. Two men opened the large doors as the figure approached, and the newcomer swept into a large hall, bustling with papers, machines, people running and shouting. The bookcases lining the walls, reaching from floor to ceiling, would've made anyone immediately declare it a library, though that would've been an understatement.

She lowered her hood and cast about, looking for someone; people lowered their gaze or gaped as she swept by them.

She reached the woman she'd singled out.

"Has it been found?"

The other woman—Head of Archives, to use her formal title—took her time acknowledging Webster's presence. She raised her dark eyes and blinked slowly, but had evidently already concluded who the interloper was, why she was here and what her purpose was. "Yes... Lady Webster."

The accent took Webster by surprise. She'd worked with foreigners her entire life, but had not expected one in this post. "Where?"

The woman jerked her head first toward a man standing close by, clutching three books and visibly sweating, then at a nearby map. It was only a few feet away from her—

closer to her than to the man himself—but she seemed unwilling to move from her spot and the man almost dropped his books in his hurry to bring the unfurled map to her hands. Webster half-expected him to bow. She rolled her eyes while the other woman unrolled the map and pointed.

Webster nodded. "As we suspected."

A nod. "We've lost contact with the crew I sent."

"How many days ago?"

"Five."

Webster sniffed. Too long. Too much depending on this.

"What are your orders?" asked the archivist.

Webster removed a glove, squeezing it. Moisture dripped on the carpet, splashing on some nearby papers. "Tell me what you know."

The other woman nodded, finally moving. "The crown was located thanks to the documents sent in last month. We took some time to decode the translations, but we had help from... a local contact." The woman looked away—someone she knew? Loved? Hated? Both? Webster didn't particularly care. "There is, however, a problem we've not been able to solve."

She led the way to an office as neat as the main hall was untidy, and closed the door behind them. Webster looked around, but the room gave away nothing about the occupant. Nothing was out of place.

"What is it?"

The woman had already begun flipping through files—she wasn't searching, Webster decided; she knew exactly where the documents were. The archivist pulled out a large folder and handed it to Webster, who untied the string and pulled out several papers.

"Professor Archimedes De Quincey?" Webster read, thumbing through the man's life. Impressive, for his age.

"He's writing a book on female leaders of ancient Egypt."

"So I see. What does this have to do with Dagan's crown?"

"De Quincey thinks he's found it, and is flying over in the next few days to retrieve it. In fact, he already has a group digging through the location he's marked."

Webster sighed. "I suspected as much when you said he was a problem." She put the folder on the desk and pointed. "What I want to know is, why is he looking for it?"

The woman sat in her chair and rocked back on it. "De Quincey has a knack for finding objects his superiors want. I... I don't think he even cares about the crown. He just needs funding for his book."

Webster had to blink. Funding. He just wants *funding*? "So why have we not reached out? We have the money."

"As you have surmised, Lady Webster," the archivist said, leaning forward and touching the folder with one finger, "he is not dim. If a random benefactor comes out the blue to give him money, he'll know we're paying him off. His curiosity is a tiny flame now; we would fan it into a bonfire. He would tear apart the world to know why. That's his job, after all." She sniffed.

"So what do you propose? You appear to know the man well."

The woman ignored the probe. "He won't be bought off. I think he should be brought in."

Lady Webster closed her eyes for a moment. Recruitment was not something she'd expected to think about this month. Another one for the Department? A stuffy, vest-wearing *professor*, no less?

"I disagree." Lady Webster stared at the file. "He must be reasoned with. He would jeopardise our operations. Besides, we simply don't need him."

"He has a great mind."

The drone from outside barely filtered into the office, but now Lady Webster felt it closing in around her. Despite their respective positions, the woman was not one to knuckle under—she needed to be persuaded, or Webster would make an enemy for life. Webster respected that, but this was protocol, and protocol existed for a reason.

Still, pushing would be as good as yelling. This woman's guard was already up; it would become a wall of spikes and thorns if Webster challenged her further.

"I agree... about his mind. We must take care, then; employ diplomacy. Still, I must disagree on recruitment."

"I'm sure you could convince Broadway—"

"Nothing to do with them. *I* won't allow it."

The archivist stood up quickly. "He won't be stopped. It would only raise more questions that you could not answer."

Webster was taken aback; the woman was talking to her as an equal, and she found herself, grudgingly, respecting her all the more. But something else was at work here.

"Who *is* he to you?"

The woman stared back, blinking but impassive as stone. She closed her eyes and breathed in. "That's irrelevant, Lady Webster."

"It's my job to determine what is and isn't relevant and act," Webster said, tapping the desk.

The door burst open and a man nearly fell over Webster. "Reports. Another attack."

The other woman flew around her desk, snatched the papers. "Where?"

The man, breathing hard, said, "Oxford."

DE QUINCEY PORED over the documents from his father's desk. Now and then a word or phrase would jump out, then fly away. He followed the text with his left hand, and jotted down his interpretation with his right. Cuneiform, Latin, Arabic: the cultures blended and clashed, obscuring his father's contention and drive. He noted strange runes and patterns, and traced them with his hand. He muttered them awkwardly, in languages he had barely understood years ago, and even less now. Speaking out loud helped him make sense of what he was reading.

He soon realised, though, that he had gained no sense of what it *meant*. It was like a code.

It *was* code. He began noticing faint traces of symbols throughout the pages, and set back to it, trying to identify the symbols, to identify a pattern.

Eventually, he sat back and sighed. He had papers to mark, lectures to prepare. This was a futile. He figured he was trying to assuage his guilt at abandoning his father, for letting him rot in a dying house. The police were investigating; what use was an archaeologist?

He rubbed his eyes and looked about the room, then froze. He slowly rocked forward, chair creaking as it hit the floor. Both hands on the desk, he leaned forward, staring at his father's ancient map. The old man's writing was still there, but now, in this light, he noticed something else in the reflection. He turned his head slightly, squinting; the window.

He got up, chair scraping, and went to touch the glass. Someone had drawn on the window in ink, he couldn't tell how recently. The pattern was similar. He turned and looked at the map. The shadows cast by the symbols fell onto a specific place he had long known about, one he knew intimately, one he was soon returning to.

He grabbed the papers again and muttered the names of what he saw. "Shadow.... Memory... heart... stone and god... lives lost... regained... grant me... the vision... to see."

He looked back at the map. That was it.

That was where his father was.

As he returned to his desk, he heard a noise outside in the hall. At first he didn't recognise it, but it grew louder, resolving into a scream. A long, unrelenting scream, rising in intensity. He watched in horror, through his office windows that looked into the corridor, as another professor ran past. He heard another sound now, another scream—no... a *howl*. Something was in the hallway, and it was coming closer.

He dove behind his desk and peered out.

He heard feet padding down the passage, slowly. He could see… smoke? Two thin plumes rising up, but they were moving. Then sniffing. A dog?

No. Something else.

His door burst in as the creature quivered on the threshold, snarling and spitting. He peered carefully from his desk, but wasn't quite sure what it was in the gloom. He stopped trying to see, moved back completely behind his desk, breathing, not daring to move. Fear gripped him, like a trap around his ankles. He focused on listening instead of looking now.

He heard the heavy footfalls drawing closer; his breathing seemed suddenly the loudest thing in the world. It neared the corner of his desk…

Footsteps, outside in the corridor. The creature's head snapped around and it ran out into the corridor, howling. Then there was nothing but silence.

What had he just seen?

HE WAS HOLDING a steaming cup of tea when Inspector Warren found him amid a gaggle of police officers. Squeezing his way through, he gently touched De Quincey on the shoulder.

"Good God," he boomed. "What a mess. How are you, professor?" He wasn't looking at De Quincey when he asked, but then, De Quincey wasn't looking at him either.

"I'm fine, thank you. Just frightened. Can someone tell me what happened?"

They were all in one of the common rooms. Some students

emerged from wherever students disappear to, clutching books and papers. He thought he recognised one of his own, though he could never really tell them apart.

"It looks like some kind of rabid creature got in," Warren said. "Unfortunately got one of your night watchmen. His name was Henry... did you know him?"

De Quincey did not want to seem insensitive—it didn't seem appropriate to tell Warren he could barely tell his own colleagues apart, let alone staff—so he just nodded. "I think so, yes."

Warren pinched his lips, still looking down the bloodied hallway. People were kneeling over patches of blood and body parts and the smell was becoming overwhelming. De Quincey went to stand, but Warren gently pushed him down.

"Sorry, professor," he said. "I'm afraid I am going to need some more details from you."

"What?" De Quincey barked. "I told... you people everything I know. Do you think I had a hand in killing some watchman I don't even know?"

Warren finally looked at him. "I thought you said you knew him?"

De Quincey blinked, cursing himself. "Yes... no. I think I did? Look, why would I... can I go?"

Warren turned to a nearby officer. They muttered things to each other, Warren jerking his head toward De Quincey. The other officer nodded and walked away with determination.

"Very well," Warren said. "Officer Addison is going to go ahead of you and check your home, make sure everything is okay."

"My home? What does this have to do with my home? Just what is going on here?"

Warren looked around nervously, and De Quincey realised everyone was staring at him. He had been shouting without realising it.

"Professor De Quincey, if you'd come with me..." Warren's voice was calm and De Quincey felt no accusation in it. It appeared Warren genuinely was concerned.

"Fine."

The two men walked outside, De Quincey yearning to smoke despite having avoided it for years. It was too close to his father, too close to being part of who that man was.

FROM A DISTANCE, Lady Webster and a few others watched two men leave the halls of the university. The police officer—she guessed—was a bear of a man, all hair and ears and eyebrows. The man next to him was obviously the professor. His eyes were distant, his skin pale and his clothes a mess. He had clearly been through some kind of horrific event. He clutched his coat as a child would its blanket. How could she ever recruit someone like this to the Brigade?

"He's stronger than he seems," the archivist said to her, as if reading her thoughts. Another man whispered into the woman's ear. "One of our informants in the police say it's a possible Ripper attack. That's two in Oxford alone."

There was the name no one wanted to speak of: Ripper. The infamous killer that had stalked the streets of London decades before seemed to have returned: the brutality, the butchery, the complete lack of evidence. Only Webster and her colleagues had managed to prevent the news leaking out wider, stopping anyone making the connections.

At the time, they had furnished the press with fake evidence—it was someone in the Royal family, a doctor, a police officer, to list just a few—and the glut of data had simply overwhelmed the hounds. They hadn't allowed the public to focus on any one suspect, and thus no one could grasp the truth. The attacks themselves eventually stopped, before the Department had worked out who—or rather, *what*—the Ripper was. She wasn't sure it had returned, but she would not be surprised.

If it was indeed the Ripper, the question was, why now? And why De Quincey? Whatever it meant, her organisation still had to cover it up. This could not get out. Explanations were necessary. Thankfully, her people in Scotland Yard had already garnered the necessary evidence for investigation, replacing them with their own narrative pieces: a wild animal of some kind. A dog? A wolf?

De Quincey got into a carriage and was off. She needed to know why De Quincey was attacked.

BEFORE HE COULD get into his own house, he had to wait while men combed through his office, bedroom and cellar. His house was modest, a mid-terrace that displayed bricks more than paint. Still, it was cleaner than most spaces and the neighbours kept to themselves. He had a tiny garden, but otherwise it was an unremarkable little house—all narrow angles and crooked walls. He had no time for repairs until it was necessary.

He spent most days either at the university preparing for digs, or out in the field. His home was where he slept—when he slept—and stored his clothes.

He actually *preferred* working at home, despite the endless books, sources and so on at the university. Home afforded him privacy—just him and the dead, ground to dust by history and waiting for him to reach in and retrace their stories.

Warren stood by him, watching the men complete their search.

"Be assured, professor, officers are patrolling this and other neighbourhoods for your protection."

De Quincey looked at him. "That's a lot of work for just some wild animal."

Warren sniffed. "We're not sure it was, yet."

"'Not sure'? I *told* you what I saw. Is this why you're searching my house? You doubt my story?"

A shout from one of the other men signalled to Warren it was safe, and the inspector turned to the professor and waved to the steps. The two men ascended.

Once inside, De Quincey began shutting doors and windows, muttering about the cold. Warren nodded and waited patiently. After a few minutes, the archaeologist made tea for both of them, and they sat down in his small sitting room.

"Lovely home you have," Warren said, looking around.

"Tell me. What's happening?"

Warren nodded. "We've seen this type of killing before."

"I see."

"A few years back. My superiors are not convinced it is a habitual killer, let alone the return of one that might not have existed, but I have my suspicions. They want very strict definitions of what constitutes a serial killer, you see. We don't want the public in a panic."

"Well, I'm not exactly calm." De Quincey looked around. "I felt targeted. It was looking for me."

"The dog?"

"The... dog, yes. The hound. Whatever it was."

"Yes, sir." Warren conveyed nothing but patience.

De Quincey looked at Warren for a while, slowly setting his cup down. "It's clear you don't believe me, Warren..."

"Now, sir..."

De Quincey held up a hand. "And yet you still post guards outside my door?"

Warren sighed. "Just because I don't believe events happened just as you said, doesn't mean I think you're out of danger. Until I know for sure what's happening, I need you to be safe."

"Very well."

The men sat in silence for some time before the police officer left, leaving Archimedes in his lounge with the soft light of afternoon fading into twilight. He eventually got up and went to his cramped study. He picked up his notes and decided to throw himself into work rather than worry. He pushed aside papers until he saw the outline of the crown of Dagan, roughly drawn by his own hand but nonetheless an impressive depiction by any measure.

He sat down. He began plotting the dig and trying to

forget that there was perhaps someone or something trying to get him, for reasons he could not understand. What would someone want—

"—WITH AN ARCHAEOLOGIST?" one of Lady Webster's younger assistants asked.

She raised an eyebrow at the head archivist, who ignored both her and the question. "It doesn't matter. We must get to him soon."

The young man nodded and whistled to the horses. The carriage was essentially invisible amidst the sea of carriages, all black and damaged. The horses' hooves sparked on the cobbles as they drove to De Quincey's home. The two women sat in silence almost the entire way.

"Are you sure you do not wish to tell me more about who he is to you?"

The other woman stared out the window. "That would take up unnecessary time, Lady Webster. Time, I believe, neither you nor he has. Perhaps one day."

Lady Webster nodded. She would have better luck drawing milk from sunlight.

Arriving at De Quincey's home, Webster, her team, and the archivist scouted the area to make sure it was secure. After a few words, the archivist disappeared back into the carriage, muttering something about important work elsewhere and a barely sarcastic mention of the Lady's abilities. Webster rolled her eyes, but let her go. Once satisfied that her people were hidden, Webster ascended the stairs and knocked on De Quincey's door.

* * *

IT FINALLY HIT him.

For hours, he had been looking at the drawing of the crown, and at the maps. Something wasn't sitting right. Now he realised he recognised the symbols: they were the marks he'd seen in his office.

The drawings were from old notes of his father's—the ones that had helped him trace the location of the crown to Iraq. He'd not mentioned them to his funders, lest they decide Mad Old De Quincey's ideas were too ridiculous to take seriously, but the younger De Quincey had been desperate—he needed progress to secure funding, and so had quietly been digging through his father's works for few years, trying to find anything substantial among the hodgepodge of nonsense and excitement and half-forgotten dreams. And he'd found the crown.

There was nothing particularly special about the crown, to his knowledge. Dagan barely registered on anyone's radar as worth the research. Sure, he had been called a God-King, but which king wasn't, at the time?

The notes and symbols were a mixture of languages, but between them they told a story. Where had his father even dug them up?

His personal library.

His father *hated* working at the university; he spent as much time as he could in his own study. De Quincey would have to return home, to find the books these symbols came from, to divine their meaning. Knowing his father, the key wasn't in the symbols themselves, but the books they came from—in them, he was sure to find—

There was a knock at the door. He blinked for a moment as reality came crashing back, and stood, his chair scraping—he hadn't even noticed sitting down again, he'd been stomping around the room, a habit from his student days. He walked to the door and yanked it open, only belatedly realising how dangerous that could be.

Before him, a hard-faced woman stared at him for a moment before turning and nodding to the dark. He registered movement in the shadows, and was suddenly confused and afraid.

"Professor De Quincey? Archimedes De Quincey?"

"Y-yes?" De Quincey's hand shook slightly, pressed flat against the door. "What's happening? Who are…?"

The woman almost slid into his house, barely touching him. The way she moved scared him more than it should—refined, graceful, yet there she was, already making herself comfortable in his lounge. He poked his head out the door, but saw nothing but mist. It didn't occur to him until later to wonder about the police patrol.

The door closed and he turned back to the lounge. He started repeating his questions, but she interrupted him.

"Don't go to Iraq, professor. You will die." The woman sat with her legs folded, showing well-worn but impressively sturdy boots. She was the most elegant person he had seen, and also appeared dressed for any battlefield.

"What? Who *are*—?"

"You are trying to find the crown of Dagan, and I am imploring you"—she leaned forward, hands pressed together, elbows resting on her knees, eyes probing—"drop it. Move on. We will fund your book. Ignore this one trip."

He closed his eyes, breathing out. "Please. Tell me who you are."

"You can call me Webster. I work for a branch of His Majesty's Government."

"Which branch?"

"I am... not at liberty to say at this time."

De Quincey had been dealing with government bureaucrats his entire life, but this was something new. He'd run into political issues, clashed with governments of foreign nations, travelled into civil wars, among people keen to convey their hatred of the colonial invaders—as much as he wanted to stay away from conflict, it was sometimes unavoidable.

He'd spent half his life digging, but he had never really wanted to take the artefacts. Not out of some moral duty or sense of compassion; they just weren't his to keep. For him, the acquisition of *knowledge* was the thing, not the trinkets he found on the way. This philosophy hardly gelled with his funders, though, who wanted things to touch and feel, who sometimes had dealings with the government themselves, who wanted riches and other nonsense to help secure power in the world.

Whatever was necessary for knowledge.

He told himself the knowledge would benefit the world, that there were bigger issues than vases or tombs. Some part of him knew it was wrong, but he'd never bothered to interrogate why—he'd leave that to his philosophy colleagues. He had books to fund.

"So I should just trust your word?" He folded his arms.

She smiled, though her cold eyes barely shifted. He blinked at the sheet of paper she was holding out, covered with familiar signatures and seals—he hadn't seen her produce it. He took it carefully, squinting at it. It signed by all his funders; his head of department, too. It indicated not only that he would still receive funding, but significantly more. More book deals, the possibility of tenure. His entire future outlined in carefully-worded governmentally-fuelled prose. Right there. Just sign. Any non-compliance would be regarded, not merely as a violation of the university's code of conduct, but as possible treason.

Treason?

"Yes," Webster said, though he hadn't said anything aloud. She was too perceptive; it threw him off. Who *was* this woman? "As I said, you may consider me a mouthpiece of His Majesty. Anything against my orders, at least in this matter, constitutes a violation."

He noticed she didn't say 'His Majesty's Government' like last time, but didn't correct her. He wasn't sure it was an omission. He didn't think she made mistakes.

He blinked at it rapidly, then returned it to her hands and looked away. Something bigger was at play here. Something buried and deep and large. Was he not tasked precisely with finding out what all this meant? For the world? Was it not his... *duty* to reveal such knowledge?

He would.

"I will." He forced a smile.

"Just like that?" She was still smiling, but he didn't think the pressure was off just yet. "That was... less difficult than I thought."

"Well," he said, taking the paper from her again and shaking it, "I doubt this was easy to obtain. Besides, digs are not my focus; the research is. Knowledge. My books. After all, I felt no attachment to the crown. It was a means to an end, and you have given me that end... and then some." He signed it and handed it back to her.

The woman stood quickly, that sureness again making him feel slightly anxious.

"I am pleased to hear it, professor." She shook his hand. "I bid you farewell."

And with that, she was gone.

He watched from his window as she disappeared into her carriage. Suddenly the police officers appeared, nodding to her and doffing their hats. The carriage disappeared.

As soon as she was out of sight, he sprinted upstairs and began packing.

WHEN HE ARRIVED at the dig in Iraq a few days later, he found his students sitting around restlessly. He kept mostly out of sight, but there was, as far as he knew, no magical technology to somehow detect his movements or his identity. Maybe there was—it wasn't his field. Who was to say what was possible? Those he dug up thought that light was magical, and the sun a god.

Marianne, perhaps his best student, had already set up the site for the dig. The students had begun digging around the edges—though "digging" was such a boorish way to convey the careful art of discovery. He rarely spoke to his students in class, and only little more when they travelled. He gave instructions where needed, but his chosen candidates were always competent enough not to need handholding. One doesn't enter the halls of Oxford if you're still expecting apron strings.

They spent days at the site, from first light to dusk. Eventually, a security detail arrived. At first he was afraid that whatever mysterious branch of government had harassed him had found him; but it turned out to be the local government, setting up blockades. He was being paranoid: he had some time before the university realised what he had done. After all, they had his plans and knew his movements. They would send someone.

ONE NIGHT, HE was suddenly awoken by a sound outside his tent. A silhouette gradually came into focus, lit by the moon. A fire blazed nearby, notes and papers flapping in the soft wind.

The shape took the form of a dog.

De Quincey grabbed his covers and recoiled. A sudden massive gust of wind tore open his tent and the roar of a beast exploded the night.

De Quincey felt himself rolling backwards, pain striking him in the forehead. The beast, wreathed in shadow and moonlight, slunk towards him, growling. He blinked blood and sweat out of his eyes.

Behind the creature, a shadowed figure had its arms raised.

"Destroy."

He wasn't sure where the word came from. It seemed to emanate from the rocks, from his own mind. He kicked his feet into the sand, scrambling backwards, feeling warmth on his head and hands.

"Professor!" He heard Marianne shouting. The creature closed in, and he watched as the security detail attempted to intervene. Blood was everywhere, screams. Someone kicked a lantern over and a fire blazed.

The creature moved through it all, a roaring, liquid darkness. De Quincey could barely see anything.

Suddenly it was on him. He screamed, raising his arm in defence, as the giant creature seized his arm in its mouth.

With his other hand, he grabbed a rock and stabbed it where he thought an eye would be. Even this close, he could barely understand what the creature was. It released him and backed off. He heard it bounding past him in the sand, more screams. It had found other targets.

Then he saw his father. He seemed older, paler. He stood in a long cloak, the wind sending ripples through the material. Blood covered his face, and in his right hand he held the crown.

"Sacrifice." His father's mouth didn't move.

He could not believe it. He *would* not. This was hocus pocus, nonsense! There *had* to be a scientific explanation.

"Father!" He tried to scream, but barely any noise came out.

He watched as his father's head exploded and the sound of a bullet richoted off a nearby rock. Suddenly, figures emerged from the shadows. He vaguely recognised Lady

Webster charging from the night, a blade in her hand. She knocked him down and the world went grey.

He watched as the newcomers slaughtered the beast; some went down, but the rest fought on, using strange weapons and... powers? He couldn't understand from his fuzzy vision.

With one last guttural cry, the beast died, and De Quincey fell into blackness.

THE HOSPITAL WAS hot, the bedsheets uncomfortable and the flies happy. He kept wanting to poke his wound, but an irritable nurse smacked his hand.

"No." That was her only English word, and he wasn't surprised it was all she needed.

He was in a cot, uncertain how long he'd been there. He could hear groaning from the other side of curtains, doctors rapidly walking back and forth. There were tubes in him, and bandages over parts of his body he'd long forgotten about.

Suddenly, the curtain was pulled aside. Lady Webster looked down at him, her hair unmade, sweat and blood covering her face. The nurse popped back and glared at her.

"No!" She pointed at him.

Lady Webster's expression was unchanged as she looked from De Quincey to the nurse, but the nurse suddenly shrunk, nodded and scampered off. Webster sucked her teeth, grabbed a nearby chair and fell more than sat. Her clothes were torn in some places and her boots scuffed, but her air of control never wavered.

"I *told* you, professor." She was dusting her gloves as she said this, the ceaseless drone of the medical facility throbbing around them. "I warned you not to come. I offered you the chance…"

"My father," he croaked. He reached for a nearby glass of water. She didn't help him, only watched as he struggled. He swallowed some water. His throat was on fire. "My father was there."

"Yes." She looked at him, her eyes narrowing. "You genuinely didn't know, did you?"

"How could I? He'd *disappeared!* He…"

"That he was possessed by the crown." She sat back.

"Possessed? How is that… It's… no. He was an old, sick man. I didn't—"

"In his desperation to bring back a wife he believed dead, your father delved into… areas he should not have. The crown was not originally a crown: it came a from a source we are still trying to understand. Call it magic, supernatural. Dagan made it his crown, but it was never really his. And when your father found it, it… awoke. Again. It whispered lies to your father. And it wanted blood. These things… these things always want blood. And yours, the son of its host, was the best kind. That is the way of magic and strange things…"

"Magic? You can't be…"

"Professor, there's a world out there you have seen, felt, *experienced* and yet refuse to acknowledge." She brought out the crown from somewhere, and he shrank from it. "Do not be afraid. It's useless now. Its power is gone."

"How could a crown…"

"You don't believe in the strange and the unexplained," she said. "Yet it comes. It comes with teeth and claws." She seemed to be speaking to herself. "Professor, I realise now I was foolish to think what you wanted was a book deal and tenure. That's not what drives you, is it?"

"I don't understand anything that's happening." He tried to sit up. "Who killed my father?"

"One of my men…" She finally looked at him. She stood up, placing the crown down carefully and leaned on his bed. "Professor. I ask you again: those material things. Those are not what drive you, is it? That's why you were willing to risk treason to come here, to dig, to find what you were told not to find. Why?"

"My father's dead and this… please. Let me be."

"You had no love for your father. You knew something was wrong." She stood up. "Face it. Look at me and tell me. Why?"

"I had to know!" he snapped. He sat up and felt a pain in his back, but he ignored it. "I had to know why! I wasn't going to be kept in the dark anymore! I will *not* be kept in the dark!"

She looked at him, his voice seeming to echo. Doctors and nurses looked over, then at each other. Some patients even stopped coughing.

Then slowly life returned and Webster smiled. "Yes."

"What is it you want?"

"Professor, you want answers? I can give them to you."

"How?"

"I want to offer you a job…"

NALANGU'S TRIALS
GAIE SEBOLD

NALANGU WAS ON her way back from fetching water when a slash of brightness caught her eye through the trees. She turned and saw glimpses of scarlet cloth and gleaming blades.

The young warriors were practising with their spears.

She moved closer. Surely it could do no harm just to watch, for a little.

The water in the container on her back sloshed reproachfully. Her mother would be waiting. *Just a little, just a little,* she told herself.

How the blades shone and stabbed. The men laughed and shouted insults, but this was serious business. The men with their weapons protected the people, and the cattle who were the wealth and gift and life of the people.

Nalangu felt a longing in her heart, and wondered what

she would do if a lion came for the cattle and something had taken all the men away; perhaps they were all sick, or gone to war. Perhaps one of them might have left a spear behind.

She imagined herself, standing between the lion and the precious cattle, holding her spear, the lion roaring and leaping and her spear *stabbing...*

But she did not have a spear. If such a thing happened she would have nothing to do but scream at the lion, and screaming was not much good with lions.

The strap around her forehead was making her head ache with the weight of the water, and there were many more chores to do today, but she kept watching. Something was wrong.

She knew every one of the warriors, they had been part of her world since she was born, but one of them... one of them was not *right*.

His face was familiar, but when she tried she could not put a name to it. It was just a face. It said, *I belong here,* but it lied.

The men leaned and turned, their backs to her, and *stabbed* forward.

And behind the wrong-face, hanging down, was an ugly hairy tail.

Nalangu gasped in breath, and clutched at the nearest tree.

Demon.

The men did not see it, they did not know it was there? What was she to do?

If she tried to tell them, they would laugh and tell her to

go help her mother. And the demon would know she had seen it and would come for her in the night.

Perhaps it meant to steal the cattle. Disguised as it was, that would be easy; it could walk one right out of the enkang. The thought gave her a cold fury. The cattle were *sacred,* given to her people by Engai's own will, every beast named and loved. The cattle were *life.*

No demon is going to take our cattle!

She clenched her hands. She had to tell someone. She could not tell her mother, her mother would be angry at her. Again. The obvious person was an oloiboni, a diviner, but there was none nearer than a day's walk away. Even if she could get permission to be out alone so long, what might the demon do before she got back?

She would speak first with yeyo Loiyan—who was kind and wise and knew almost as much about medicines as the oloiboni. Maybe she would know a medicine for this.

Nalangu moved away as stealthily as she could, so that the water she carried would not slosh and betray her, and as soon as she thought the demon would not hear her, she ran.

As she pelted through the enkang people cried out after her, laughing.

"Shake that water all you will, it won't make butter!"

"Hurry, hurry, your mother is waiting!"

"Yeyo, please, may I come in?" She said, panting, at the entrance of the hut. "It's Nalangu."

Loiyan came to the entrance. She was an old woman, very straight, with eyes as bright as an eagle's, her long earrings clicking against her broad beaded collar. She looked Nalangu over, beckoned her in, and gave her milk. "Now," she said. "Tell me."

Other than the door there was only one small opening at the back of the cooking area, to let light in and smoke out, but Nalangu could see Loiyan quite clearly. She did not look as though she were about to scold.

Nalangu took a deep breath. "I saw a demon. I stopped—" Nalangu unhooked the headband, and stood holding the water-carrier in her hands, lowering her head. "I stopped to watch the men practise with their spears, and I saw a demon."

For a moment Loiyan was silent. *Please, yeyo, believe me.*

"Put the water down and come sit with me," Loiyan said.

Nalangu did as she was told.

"Look at me, child. Is this a true thing you are telling me?"

"Yes, yeyo."

"Tell me what the demon looked like."

Nalangu did her best, though apart from the tail, it was hard. "It looked like all of them," she said. "It had no face of its own."

Loiyan said, "Wait here for me. If anyone comes in, you must say nothing of this. That is very important. You understand?"

"Yes, yeyo."

Nalangu sat smelling the comforting smells of milk and meat and leather and smoke, and the mud mixed with cattle-dung that made the roof and walls. Outside, people were laughing and arguing and building and carrying and mending, and the children who were too young for chores were running about and shrieking, and she felt strange and far away from all these things, knowing there was a demon out there.

Loiyan came back with a young woman called Nkasiogi, who was only a little older than Nalangu herself. She was quick and strong and often seemed angry.

"Tell her what you saw," Loiyan said. Nalangu did.

Nkasiogi did not look angry at Nalangu. Instead, she gave a hard fierce grin, and left the hut.

"Don't worry, child," Loiyan said. "There are people who know what to do about demons. Have you seen one before?"

"Not like that." Nalangu told her about the time she had seen a shadow that hovered about one of the cows, but had been too young to explain what she saw. The cow had gone mad and killed its calf. It had to be slaughtered, with swift brutality instead of the normal loving care and respectful ceremony. The whole enkang had been miserable over it.

"Yes, I remember that cow," Loiyan said. "That was very bad. And have you seen other things?"

"Yes."

"Why did you not tell anyone?"

"I told my mother, but..." Nalangu did not want to be disrespectful to her mother, but speaking of what she saw got her nothing but scolding and extra chores, for trying to make herself important, so she had stopped.

Loiyan asked her many things, and Nalangu found

herself confessing how she had imagined defending the enkang. Loiyan smiled, but did not laugh at her.

Nkasiogi returned. "They are ready," she said.

"Good," Loiyan said. "Listen, Nalangu. You know that Black Engai is kind and generous, she gives us cattle and water and good pasture. You know that Red Engai is vengeful, and punishes wrongdoers. You are ilkonjek, one of the People of the Eye. You can see things other people cannot see. And sometimes when women are ilkonjek, and if they have the spirit and the heart for it, Engai chooses them to become Sisters of Night. The Sisters embody both aspects of Engai, to protect the people. Not against the lion, not against those who deny us our pasture or take our cattle, but against other enemies, that cannot be defeated except by those who know how to hunt them."

"How?" Nalangu said. "How are they defeated?"

"With skill, with cunning, with stealth."

"And with seme and spear," Nkasiogi said.

"With *spear?*" Nalangu's shoulders straightened.

Loiyan leaned forward. "Tell me, when you dreamed of defending the enkang, did you imagine that people were watching?" Loiyan said. "Did you get praise and presents?"

"No. I just killed the lion."

"That is good," Loiyan said. "That is very good. Because if Engai chooses you, and you succeed at the tests, then it is a hard trail you will walk. You will know what the people cannot, and you can never speak of it. Your duty will be to the people, but you will be always a little separate from them."

And Nalangu, who had always been close-woven in her tribe as a thread in a cloth, felt a shadow on her heart.

"Engai is asking you to be as the thorn fence around the enkang," Loiyan said. "The cattle do not know how the fence is made, they only know that they live through the night."

"The cattle at least know the fence is there," Nkasiogi said, her voice sour.

"Our pride is in *not* being seen, *not* being known; we do what we do, and the people are safe even from knowing that they were in danger," Loiyan said. "Nalangu, understand this. You can still refuse, but if you do, or if you fail, then the tigir will be put on you, so that you may never speak of what you know. The memory may seem like a dream that troubles you often, and it may leave you restless with your life, but you will not know why. It must be so, to keep the Sisters safe.

"If you succeed… you will face great terrors. The teeth of night will tear at you, and if you are defeated, you may lose far more than your life. This is the truth of it, bare as a bone."

"But"—Loiyan grinned, fierce and hard, and looking at once young and full of blood and old as the moon—"if you pass the tests, you will be, with your sisters, the fence around your people. You will hear the warriors boast of their kills and their courage, and you will know that what you have faced is far worse than lions. *If* you pass the tests."

"What are the tests?" Nalangu said.

"First there is training. Nkasiogi will train your hand. I will train your Eye. Are you willing?"

"Yes," Nalangu said, joy rising in her like a flight of birds.

THE TRAINING TOOK two years, sneaked in around chores, the Sisters of Night arranging things so Nalangu's absences from her work and the enkang were not noticed.

Loiyan taught her to see around the edges of things, to notice shadows that fell against the light, and breezes that moved against the wind, and darkness that slid up the legs of the cattle or crouched in the branches of the acacia trees, and to watch the little serval cats who could sense things people could not. Loiyan was patient and kind and utterly, utterly immovable. Nalangu worked to please her until her eyes swam and her head ached.

Nkasiogi taught her the spear and the seme, and how to fight when neither was to hand. She was impatient and unkind and just as immovable. Nalangu worked, never expecting to be praised, until even the smallest of her bones ached. On the day Nkasiogi said, "good," Nalangu drank it down like sweet fresh milk. The next day Nkasiogi pushed her harder than ever.

One day, after two years, when training had become so much part of her life that Nalangu had almost forgotten its purpose, the enkang woke to wailing and shrieking. Loiyan came to Nalangu as she set off to milk the cows, and said, "Kingasunye *Kanunga* is missing. One of the others will do your milking. Come with me."

Kingasunye was no more than two, a swift-moving little creature of great charm. Her mother, Naeku, shed slow, almost silent tears as she moved about the hut. "She was sleeping right beside me. I woke and she was gone, as though she had never been there at all."

"You are sure it was not a leopard?" Loiyan said. That had been Nalangu's first thought, too. Leopards were very skilled, and could take a grown man in the night without a sound.

"That is what everyone says, but there is no blood— none—and the dogs never once barked." Naeku's voice was low and weary, and she picked up a piece of clothing, as though to mend it, but only sat with the cloth limp in her lap.

The hut seemed very dark to Nalangu, who saw better in darkness than most people did. Even the air seemed dirty. She looked about while Loiyan talked comfortingly to Naeku.

Nalangu peered until her eyes ached. *What has Naeku been burning, to make such a smoke? I can hardly see anything, certainly nothing that is out of place...*

There was no curse-medicine smeared on the doorway. The hut was as clean and tidy as a hut could be, except for the air...

Stupid. Nalangu shook her head at herself, and looked again, at where the darkness in the air curled thickest, beside the bed that Naeku shared with her children.

If she had not been looking very hard, and had not been blessed with slightly more than natural eyesight, she would not have seen it.

On the floor beside the bed was the faint, blurred mark of a leopard's paw.

She signed to Loiyan that she had found something, and they went outside to speak together.

"I am sorry, yeyo," Nalangu said. "I thought something evil had come there, because the air was so thick and dark, but there was nothing but a leopard's pawmark. So it seems the child was taken by a leopard, after all. I cannot explain the darkness."

"I can," Loiyan said. "And you were right. The one who took the child left that deception of the eyes, meaning to hide its presence, but it was too clever, and instead showed very clearly that there was something there to hide. But it did not reckon with your eyes, and your Eye, Nalangu."

"Did I make a mistake? Was it not a leopard's print?"

"It was. Some leopards are not always leopards," Loiyan said.

That meant it was one of the cat-people. Nalangu felt a cold excitement in the pit of her belly. So far in her training she had dealt with small things, little demons that spoiled meat and sent flies to bite the cattle and stones to trip the feet: tricksters and mischief-makers, nasty, but weak. Cat-people were a different matter. All the speed and strength and stealth of a leopard, and all the cunning of a human.

"Go look for the trail," Loiyan said. "Follow it no farther than the edge of the enkang, then come to my hut."

Nalangu did.

The creature had come into Naeku's hut as leopard, but had left as a person—though its human footprints were slightly too wide, and with almost no heelmark, as though they walked always on the balls of their feet.

And why would they leave in that shape? It had been

night, the dogs had not scented them, a leopard's form would be far swifter and more silent, and a leopard carried both its prey and its own kittens easily in its jaws.

But leopard kittens had soft loose skin at the neck, that made such a thing easy, and when picked up in that way knew to go limp. A human child, even if picked up by its wrappings, would not be accustomed to it, might be frightened and cry out. Arms would be better... for a child the kidnapper wished to take away swiftly, silently, and still alive.

At the edge of the enkang the trail was fading, but still there. Nalangu left it reluctantly—soon it would be lost as people and cattle and dogs passed over the ground—but Loiyan had told her to come back. And what could she do, alone, and only partway through her training?

Nkasiogi and several of the other Sisters had joined Loiyan when Nalangu returned. Nkasiogi looked angry, but then the thought that the cat-people had walked into the middle of the enkang and stolen a child was enough to make anyone angry.

Nalangu told them what she had found.

"You are right," Loiyan said. "It seems they want Kingasunye for some other purpose than food. Well," she said, "it is time."

The other Sisters nodded, looking solemn. Nalangu felt something gathering in the air.

"Nalangu," Loiyan said. "This will be the first of your Great Trials, the Risking of the Flesh. You will find their lair, and you will find Kingasunye, and do what you must."

"It is not time!" Nkasiogi said, loud enough that the chatter outside paused a moment. Loiyan frowned at her.

Nkasiogi lowered her voice, but it still rippled with fury. "She is not ready."

"She is ready," Loiyan said. "You were, at her age, and have you not been her teacher? Have you not prepared her well enough?"

This exchanged passed by Nalangu almost unnoticed, as her thoughts ran to sharpening her spear and gathering her provisions and whether she was afraid.

But the first thought, and the clearest, came to her in the voice of a younger girl, who had watched, from hiding, as the warriors trained with their spears to protect the cattle and the people, and that thought was *Yes!*

NALANGU SMEARED HERSELF with a mixture of unpleasant ingredients to disguise her scent, and filled gourds with meat and milk and salt and water, and the honey-beer infused with herbs and spices that would give her strength and help heal wounds. She wrapped the gourds so they did not rattle or slosh (it made her think of how carefully she had moved, with the water on her back, the day she had learned of the Sisters), and bound fine strong rope under her shuka. She would collect her spear from its hiding-place outside the enkang.

She had been given a dose that gave her symptoms of fever, and one of the Sisters had told her mother she was taking Nalangu to another enkang, to see someone who was very skilled in medicines. If Nalangu died, everyone would be told the fever had killed her. No-one would ask to see her body, it was not the way things were done. Bodies, emptied of their spirits, had little significance.

But Nalangu knew that her mother, though she scolded and fussed, would grieve for her, and felt sorry that she could not know the truth.

The Sisters murmured advice and blessings. Nalangu felt their strength lift her up.

Loiyan said, "The leopard-people were once solitary, like ordinary leopards. But they have learned to live together. Like us, they understand that it gives them strength. Remember what they are. *All* of what they are. And remember all of what *you* are."

Nkasiogi said, "I am the one who taught you to fight; do not shame me by getting yourself killed."

Nalangu chose her moment to slip away, and followed the trail.

SHE FOUND THE entrance to the lair in the foothills, a gap between the rocks, invisible from more than a few feet away.

For some time she lay downwind and watched, thinking.

She was one, and they were many. They knew what lay inside, and she did not.

One person alone, or with companions, could fight and kill a leopard... if they saw it coming. Most never did.

One person alone against *many* leopards would die.

If she died before she reached Kingasunye, the child would be lost. She had to stay alive to get her out.

Remember all *they are*. They are leopards, but they are also people. They are people, but they are also leopards.

There was at least one thing that both cats and people shared: *curiosity*.

Nalangu searched until she spotted a rock-hyrax den. It was the right time of day; soon they would be coming out to eat. She set a grass snare and waited, still as a rock among the rocks.

Eventually a small black nose appeared, then a grey-brown muzzle, a pair of eyes shiny as beads with white flashes above them, upstanding ears aquiver for every sound. The eyes passed over her, the ears did not find her, and the hyrax crept forward and into the grass snare.

It writhed and snapped as, avoiding its frantic jaws, she took one of her own necklaces and fastened it around the beast's body, the beads and pendants glinting. She also fastened a long, strong thread around its neck, and when she had done, she crept as close as she could to the mouth of the leopard-people's lair, tied one end of the thread to a nearby tree, and released the hyrax.

For a moment it crouched, quivering, then it darted across the front of the lair. When the thread brought it up short, it darted back again.

After a few minutes of this, Nalangu saw movement at the entrance to the lair, and soon after that a woman emerged. She was naked and moved with a leopard's sleek, lethal grace. She watched the hyrax, her head tilted, and called over her shoulder, "Come see this. This is a very strange thing."

"What is it?" said a voice from inside.

"It is a hyrax in a necklace!"

"Truly?"

Another woman came out and the two peered at the hyrax, grinning, and although they were in human form, Nalangu could almost see their tails twitching.

"Well, I have never seen such a thing. How did it get a necklace?"

"See how it runs about, showing off its splendid jewellery!"

They laughed, and in their laughter was a low growling note.

Nalangu waited until the hyrax was at a distance from the lair, took the end of the thread, and moved it to a tree a little further away. The hyrax ran back and forth. The leopard-women followed. And so they went until the leopard-women were a good distance from the lair. Nalangu cut the thread, and the hyrax ran, with the women running, laughing, after it. Nalangu slipped into the cave.

She stepped to one side so she would not be outlined against the entrance, and stood for a moment to let her eyes adjust. Beyond the entrance, the lair was lit only by a trickle of sunlight through cracks in the rock.

She crept deeper in. The air grew cool. The powerful smell of leopards was everywhere, but so were human smells—fire and cooked meat.

The guards—if that was what they were—would soon either realise they had been deceived, or catch the hyrax, or become bored—and then they would come back. Nalangu's eyes, her ears, her very *skin* were alert to every sound and shift of the air.

Light bloomed along the wall. She could hear conversation and movement, and she tightened her grip on her spear.

The passageway began to widen out. Nalangu tucked herself behind a projection of rock and peered around it.

Before her was a wide cave. There was a fire-pit in the centre, and a hole in the roof overhead. Grass had been dragged into mounds all around, and covered with hides and bright cloth; and on them sprawled the leopard-people, in fur or in skin. She saw a woman drinking blood from a gourd as one of her own people might, and another gnawing on a raw kidney. She saw a leopard tucking a piece of hide more firmly under its mound of grass with its foot, and another with a baby that looked human— not Kingasunye, this one was barely a week old—lying sleeping against its side.

She could not see Kingasunye anywhere. There was a side-passage leading away to her left, and she crept down it. There was almost no light, she moved in a world of grey and darker grey, black and lesser black.

Down the passages came stinks and breezes and purring and growls and then, unmistakably, the giggling of a small child. Nalangu moved towards the sound, seeing firelight glimmer on the wall.

A small cave, lined with hides and grass. A fire, a smokehole. And Kingasunye, quite unharmed, playing with the tail of a she-leopard with a torn ear who lay curled about her.

The leopard leapt to her feet, snarling, putting herself between Nalangu and the child. Kingasunye, disturbed, wailed and clutched at the leopard's leg, and in that moment's distraction Nalangu could have speared it, but something stayed her hand.

A change in the air behind her brushed warning across her skin and sent her diving out of the way as another leopard, silent as smoke, leapt from the passageway for her throat.

She spun and stabbed, and the leopard slid out of the way of her spear, and came again, and Nalangu ducked, feeling its hot breath on her shoulder, and stabbed, and a claw scored her side, and her blade struck nothing but the wall, and she dropped the spear—no use in such close quarters—and grabbed her seme, and heard the roar of pain and fury as it met its mark, and she and the leopard danced their deadly dance and the firelight flickered and now there were others, not fighting but only leaning against the walls of the cave, watching, some as leopards and some with everything about them human but their bright, green-golden eyes.

In the brief glances Nalangu dared to snatch, she could not see any of them moving towards the fight, though all of them were watching.

There was no time to think of grief, or regret, or failure, or how she would get the child out. There was no time to feel the pain of her wound—or the next, or the next.

There was only time to move and stab and slash and dance.

Blood was running down her shoulders and breast, and she was tiring, but her opponent, too, was tiring, its fur streaked dark with blood, its mouth panting meaty gasps.

It leapt again, so close its fur brushed her. She went down onto one knee, rolling aside, back up. The leopard slammed into the wall, grunted, turned, and her seme grazed its side.

"Enough!" The voice cut between them like a blade.

The leopard dropped back, snarling. Nalangu almost went after it, but pulled back. She was alone, blood-sticky, exhaustion and pain surging. Her opponent collapsed to the ground. Others surrounded it, licking its wounds, bringing water.

Kingasunye was bawling. Where the she-leopard with the torn ear had been was now a woman, still with a torn ear, glaring at Nalangu, holding the little girl tight in her arms.

"A good fight." It was the voice that had said *enough*. A woman, tall and straight, with a great thick scar running below her breasts like a rope around her ribs.

"It scared the little one," said torn-ear, in a growl.

"But it did not scare *her*," said the tall one, looking at Nalangu with her head cocked.

"I did not have time to be scared," Nalangu said, trying not to sway. "Give me the girl."

"Bring water, and binding," the scarred one said. "She is interesting."

"Will you let me take the girl?" Nalangu said.

The woman said, "If your wounds are not treated you will die. Perhaps even if they are. What we bite often dies."

"Will you give her to me, or not?" Nalangu said.

"Bind your wounds," the leopard-woman said. "Eat with us. I am Crocodile Dancer; there, I make you a gift

144

of my name. Now look to yourself, and drink water, or you will die, and that would *not* be interesting."

"She cannot have her!" said torn-ear. Human, she was lean and strong. Her stomach bore the marks of pregnancy and her breasts were milk-heavy. She clutched Kingasunye to her so that she squirmed.

Crocodile Dancer did not answer her. Others came with water and bindings and Nalangu treated her wounds as best she could, salting water to wash them with and keeping the pain behind her teeth, while they watched her with their green-golden eyes.

Crocodile Dancer sniffed at the gourd. "Why do you salt the water?"

"It cleans the wound better," Nalangu said, "and it is less likely to fester. Now you know what you did not before. *I* have made *you* a gift."

Crocodile Dancer smiled. "Here, you have missed one," she said, and washed and dressed a wound on Nalangu's back that she could not reach herself, and Nalangu sat feeling the sure movements of the leopard-woman's hands and considered how strange her life had become.

They gave her meat and water. She drank the water, and not being sure of what it might be, hid the meat in a gourd. She drank her honey-beer and offered a taste to Crocodile Dancer, who wrinkled her nose at the smell and refused.

"Tell me why you took Kingasunye," Nalangu said.

"I did not take her. Catches Crickets took her," Crocodile Dancer said.

"Then tell me why Catches Crickets took her."

"She lost her cub. A lion killed it."

"And now another mother has lost her child."

"Did you wonder," Crocodile Dancer said, "why Kingasunye did not cry out when she was taken? Did you wonder why she sits so happily at Catches Crickets' side, playing with her tail like her own cub?"

"She is very young. She does not understand the danger."

"No, she does not," Crocodile Dancer said. "But we do."

"What do you mean?"

"Her father was one of ours, and so is she."

Nalangu opened her mouth, and closed it again, having nothing useful to say. No-one paid much attention to who fathered a child, so long as the father belonged to the right ol-aji, but *this*...

Crocodile Dancer said, "It does not happen often that there is a cub, from such a mating, and sometimes the cub is just human. But this one has the scent of us. Last year when you built your enkang in this place, she was too young for us to be certain. And now, we are. So Catches Crickets took her."

"She was not hers to take."

"Was she not?" Said Crocodile Dancer. "Now, she seems a child like yours. And when the change comes on her, what then?"

Nalangu looked around at the cave. Everything was strange, and dangerous; the eyes of the leopard people like burning jewels, the stink of their kills, the claw and muscle of them, their beds of rock and grass, Crocodile Dancer's chilly amusement. This was no place for a child of the tribe, surely it was not.

"It is my duty to take her back to her mother," Nalangu said.

"Then you must fight Catches Crickets. And this time I will not stop it."

"Then I must." Despite the honey-beer Nalangu felt the pull of her wounds, and the weariness in her muscles, but this was her duty and she would not shirk it.

The leopard-people pulled back from a space in the centre of the cave, in front of the fire-pit.

The light was bad, the ground unfamiliar. But this time Nalangu knew what was coming. To watch a leopard kill and to know what it is like to be prey, these are very different things. *Remember what they are, and what you are.*

She picked up her spear and her shield.

They watched. As humans, they were very still. As leopards, their ears flickered, their tails twitched.

Nalangu watched Catches Crickets return to leopard form. The transformation made her eyes wince and sat unpleasantly in her mind, and she wondered what such a thing felt like, especially the first time.

"Go, then," said Crocodile Dancer.

Catches Crickets came in with deadly speed, straight for the throat.

Nalangu was ready. She blocked, knocking Catches Crickets aside. The leopard came again; again, she knocked her aside. Again, and again, and again. The leopard was tireless and terribly fast.

But she is not truly tireless. Not truly.

Nor am I.

Months and months of training. The dust and hard-packed dirt, Nkasiogi's voice, saying *Again*. And *Again*. And *Again*.

Loiyan's voice, saying, *Use your Eye. Do not just see, but always* perceive.

Catches Crickets was all drive and fury and fear, wanting to save this cub as she could not the one she had lost. *Remember what they are, and what you are.*

The burn of claws along her arm, the hot stink of breath, one glinting fang so close to her eye she felt it brush her lashes.

Turn and jab and block and thrust. They locked together, trembling with tension, each waiting for a moment of weakness that would leave an opening.

A red line down the spotted hide and a roar of pain.

Remember what they are, and what you are.

Nalangu blocked. She jabbed. She blocked. Her wounds reopened, and she slipped in blood and fell and only just rolled out of the way; and she was back on her feet, and they were both panting, and tiring.

And, oh, her blood sang even as it spilled, and she was *alive* and all her senses sharp as blades.

She was alive because Nkasiogi had trained her.

She was here because Loiyan had believed her.

Nalangu could see Kingasunye watching the fight, her eyes wide and afraid, and were they tingeing gold already?

She knew how the girl moved, lithe and quick, not like a toddling child still finding its feet, but like a leopard-cub. And where, back home, was her Loiyan? Where was her Nkasiogi?

Nalangu looked into the green-gold eyes of the leopardess,

so hot and furious, she *felt* the desperation of the coming lunge—*I must finish this, now*—and Nalangu twisted and took her spear in both hands and swerved and *spun* and the shaft of her spear was across the leopard's throat and she *pulled*.

And Catches Crickets writhed and choked and heaved her shoulders and tried to rub Nalangu off against the rock, and she clung on with hands and thighs and feet, and finally Catches Crickets dropped to the floor, and Nalangu with her, rolling so she was on top.

She extracted her spear, stood, backed away, holding it ready. Catches Crickets lay limp.

Kingasunye, wailing, ran across the floor and flung herself on the body. An ear flicked, the tail twitched.

"You have not killed her," Crocodile Dancer said.

"No."

"Why not?"

Nalangu said, "If I take the child back to my enkang, what will happen?"

"If she is lucky," Crocodile Dancer said, "when your people begin to realise what she is, they will kill her quickly. If she is not lucky, they will try to drive the leopard from her with fire and iron, with pain and terror, and when that fails, they will kill her."

Nalangu said, "Give her foster-mother some of this"— she held out the gourd of herbed honey-beer—"and make her drink it, even if she spits. It will help her heal. And when the child is old enough, tell her that her birth-mother is Naetu *Kanunga*. She has a right to know that."

She picked up her spear, and turned away.

"You have earned the right to take her," Crocodile Dancer said.

"Yes," Nalangu said. "But I will not."

Crocodile Dancer tilted her head. "A gift for a gift. What would you have?"

"Keep your people from our cattle. And your men from our women."

"I will do what I can," Crocodile Dancer said. "May you always catch what you hunt."

"And so may you," Nalangu said.

She felt their eyes on her back as she walked out into the night, but when she reached the entrance, and looked behind her, there was no-one there. The crack in the rock might have been no more than the lair of a rock-hyrax; or of nothing at all.

She did not want to go back to the enkang—and face Loiyan—and because she did not want to, she put up her chin and straightened her back and walked as fast as her injuries would let her, and went into the enkang by the secret way, so no-one would see her injuries and question her, and she took her spear, to hold onto it a little longer.

"I did not bring her back," she said, in the dark hut smelling of herbs, where the light gleamed on Loiyan's beads and teeth and eyes. "I could not. I have failed." And she knelt down and held up her spear in her two hands, for Loiyan to take from her, and her heart ached at it.

"Put down your spear and tell me," Loiyan said.

So Nalangu told her. And afterwards Loiyan re-dressed her wounds and gave her stronger medicine to drink, and told her to rest, and went away.

Soon after, she came back with Nkasiogi, who scowled and said, "Well, you are not dead, at least. Don't lie too long without stretching, or your muscles will stiffen. Oh, don't look so miserable, I am not going to make you train for a few days."

Nalangu blinked and looked from one to another.

"You did what was right," Loiyan said. "The trial was of your sense as well as your strength—they always are. You passed."

"What of Naeku? What of her grief?" Nalangu said.

"What would her grief be, if you brought the child back to suffer and die for what she is? Naeku must live with loss, and you must live with the knowledge she is denied. Even the right decision does not come shadowless like a bright noonday. Always you must choose, and with every choice made another is lost."

Loiyan laid a hand on Nalangu's head. "Now you must rest and grow strong, and when you are well, we will begin to prepare you for the Risking of the Soul."

NALANGU SAT WITH her spear across her knees, smelling the herb-thick smoke and the bitter fumes of the brew she would soon drink, breathing steadily, trying to calm her mind.

Yet again, she had taken the medicine to give her symptoms of fever, and had been whisked away to the secret hut of the Sisters.

Yet again, she wondered if she would ever go home.

It had been two seasons, between the last Trial and this

one. She had trained until her spear and shield felt like extensions of her limbs. She had trained until the smallest breath of the other world sang in her ears like a lion's roar. She had learned the nature of every type of demon the Sisters had ever encountered, and some that were only rumours.

She was still not sure it was enough.

Loiyan, Nkasiogi, and five more Sisters of Night sat around her. They would guard the way, if she failed, in case any of the demons decided to try and follow her trail back to the upper world.

The Sisters, seen together, had a look about them that was almost like a family, though not in their features. It was in the way they moved, the way they spoke, the threads of understanding that bound them together in word and gesture. They were the hide and stitching and frame of a shield, strong against all that threatened the people.

If Nalangu succeeded, she would be bound together with them, to stand against darkness. If she failed... but she would not think of failure. Thinking of it would make her weak.

"Once you drink, it will be very quick," Loiyan said. "You will land hard and sudden, and the demons will scent your spirit and come fast. Be ready."

Nalangu grasped her shield and her spear, feeling the shape of them, familiar as the lines of her palm. If she did not know them well enough, remember them well enough, she would be unarmed when she faced the demons, and they would tear her soul to shreds and gulp it down, and her body would die.

Even armed, that was a good possibility.

If she survived, she would gain the knowledge the demons guarded. She would see visions that would help her protect her people. She would return as one of the Sisters of Night.

There could be no bargaining, though the demons would attempt it. There could be no compromise, though they would lie and promise it. There would be only success, or failure.

And she would get only one chance.

The drink was thick and bitter. Her tongue curled at it, her throat tried to close. She gulped it down.

"Close your eyes, and lie back," Loiyan said.

She did. The blanket beneath her was soft and thick. Nalangu wondered briefly who had woven it, and if they knew how it would be used.

The women began to hum, a low tune that was simple on the surface and complex underneath. Nalangu found herself trying to follow its harmonies, tease one individual voice out from the others. There was Nkasiogi, her tones rich and sweet, as different from her acrid words as possible, yet unmistakably hers.

Nkasiogi's voice became a thread, shining silver, among the other threads, a complex plait of light and colour, leading into the dark. Nalangu pulled away after it...

The separation from her physical self was sudden and soft as the tearing of tender meat. The very ease of it was somehow horrible. Nalangu tried to ignore the feeling that half of her was hanging in tatters over the void, and followed the voices, the shining interwoven thread, down and down and down.

Her descent sped, now she was *falling*, tumbling over and over, spilling helplessly into the dark. *Where are my spear and shield?*

She grasped them, and they became themselves, solid in her hands, the moment before she hit the ground with a jarring force that almost tore them out of her grip.

Nalangu bounced upright. The landscape around her was all dimness and smokes and sullen glows, like the aftermath of a bush fire.

The first shape came at her with such terrible speed that she only just got her shield up and her spear in front of her in time; the blade of the spear was scarlet in the dimness, the colour of courage and blood. It sank into shadowy substance that coiled and grasped at it.

The demon shrieked inside her head, the noise clawing at her mind. It moved with slick uncanny speed, pulling itself away from the spear, but she could see it was wounded. Darkness seeped from it, vaporising as it flowed. Again she stabbed, and the demon writhed and howled and was gone, but her senses spun her about and there was another, this one more substantial, its matter shifting and bulking to suggest muscles, fangs, claws. It had many eyes scattered about it, some as blank and glittering as the eyes of locusts and others horribly human. It gibbered as she sank the blade into it, the sound creeping over her soul like an infection, and faded away.

There were more.

There were things that crawled and things that skittered and things that stank like dead flesh. There were things that giggled like children and promised her horrors that she would always remember even if she never found the words to describe them. There were things that sang sweet harmonies, and promised her glories that made her ache with longing, even as she knew they were lies.

There were more, and more: an endless, dreadful horde of them. She fought and fought, her mind, her spear, her limbs, her soul, all one, all resisting, and weakening, and wearying.

Suddenly there was a space. Nalangu leaned on her spear, panting, knowing this was only her mind's vision, but feeling every searing breath, every welt and rip and aching muscle and poisoned barb sunk in her cringing flesh. Every lie and promise and twisted thought that wrenched and sickened her weary spirit.

They must be gathering their forces for another attack. She searched for the thread of the women's voices, that multi-coloured shining rope, and wondered if she would ever find her way back, or if the Sisters would—with regret, with sorrow, yes, but without a choice—leave her here to be ripped into screaming shreds that might survive in suffering for dreadful ages.

The thread, her guide home, turned and shone and sang in the darkness.

And suddenly she could hear Nkasiogi's voice, rising clear from the rest. "*Enough,*" she said. "*They are finished. You have done well. Come back now.*"

Oh, she wanted to, so very badly. She had never felt so tired and sore and near to broken. "But I have not had the vision," she whispered.

"No, *that is a great pity, but you have fought well, and*

it has been decided that you do not need to have the vision to be accepted as one of the Sisters of Night. The vision can wait."

To go back, to rest, safe and honoured with her beloved Sisters. She stretched out her hand, to touch the strands, and the voice said, "*You have fought the best of all, you have no more to learn. Come back, and lead us.*"

And Nalangu snatched her hand away, and for all her weariness, laughed. "Crawl away, demon," she said. "The Sisters have no leader, the Sisters are one. And there is *always* more to learn." And she thought what Nkasiogi would think of her voice being made to say these words, and laughed even harder, and some of her strength returned to her.

The voice spat and swore terrible curses, and Nalangu grinned and gripped her spear tightly and was ready when the demon came.

It was the strongest yet, dreadful in its speed and its absolute fury and its utter violence. It tore at her until she cried out, taking great mouthfuls of the flesh of her spirit body, sinking its fangs into her mind, but she would not yield. It had tried to make her falter—had tried to avoid this fight—and that meant it feared her. She hacked at its shifting limbs and stabbed the reeking, shadowy mass of its flesh, until its poisonous ichors spilled and ran and its curses weakened, until it turned and fled. But it cried out to her one final time. "You have won your vision, warrior. I hope it pleases you well." And, cursing and laughing, it was gone into the smokes and glooms.

And then Nalangu heard a strange ripping sound,

like something tearing open, that was at once quiet and profound, and the gloom around her lightened and shifted and became daylight.

But what daylight was this? Dull and grey, and as full of smoke as the demon-realm. She stood on a wide path, covered in small round stones half-buried in the ground. It ran ahead, straight as a spear-haft, ending abruptly at a wall, built of regular red stones, smeared with black. To either side were buildings, like canyon walls, absurdly tall.

"*Keep your eyes open,*" someone said. It was a white man, paler than a lion's pelt, only the second one she had ever seen. He was not speaking Maa, yet she understood him. And she understood his name was *Frank,* a name cold and sharp as himself. "*It came down here.*"

"This is too good a place for a trap," Nalangu said. And *she* was not speaking Maa, either.

"*But there's nowhere it could have* gone," said another man, huddled in a great thick wrap. His name was *Archimedes.*

"*Coal cellar,*" said a woman—*Gracie, she is Gracie*—pointing. "*Look.*"

Nalangu could see where she was pointing, a small round opening set in the ground, rimmed with metal. Smeared on its rim was some thick gleaming stuff. *Spoor.*

"*How the devil could it fit in there?*" said Archimedes. "*And how are we supposed to follow it?*"

"*Don't look at me,*" said Gracie, "*that thing looks tighter than a duck's never-you-mind.*"

Nalangu, impatient, and aware that her feet in their heavy boots were going numb with the cold, said, "The cellar belongs to that house. I am going to knock on the door."

"*Wait...*"

And the vision changed, and she was in another strange place, even colder than the last, snow everywhere. She had seen snow before, in the mountains, but never so *much*, lying everywhere thicker than the length of her arm, white where it topped walls and roofs, grey where it was churned by passing feet. The air was like metal in her lungs. To her right a building rose to a dome topped with a point, showing gold where it wasn't covered in snow.

The same group of people stood with her—Frank had a bandage around his head, Gracie an ugly wound down her arm where something had ripped through layers of cloth—and there was shouting and the bellowing of terrified beasts and two horses were belting towards them, dragging behind them a sort of wagon that ran over the snow on wooden blades—the driver's seat empty, a screaming fur-clad woman in the back clutching two screaming children, and something like a cross between a snake and a crocodile but huge, each great scaled leg as tall as Nalangu, that whipped along behind with appalling speed, and its head turned and she saw its eye, the slit pupil lit with unearthly fire, and Archimedes shouted *now* and the weapon bucked and roared in Nalangu's hand...

And there was a place of glimmering light and buildings that stood with their feet in water, and cats everywhere, smaller even than servals, grey or striped or black and white like zebras. She and her companions were sliding along on the water, in a boat propelled somehow by a man with a pole, dressed in striped garments and a strange pale hat with ribbons trailing from it, and Frank, peering over the side, said, *"Pretty place, but be glad we're here in winter. In summer it stinks."*

Nalangu pulled her heavy coat tighter around her. The breeze whipping along the water had ice in its breath.

"Are there demons in the water too?" Gracie said.

"Only sewage, so far as I know," said Archimedes. *"Just don't drink it or swim in it, or you'll be longing for a demon to put you out of your misery."*

"Swim, in this weather? No thank you…"

Something caught Nalangu's eye. "Look," she said. An old archway, and a dozen cats bursting out, ears flat, tails puffed, streaking away in all directions, while passers-by cursed and laughed.

"Pull up here, thank you," Frank said and they scrambled out of the boat while coins changed hands and the boatman's thanks faded behind them.

"Yes, look, it's left its prints on the sill there. We'd never have spotted them otherwise. You said to watch the cats," Archimedes said, grinning at her, and Nalangu grinned back, and they went shoulder to shoulder into the tiny stone square where something writhed and gibbered and dripped…

And then the world sealed itself shut, like the closing of a mouth, its secrets told, and she was alone in the void for a moment before the voices of the Sisters were around her once more, cradling her, drawing her up, back to herself.

*　　*　　*

NALANGU OPENED HER eyes to the familiar darkness of the hut, and shivered all over, as the welcome heat of home seeped into flesh and bones that were still cold with the air of unknown places.

She blinked and looked up at the faces of her sisters in arms.

"The visions..." she said. Her throat was too dry for more.

Someone passed her a gourd of fresh milk, and she drank, and even as it soothed her, she could feel things she had understood sliding away. The names of those she had fought beside.

But she remembered enough to know her vision was wrong.

It *had* to be wrong.

It wasn't just that the places she had seen were so completely strange, places that could never be reached by walking, far from any grazing ground the people had ever seen.

None of her people were there.

None of her *Sisters* were there.

When she could speak, Nalangu told them, hesitant, pulling the scraps together, scattered beads of a broken necklace.

And the Sisters listened.

"You saw *nothing* you knew," Loiyan said.

"No. Even my clothes were different, because it was so cold."

"But you were fighting demons," said another.

"Yes."

Then there was a long silence, and they sighed, and shook their heads.

"There is no doubt," Loiyan said. "I am sorry, sister, daughter. You are my heart's child, and you are a warrior. But there is no choice."

"No!" Nkasiogi said. "No. There must be another way."

"You know there is not," Loiyan said.

"I have failed, then?" Nalangu said. She thought of the tigir, the silencing, and her stomach quailed. She looked at all their faces, feeling their warmth, their companionship, their bravery, desperately trying to brand her memory with their faces, so that once the tigir had been laid on her, perhaps she would remember how it had been to be one of them. They looked at her with no sign of disappointment, only with a compassion as deep as the earth. Apart from Nkasiogi, who looked both furious and miserable.

"You have not failed," Loiyan said. "But your fate does not lie here. You must seek it out. You must travel to where it waits."

"Travel?"

"Yes. You must find these lands and these people and stand with them, and not with us."

"Why should she?" Nkasiogi burst out. "Why should she help strangers, instead of her own people? Even if they are there! Will you send her out alone to look for something that may not exist?"

"It is the custom and the law," Loiyan said. "Nalangu, you must travel towards your destiny, carrying only your weapons and what will sustain you; and you must go today."

Nalangu blinked. Everything had changed so quickly. She had been, she thought, prepared for failure. Perhaps even for success. But this... to leave *everything*? To leave her Sisters, her family and their cattle, her people, her *land,* to go among strangers in the cold...

"My mother?" she said.

"We will tell her you have died of the fever," Loiyan said gently.

She knew that, of course.

"And where is she to go?" Nkasiogi spat. "No-one even knows where these lands are!"

"North," Nalangu said. "I must go north." And with those words, she knew she had accepted it, even as her heart was breaking.

As NALANGU SET out on the road, she did not look back; she did not dare, for fear she would never be able to go on. The Sisters had all wished her well, given her gourds of milk and meat and blood and herbs. Except for Nkasiogi, who had stalked from the hut as though if she stayed she would kill someone. Nalangu tried not to let it hurt her too much, but that was the bruise she thought would last the longest.

Then as she passed out of sight of the enkang, beyond the trail that led to the cave of the leopard-people, Nkasiogi was there, standing by the side of the road.

Nalangu stopped. Nkasiogi glared at her. "Well," she said.

"Well."

Nkasiogi held out her best seme. The blade gleamed in the sun. She had never let Nalangu use it. "This is better than yours. Take it. Do not shame it, or me."

Nalangu took the seme, and gave hers to Nkasiogi. "I will not shame it, or you."

Nkasiogi looked her long in the face. "No," she said. "I do not think you will. Travel well, Sister."

"Fight well, Sister," Nalangu said.

And Nkasiogi clasped her arm, hard enough to mark, and Nalangu did likewise, and then Nkasiogi walked past her, back towards the life that Nalangu was leaving.

Nalangu did not turn. She did not watch. She slung the seme, and kept walking.

The sun set, red and shimmering, and Nalangu kept walking. The dark came with the whispering song of insects and the coughing grunt of a lion, and Nalangu kept walking. Once a leopard cried near her in the night, and once something whipped across the path too swift to make out, and Nalangu kept walking.

The drug, the fight, the visions, the leaving had left her light and hollow as an empty gourd, and there was so little left of her that it hardly seemed any trouble to just keep going, as the night ended and the sun rose again, painting the land bright.

But eventually her body gained weight and substance and need, and she stopped and made a rough shelter, and built a fire, and ate.

And so the days went on. Twice she saw leopards. They did not attack her, but only watched, and she thought they might be of Crocodile Dancer's people, for what other leopards would stand so and let themselves be seen, watching? The thought gave her a strange comfort, and she nodded to the leopards, who flicked their ears and stared with their green-golden eyes. Nalangu walked on.

Once she crossed the trail of a demon, but it was old and faded, so she walked on.

And one morning she saw something strange in the sky, some terrible new demon, out in the waking world, bold and fearsome, a great noisy thing that floated on the air, with bulging sides and fluttering limbs.

Nalangu saw it turn towards her, and begin to descend, and gripped her spear and Nkasiogi's seme. The demon was huge, but it was slow.

And if she did not survive this, then she would at least die following her fate.

But as the demon drew nearer and lower, she could see that it was a *thing*, a built thing, a great long swollen bag with something slung below it. Something that reminded her of wooden buildings she had seen in her vision.

And she could see *people*, leaning out and pointing at her.

She did not put down her weapons, but stood, waiting. Her heart panted in her chest, but she was not afraid.

The thing came down in the road, scraping and roaring and sputtering and sending up great clouds of dust, and a figure emerged, coughing, and Nalangu knew it was not a demon; for whoever heard of a demon that coughed at the mere dust of a road?

The figure came towards her, and its clothes were strange and it wore a hat that shaded its face, and then it pushed back the hat, and there was a face she recognised. A man, pale as dust, who looked into her face, and smiled, and said, in clear but strangely spoken Maa, "Hello. We have been looking for you. What is your name?"

"Nalangu," said Nalangu.

"Nalangu. I am Archimedes," said the man. "You look well prepared."

"Not for this," Nalangu said.

"None of us were," said Archimedes. Then he said something over his shoulder, and the rest emerged.

She knew them, they were utterly strange and yet she knew them, though only one name came back to her. "Frank," Nalangu said, pointing at the man in the scarlet jacket.

He blinked, and laughed, and held out his hand. She put the seme away and reached out, and he took her hand in a brief light clasp.

And one by one they took her hand, and with every clasp it was a little less strange. And there was the woman, *Gracie,* and that helped a little too.

They waited as she readied herself to step into this thing, this demon-bodied craft, feeling the earth beneath her. Home. A little step, and the land that had borne her would no longer be under her feet. She took a breath, and stepped.

Nalangu watched, as it all fell away. How strange everything looked, so far and small. She turned away from the window. "Where is the demon?" she said. "Do you know its weaknesses?"

Archimedes translated, and there was laughter. "They

think you're going to fit right in," he said. "I have to say I agree."

Nalangu looked at her new companions. They were not the Sisters. They would not ever be the Sisters. But they were warriors. They were the fence around the people, *all* the people. The enkang had been her world. Now the whole world would be her enkang.

"Show me what we hunt," Nalangu said.

Nobody can say he is settled anywhere for ever: it is only the mountains which do not move from their places.

Maasai Proverb

WHERE YOU BURY THINGS
GUY ADAMS

THERE IS A quality to the light of a Calcutta sunset that is quite the most delicious thing. One could almost imagine the buildings to have been bathed in syrup.

"Mr. Bey?"

I took a last sip of my brandy—if I have a credo in life, it is to always enjoy the moment—placed the glass on the table next to my armchair and feigned the sort of relaxed indifference people rightfully expect from an old Etonian. If I learned one thing in that noble establishment, it was the art of insouciance.

"Miss Collins," I replied. "What a charming surprise. I was led to believe you were dead."

She fluttered like a moth searching for an open window. It was positively draining keeping an eye on her as she gadded about on the rug before me.

Her behaviour was antagonising some of the other residents. Those who stay at the Auckland Hotel do so with the specific wish to avoid excitement. It is a little piece of England dropped here in the heart of a bustling city. That is to say, a place where a certain kind of traveller can pretend to have enjoyed a city without actually having experienced it.

At the far end of the room, a brutish pianist was doing unkind things to Beethoven. To my left an old soldier snored, his nasal rumbling a memory of barrages gone by. To my right, a dowager of some distinction was complaining to her companion that the heat was proving disagreeable to 'Sir Henry,' said person being— horrifically—her Pekingese dog. Beyond her, a pair of young sisters stared out of the window, horrified that they were no longer looking out at the reassuring, aseptic vistas of Eastbourne. Earlier, one of the staff had dropped a tray of Chai and the resulting noise had sent the room into the sort of panic one might expect to result from a stick of dynamite being hurled through a window. One elderly couple had actually retired early to their room following the incident, 'darling Nigel's nerves not being what they once were.'

In short, this was not a room in which exuberance should intrude. Miss Collins may have only been pacing— if rather erratically—but her presence was as unwelcome as the sudden appearance of a marching band. I should had invited her to sit, but I didn't.

"Dead?" she said. "Whatever made you think that?"

I could have mentioned the considerable quantity of

blood on the rug in her bedroom, or the dainty, severed hand sharing pot-space with a decorative aspidistra; but, frankly, either seemed vulgar.

"Confusion on my part, I'm sure," I replied, shifting slightly in my seat, slipping my hand down the side of the cushion to retrieve the object I'd hidden there.

"Clearly, I am *not* dead," she insisted.

"Clearly."

She stopped pacing and smiled. She was the most remarkably beautiful young woman, but then, I was always sent weak at the sight of auburn hair.

Such a shame I was going to have to kill her.

I HAVE BEEN all over the world, and there are only two places I would avoid returning to: Aberystwyth and central Australia. I have no problem with rough living; I have endured in jungles, deserts, ice floes and English market towns, and can make my peace with the absence of most simple comforts. But certain parts of Australia really do take frugality of pleasure to bloody-minded extremes.

"What are you doing?" asked Nowra, my aboriginal guide, a young man so sharp I could have used him to chop an onion.

"I am sitting in the river to cool off," I explained.

"Idiot," he said, demonstrating, as he frequently did, how encouraging one's staff to ignore social protocol and speak their mind can lead to irritation. "That's Lhere Mparntwe, what you call the Todd River. It's dry."

"If you ask me," I replied, tossing a handful of dust

into the wind, "the responsibilities of a river are generally light. Being wet might be considered the most basic requirement."

"It floods at some points during the year."

"What with? Rocks?"

I stood up, deciding it would be quicker to walk rather than swim.

"The white settlers made the same mistake," said Nowra. "They set up their telegraph station here because they thought it was a watering hole. That's why they called their town Alice Springs."

"One can hardly call it a town."

"*They* do."

"They're excessively ambitious. It's another white man's trait. We do love putting up buildings and owning plots of dirt."

"It makes me laugh."

"No Englishman will tolerate being laughed at."

"Then they shouldn't be so funny."

"Define 'funny.'"

Nowra pointed at my equipment. "Messing about in the dust, trying to find gold."

"Gold, diamonds, *anything* of value, Nowra; one cannot afford to be picky. In fact, one cannot afford much at all, which is precisely why I am doing it."

Nowra sniffed; one presumes it was derision rather than catarrh. "White man and his money."

"Watch who you're calling a white man, I'm half Egyptian."

"You cannot tell."

"Is that an insult?"

"It is whatever the white man wants it to be." Nowra smiled. He really was most tiresome. "When white men need money, do they not normally get a job?"

"Like leading idiots around deserts in Australia, for example?"

He nodded. "Idiots are easier to find than diamonds."

"I have other reasons to avoid the civilised world at the moment. I needed somewhere remote and unpleasant to escape to. I chose your home."

"It welcomes you and the little money you have. What is it you're running away from?"

"That, my dear chap, must remain my business."

I HAD BEEN here for two months now and was finding it increasingly difficult not to consider it a prison sentence. The Australian desert had no need for iron bars, as there was nowhere to escape to. I am a well-travelled man, as I trust I have made clear, and rarely while marching across the soil of the world did I find myself hankering for the comfort of Piccadilly, or Regent Street. While London may well have become my home, it is not somewhere I ever wanted to stay in perpetuity. My Mayfair flat was a place to store my books; all decent men require a library, but few choose to live in it. London is a place to start from.

Now, for the first time in my life, I missed it deeply. But there: I'd made my bed, and it was a thin bedroll in Alice Springs, a town that hadn't quite got the hang of being a town yet.

There was a telegraph station, and around it a slowly—oh, so slowly—growing camp of settlers, here to seek their fortune. Gold had been found near here, and where there's gold there will always be delusional people with sieves.

I was, of course, one of them.

My reasons were, perhaps, a little more complex than the others who had come here—or maybe not. I got the distinct impression most of them were on the run from some transgression or another. The essential details remained the same, however; my finances were at an all-time low and I very much needed a fresh start in life.

NOWRA AND I chose to have lunch beneath a desert bloodwood tree. The shade it offered was purely notional, but at least it felt like a proper place to sit as we ate our provisions.

As we sat and chewed miserably at something that was not so much cooked as mummified, we saw a group of strangers crossing the desert a couple of miles away. Honestly, I was interested in them as much for the change of subject as anything. Nowra had been once more prying into whatever recent misfortune it was that had driven me to this godforsaken country of dust, impoliteness and murderous wildlife.

"Who are they, do you think?" I asked, gesturing towards them with the remains of something roasted.

"More idiots," Nowra replied. "I told you they were plentiful around here."

There were four of them. Two men—one young, with

a military bearing, the other considerably older, his grey hair wafting in a breeze he was lucky to have found in this baking, infernal place—and two women, one of whom appeared to hail from Africa, given her warrior's dress and the spear she was carrying. I will admit to being positively intrigued by the latter; I had met few women so interesting as to be carrying a spear.

"Their idiocy aside," I said, "might you know any more about them? One presumes they're not also on the hunt for gold or diamonds?"

"Who can tell?"

"One doesn't dig for diamonds with a spear."

"Idiots might. Idiots are capable of anything. Anyway, they are of no importance. Tell me more about what happened to you in India."

"You're a nosey beggar."

"I am no beggar, I earn my keep."

"And you are perfectly aware of the point I am—quite bluntly—driving at. Why are you so infernally interested in finding out about my recent misadventures?"

"Idiots tend to repeat themselves. I don't want trouble."

"Who does?" (Well, me, perpetually, but I thought it imprudent to mention the fact.) "As delightful as all this chewing has been," I continued, "and one can hardly grace it with so lofty a term as 'lunch,' I think I should like to follow those people and find out what they're up to."

"Is that because you are—and correct me if I am wrong, I am keen to learn your language better—a nosey beggar?"

He really was the limit.

*   *   *

WE FOLLOWED IN the footsteps of this intriguing foursome. I will confess I was instantly rather jealous of the fact that they hadn't thought it necessary to hire a local guide.

"They are cleverer than you, I think," said Nowra.

"You'll get no disagreement from me."

The landscape close to Alice Springs was by no means completely sparse. Aside from the previously mentioned bloodwood trees, clumps of wispy silver cassia dotted the red earth, alongside occasional plumes of dry grass. It wasn't what one could call lush, but it was something to break up the view. As Nowra had said, for a short time every year, the dry river would flow, the water seeping into the earth to sustain the plant-life. A whole ecosystem living on so little, surviving the drought just for the faint promise of water to come. The plants and the people were not so different around here, I decided.

Even with these valiant attempts to offer more than baked clay and misery, there was little to obscure our view of the travellers; and it was clear they were heading towards the mountains—or, rather, between them.

"Ntaripe," said Nowra.

Or, in the language of Idiot White Men, Heavitree Gap, the gap through the MacDonnell Range that led to Alice Springs.

"It is an important place," said Nowra, "according to the old men of the Aranda."

"It's important in that it's the easiest place to put a road, certainly," I agreed, though, as those who know my history will attest, I was by no means so blind to superstition as I sometimes like to pretend. How could I be, after what had happened to me in Calcutta?

If the group ahead were aware of us—and I wouldn't do them the disservice of assuming not—they gave no sign. Clearly whatever it was that brought them here, the presence of a couple of prying strangers was no deterrent. No doubt they assumed we were harmless. I could have corrected them of that assumption, but, for what it was worth, I hoped the need wouldn't arise.

As they approached the gap, they moved to the left and began heading into the mountains, scaling the rocks, a cloud of orange dust trailing behind them.

"Lovely," I said. "A climb, and on such a cool day."

Nowra was getting surlier by the moment, even more irritated by this sudden excursion than he'd been with my pathetic attempts to pry fortunes from the earth. "I begin to realise what it is you are running away from, I think," he said. "You stuck your nose where it was not wanted."

It was the habit of a lifetime, I couldn't deny that, but Calcutta had been more complicated.

"MR. BEY," SAID Miss Collins, "have you been sitting on that all this time?" She was staring at the revolver I had withdrawn from beneath the chair cushion with rather more composure than I would have liked. I dislike guns. I respect them, they can be terribly useful—even necessary—but I treat their presence much in the way I treat the arrival of distant family members visiting my home: they've turned up, they're staying, and won't it be simply delightful when they've gone away again?

This is not to say that I am entirely incapable in their use. I have had a number of careers over the years: explorer, prospector, spy, journalist, all trades in which someone or something may try and kill you. Therefore, a familiarity with firearms is positively encouraged.

In fact, I once had something of a reputation as a crack shot, predicated entirely on one rather boisterous evening culminating on Bank junction that resulted in the statue of Duke the Wellington losing his nose. I wouldn't need such questionable skill here; she was only a few feet away and quite impossible to miss, if only thanks to that radiant smile.

"I had a feeling it might be necessary," I replied. "The residents here get surly when afternoon tea is pending."

"And why are you pointing it at me?" she asked. "Surely I am not that intimidating? Are you so terrified of a young woman on her first trip abroad?"

"Of course not," I replied, shooting her right in the forehead.

"YOU SHOT A woman in the head?" Nowra asked. Which surprised me rather as I had no idea I'd spoken out loud. It says a lot about the state of a man's mind when his surface thoughts start leaking out of his mouth. I'd have to watch that. In my old espionage days, a slippery tongue would most certainly have cost me my life.

"It was a trifle more complicated than that," I told him. "And now is not the time to discuss it."

"If I am in the company of a man who would kill an innocent woman, I would like to know."

"'Innocent' doesn't come into it. 'Woman' either, for that matter. Where do you think this leads?"

I was looking at the cave entrance into which the group we had been following had vanished. I was also changing the subject, quite definitively. "Do your people know about this?"

"My people know everything," he replied.

"So answer the question. Where does it lead?"

"I don't know." If he saw any contradiction in his statements, he didn't let it bother him. "Nowhere important."

"Important enough for our four friends to trek for miles in order to enter it," I pointed out.

"They are—"

"Idiots, yes, let's not go through all that again."

"We should not go down there. You won't find any diamonds, isn't that what you're here for?"

"Why are you suddenly so concerned?" I asked. "Your indifference to the matter earlier couldn't have been more pronounced."

"I have realised I would like to continue getting paid."

"Then kindly stop being so obstructive and follow me."

I entered the cave.

THERE ARE PEOPLE who positively rejoice in holes in the ground. Personally I'm not that enthused by them. Holes in the ground are where you bury things.

The entrance was a narrow crack in the rock and necessitated abandoning my pack. I removed a lantern and my revolver and hid the rest of my meagre possessions behind a rock. It wasn't much, but it was all I had; it would be a shame to lose it.

The narrow gap opened out into a much larger cavern. I crossed the dusty floor, the scuffle of pebbles beneath my boots echoing from wall to wall.

"Impressive," I said, more to announce my presence than anything else. While Australia is full of things willing to end your life, most of it had the good sense to leave you alone if you went loudly about your business. I hoped my stamping feet and loud voice would send things away into the shadows where they could wait for me to be elsewhere.

Moving around the cavern, shining the lantern on the walls, we discovered an exit leading further into the mountain. A passage that would just about allow us to pass single file (as long as I was prepared to angle my head rather too far to the side for comfort).

"I suppose you will want to go in there?" asked Nowra.

"There seems little point in staying here," I replied.

"There seems little point in going in there either," he said, "but you will do what you will do, and I suppose I must come with you."

"Clearly the passage leads somewhere of interest," I pointed out. "Again, four people would hardly go to the effort of traversing it on a whim."

Nowra said nothing. I decided that was close enough to acquiescence and we entered the tunnel.

* * *

IT WAS, AT least, somewhat cooler down there than it had been above. Five minutes ago, had you asked me whether I would have suffered a cricked neck for the sake of a little less heat, I would have asked where such a deal could be made. Now, having bumped my head so often I had serious doubts I could ever find a hat to fit again, I yearned once more for the open air. If that meant a hostile sun, so be it.

Nowra, who had the fortune of being a good foot shorter than me, bore the journey with his usual smugness. "You are the one who wanted to come down here," he said. "You should be enjoying yourself."

"I am in a state of near bliss," I told him. "Now, be quiet and keep your eyes peeled for snakes."

"No snake would bite me," he said, as if I had only been concerned for him. I suspect he was right, though, it would take a decidedly impressive set of fangs to puncture that sunburned skin of his. The fact that one so young possessed such a leathery exterior said all that needed to be said about the local climate. If he made it to forty, he would look like a rock.

"That's a relief," I said. "Nonetheless, if you should spot one, feel free to mention it, since *I* may be seen as fair game."

Given the winding nature of the passage, it was hardly surprising that there was no sign of the group we had been following. What *did* surprise me is that we couldn't hear them. Certainly they had a considerable lead on us, but one would have thought their footsteps would echo back towards us—and ours to them. Again, if they cared that they were being followed, there was no evidence of it.

I noticed some drawings on the wall and pointed them out to Nowra. "Your people have been down here, then?" I asked.

He shrugged. "We get everywhere. It is our land, after all."

He made no attempt to translate the figures for me. The illustration was of a man, his head surrounded by serpents. My limited experience of the Aranda people led me to believe they weren't in the habit of posting warning signs; the illustration likely had a greater significance than simply: *Caution—Here be Snakes*.

"What does it mean?" I asked him.

"It means you have to be careful of snakes," he said.

"Oh," I replied, rather disappointed. "Any particular type of snake?"

"Snakes come in all forms," he said. "It depends on how literal you wish to be. For example, would your people not call you a snake for what you did to that woman?"

Back on his favourite subject again. How tedious.

"Those that knew the circumstances—of which there are precious few, one of them the Foreign Secretary of England—called me a hero."

"For shooting a young woman? What strange people you are."

"I told you, it was more complicated than that."

"So explain."

"I don't want to. I would have thought was obvious, from the way I keep changing the subject."

"You're ashamed?"

"Not in the least. I simply do not wish to discuss it."

The passage grew narrower.

"How adorable," I said, "if this passage gets any tighter we'll have to crawl along on our bellies."

"Like snakes?"

IT WASN'T LONG before my prediction was proven correct. The one consolation as I scuffled along in the dirt was that at least Nowra had to suffer the same indignity. It may seem churlish of me, but he'd been so perfectly annoying that I took my revenge where I could.

"I hope this passage widens again soon," I said. "I have no great desire to try turning around."

"The others have not returned," he pointed out.

This was a surprisingly positive statement from Nowra. "Well observed," I said. "So we can assume our confined state won't be permanent?"

"Either that or we will be stuck here," he said, "no longer able to move in either direction."

I should have known.

"Trapped," I said. "And to think I came to your delightful country with the explicit intention of avoiding such an eventuality."

MISS COLLINS TOPPLED backwards onto the rug, her face a perfectly pathetic, slack image of confusion. In this, of course, she wasn't alone.

I will not deny that in my youth I often enjoyed being the centre of attention. It must be said, however, that there is a great deal of difference between captivating a room with your flair for the Schottische and standing over the body of a young woman with a smoking revolver in your hand. I couldn't reasonably expect anyone to start applauding.

Miss Collins' body twitched and, deciding I might as well be hanged for a sheep as a lamb, I put two more bullets into her. That, I believe, was the point at which the residents *really* started to panic. Sir Henry, that most noble animal, had already fled the scene, startled by the sound of the first shot. With the second and third, his owner and her companion followed him. The room became a mass of screaming and running feet.

Unfortunately, not everyone ran away. In my experience there is nothing quite so awkward as a male in company. A man on his own does what he thinks best, but put him in a group of other men—or worse, under the gaze of a woman—and an irritating inclination towards bravery arises.

"Now see here," said the old soldier, woken by the gunshots, "there's no need for all this foolishness."

Foolishness. As if I had just executed somebody in a fit of high spirits.

"Put the gun down," said a man towards the back of the room.

"You can't shoot us all," said another.

"Probably wouldn't dare," said another. "*We're* not defenceless women."

Oh how tedious this was going to be. It was clear I wasn't

going to be able to leave the room without a fight, and despite current appearances, beating innocent people was not something I was inclined to do. Nor, however, was I willing to be on the receiving end of whatever rough justice these chaps had in mind.

All of which left me with only one option that I could see.

I jumped out of the window.

To MY DISTINCT relief, Nowra and I found ourselves in a cavern. Like a pipe feeding into a tank, the tunnel emerged through a ragged hole in the rock and we pulled ourselves through and dropped down into the dust below.

There was still no sign of the party we had been following, and there were three possible exits from the cavern. Holding the lantern to the ground, I observed the dust in front of each possible exit and was soon able to discern which tunnel they must have taken.

"I am wondering," said Nowra, "if there is *anywhere* white man won't go."

"We approach the world with curiosity," I admitted. "Some of us, anyway. I should introduce you to an old colleague of mine, Travers, you would have liked him. He works in the Foreign Office and yet has never set foot in another country. Exists entirely within the small triangle formed between his office, his club and his lodgings. I once asked him whether he wished to accompany me to a violin recital in Ealing; he blanched at the thought of travelling so far out of his way, and refused me in something approaching panic."

"Is Ealing a dangerous territory?"

"That depends entirely on your opinion of suburbanites."

"I don't know what they are."

"Creatures born and raised to clean air, leafy avenues and boredom."

"They don't sound threatening."

"Try attending a dinner party sometime."

We followed the group's footprints through a tunnel, and it swiftly became clear we were approaching our destination.

"Turn out your lantern," I told Nowra.

"Why?" he asked.

"Because we won't need it." I extinguished my own lantern—true enough, a faint light was now discernible further along the tunnel. I could only presume we had finally caught up with the other party. I bore them no ill will, of course. How could I? I didn't know them. But I couldn't be sure we would be met with the same equanimity. We would advance carefully, we would observe, and then, once assured that they meant us no harm—or at least, as assured as we could be—we would present ourselves. In hushed tones, I explained as much to Nowra. He didn't argue, just nodded.

We moved as silently as possible, not difficult in the soft, dry earth lining the tunnel. Working our way towards the light, which brightened with every cautious step. It was clear that the source of the light was something significantly more impressive than a few lanterns. It had an emerald quality, shimmering on the cave walls like sunlight through stained glass.

The tunnel opened onto a wide plateau at last.

Beneath us, far bigger than one could imagine, even here in the heart of the mountains, lay a city.

I CAN'T REMEMBER when I first got into the habit of always checking the windows of any room I intended to spend time in. I suspect it goes all the way back to my unpleasant time hanging from an upper window of Lupton Tower during my schooldays.

It was a quite remarkable dawn that morning, I recall, though its beauty was somewhat wasted on me, my mind being elsewhere at the time. I had no interest in curtailing my schooling by plummeting to my death; but then I had no great desire to come face to face with the French master either, not considering the relationship I was enjoying with his wife. I did, finally, manage a controlled descent to the floor below, but being aware of fresh-air escape routes is a sensible precaution, and these days I make a point of it.

The main window of the Auckland Hotel's lounge led out to a short balcony. From there, residents could look down on Calcutta—in all possible senses of the term—like an ancient monarch contemplating their province from the safety of the battlements. In itself, the balcony was no great escape, but as long as one doesn't lose momentum I am gratified to report that it is entirely possible to leap from there and catch hold of the Union flag hanging from the front of the establishment.

I am no great patriot, but I will not deny the sight of that noble banner will forever trigger a warm, fond glow since that evening. It may sound absurd, but those few seconds swinging back and forth to reach the safe embrace of the park across the road were, by some measure, the most relaxing and pleasant of my day thus far.

If the cab drivers of that noble city were alarmed at the sight of a gentleman adventurer flying over them, they showed no sign. In truth, India has always been full of surprises; no doubt my aerial acrobatics ranked low amongst the spectacles that had already filled their days.

Coming to land in a thick hedge of Japanese boxwood, I could almost imagine the racket from the balcony behind me was applause. I was not, however, so egotistical as to luxuriate in the moment; in situations like that one doesn't waste one's hard-earned freedom, one can never tell how long it will last. I took to my feet and sprinted down the street, plucking foliage from my clothing.

Within a couple of hours I was on a ship heading back towards England.

I AM A lucky man. These eyes have seen sights most could not begin to imagine, and moreover, they have survived the experience. Nonetheless, that city in the mountains ranks amongst the strangest things I have ever seen.

In construction it called to mind a hive. The buildings were hewn from the rock so as to seem a continuous part of it, nature chipped and moulded to practical use. Not that the city's aesthetic was entirely functional. Its makers had not downed tools the moment they had achieved a viable habitation: they had finessed and decorated. There were domes and minarets, courtyards and terraces. Many of the buildings had been decorated with precious stones—no wonder I hadn't found any, the builders of this miraculous place had conscripted them all in the name of beauty. There was even fresh water, a river running through the heart of the city, culminating in a waterfall that glittered just as brightly as the precious stones. The source of the light was also now apparent. Strings of glowing cages filled with some form of phosphorescent material dangled above and between the buildings; hundreds of tiny light sources that, together, provided a green glow as bright as a summer dusk.

"Beautiful," I said, because it felt necessary that this sight should be marked by speech, even though no words truly felt up to the task.

"For once we agree," said Nowra.

But where were the people? By which I didn't mean the party we had been following—though certainly there was no sign of them—but rather the inhabitants of this hidden world. It was a city of size and complexity, and yet the streets and alleyways that ran between the buildings were empty. Nobody looked out of the arched windows, nobody drew water from the river. While the city showed no sign of neglect, was it possible it was an artefact of history, a place no longer inhabited?

With that thought, I was suddenly struck by dizziness. It was a momentary spell, not unlike a bout of vertigo—which, I might note, was a condition I rarely experienced. In that moment, nothing around me seemed entirely fixed: not the walls of the tunnel mouth around me, not the buildings of the city before me, not even Nowra, that most solid and permanent figure—as fixed in my life these last few weeks as the grit in my boot. None of it seemed substantial.

I reached out to the rock wall of the tunnel, seeking to steady myself, but it simply wasn't there. Stranger still, although my balance was lost and I felt myself toppling forward, I didn't fall. No, that isn't entirely accurate. I fell, but I did not land, just a lengthy sense of being outside the physical world entirely, adrift in some insubstantial plane.

It took a considerable effort to reassert myself. I insisted on the solid feeling of stone beneath my boots, and eventually found it once more. I insisted on the taste of the slightly stale air in my mouth, refusing to take no for an answer, and there it was. I insisted on the sight of that impossible city, glowing green in the heart of the earth, and once more I looked down upon it.

"Are you alright?" asked Nowra.

"Perfectly, thank you," I replied. Which was true, because in that moment of dislocation I had remembered something terribly important. "Just a moment of dizziness."

"So now what do you want to do?"

THE QUESTION SEEMED somehow insulting. I turned to the Foreign Secretary—or Grunter, as I had called him ever since our days at school together, for reasons that shall remain indistinct for the sake of decorum—and fixed him with my most despairing look.

"What do I want to do?" I asked. "I want to return to some form of normality, Grunter; I wish to sit in a restaurant without fearing the forces of law and order will descend on me at any moment. I want to stop seeing my name written on the front page of the *Times* right next to the words 'ruthless' and 'murderer.' Perhaps most of all, I wish to stop wearing this blasted wig and false beard. It itches."

"Naturally," he replied, sighing. "But it's all rather complicated. You did shoot a young woman in front of many witnesses."

"She wasn't a young woman, Grunter, she was a rakshasa, a shape-changing demon bent on infiltrating the British government. The real Miss Collins was dead before I even arrived in Calcutta."

"I know all that, Winnie," he said, "but there's simply no way we can inform the British public of such things. If you had been able to kill the demon with a tad more subtlety... we never imagined you'd just *shoot* her in front of an audience."

"I took the opportunity when it presented itself."

"Please don't think me ungrateful, I am simply drawing your attention to the awkwardness of the situation. Roughly thirty people—including several minor aristocrats—saw you kill what *appeared* to be a young woman. The only way of clearing your name would be to admit what she really was, and the ministers—the few who even know the truth—are simply not willing to do that."

"So you leave me to the wolves?" I couldn't believe

Grunter was doing this to me. Surely there was some way out of my current fix?

"Not if we can possibly help it," he said, "but any solution is going to take a certain amount of time and a great deal of careful thought. Winston Bey must vanish for a while."

"But I have no access to my assets! I can't set foot near my home, let alone a bank. I've been sleeping rough since my return."

He wrinkled his nose. "I am only too aware of that. Look, I can get you cleaned up, buy you passage somewhere— and that will be out of my own pocket, Winnie, the government can't be seen to be involved—and, while you keep out of sight in some distant corner of the globe, I will do all I can to think of a way to clear your name. Or if not that, then to create you a new one."

"And where exactly do you think I should go?" I didn't like the sound of any of this, but I was enough of a realist to accept it. This was the only offer on the table, and in my current circumstances, beggars could not be choosers.

"Have you ever been to Australia?" he asked.

"WHAT DO I want to do?" I said. "Why, get to the truth, what else?"

Carved stone steps led down from the plateau.

"What truth are you seeking?" asked Nowra as we descended. "Something to help you return home to your old life? Perhaps if you destroy this place, they might welcome you back."

"Destroy it?" I asked. "Is that really what you think of me? A blunt instrument, deployed against all the strangeness of the world? A hammer, to pound the unknown into dust? I am all that I have ever claimed to be, Nowra; a man wandering the world, seeing what may befall him."

"You deny that the English government sent you here for a reason then?"

"I do." Although it occurred to me that Grunter was perfectly capable of sending me here with an ulterior motive. Like all Whitehall creatures, that sort of thing amuses him sometimes.

The steps ended at a wide path into the city, and we wandered between the buildings. I didn't waste time looking through the windows or exploring deeply. I knew where I was going.

"And the others?" asked Nowra. "Who sent them?"

"You'd have to ask them." I smiled. "But then I imagine you already have."

We'd arrived at what I had been aiming for, a small round building with a dome of red quartz. Entering, we stepped into a warm yellow light, bathing the five sleeping bodies we found lying on the floor: the four people we had been following, and, of course, myself.

"You are aware that you are dreaming?" Nowra asked.

"Yes. I wasn't to begin with, but eventually... You wanted to know me. To understand me."

"I am still not sure that I do," he admitted.

"Can't help that," I replied. "You know me as well as I know myself by now, and—well—now we're getting into a philosophical minefield, aren't we?" I gestured to the other four lying before us. "And them? Do you understand them?"

"They say they are only here to investigate. If we present no threat, then they will leave us in peace." He looked at me and I was relieved to note that the false image I had placed on him, humanising him, reducing him, was now gone. Because Nowra was many amazing things, of that I had little doubt, but the last thing he could be considered was human. That thick skin? Scales. That sharp tongue? Forked. Beware of snakes, the cave painting had suggested, especially those that can wrap themselves around your mind. He walked upright, possessed the four limbs we humans take as read, but I had been warned of snakes and found myself bitten anyway.

I thought about what he'd said, that these four had been sent to investigate this strange subterranean world. Was I seeing the hand of Grunter here? I suspected so. No doubt I was intended as an ace hidden up the sleeve. An extra pair of hands should it be necessary. Of course, if he'd bothered to tell me I could have saved myself no small amount of bother but that's spies for you, consistently playing a game and refusing to explain the rules. It's all terribly tedious.

"And you doubt them?" I asked. "You can see inside their minds, just as you've seen inside mine."

"The young woman you killed was what you would term a monster."

"Yes, she was."

"But that is what concerns me. If you viewed her in such terms, how do you view me?"

I sighed. "My dear Nowra, you've been an exceedingly irritating guide, but that's no excuse to put a bullet in your head. The creature that killed and copied poor Miss Collins had designs on conquest. It—and the rest of its kind—was attacking us. I was simply returning fire."

"My people will be seen as a threat. You will hunt us down, you will try and destroy us."

"Will we?" I thought for a moment, then asked the only thing I could think of. "Show me."

"Show you?"

I gestured towards the city outside. "No more hiding. Show me it all."

He inclined his head, tongue slipping in and out between dry lips. "Very well," he said.

We stepped back outside, and streets that had been empty before now teemed with life. Nowra's people, these beautiful amalgams of human and serpent, were everywhere. I saw them leaning out of their windows, running along the streets, bathing in the river, gathering in squares.

It would seem they had the best of both worlds: walking as we do, slithering up the walls of buildings, scrambling along the roof of the cavern.

From somewhere I could hear music, a low, hypnotic melody that sounded like the wind through narrow tunnels. I stepped a little way up the street, trying to find the source. It came from one of the squares, where several of the snake people were gathering around a large rock, honeycombed with holes. They moved around it, blowing into the holes, the whistling sounds rising up and blending with their echoes high overhead. Around these musicians, a crowd danced. Entwined in couples, they swayed and glided around the square, eyes closed, lost to the music.

"You're still in my mind," I said to Nowra.

"Yes."

"So what do I think?"

He paused for a moment, closing his eyes and trying to decide. All he had to do was look at my face. Finally he opened his eyes, and there was softness there.

"You think we're beautiful."

"Yes," I said, "yes, I do. And I can assure you that I could never destroy what you've built here. Quite the reverse: I would defend its safety until my dying day."

"Yes," he said, "I believe you would."

"How long have you been here?" I asked him.

"Always." He said. "Longer than you. Much longer."

"I can believe that."

Nowra and I were silent for a short while, the two of us walking the streets of his home, occasionally meeting with people he knew. Eventually we turned our attention to the pressing question.

"What about the others?" he asked. "How can I know whether they're to be trusted?"

"You can't," I said. "But I've had a thought about that."

"RUN!" I SHOUTED, as we burst from the mouth of the cave. "The fuse has only a few seconds left."

"What do you *think* we're doing?" asked Ms Braithwaite, "we're not bloody *idiots*, you know!"

"Now, now, Gracie," said De Quincey, rather breathless.

"Rocks, to the left!" Fairburne shouted. "They'll provide cover."

"Down!" shouted Nalangu, pushing me forward with the more tolerable end of her spear.

We threw ourselves behind the rocks that Fairburne had suggested, just as the sound of dynamite tore through the early evening. A shower of stones, a wall of hot air and, for a moment, all of us blacked out.

"At least that's what they think," I told Nowra. "Look after yourself, old boy."

"And you," he said with a smile, "the world needs idiots, after all."

With that, he and the handful of his people that had helped carry the four strangers out retreated back to their beautiful world.

After a while my new companions woke up.

"How much dynamite did you use?" asked Fairburne, rubbing at his ears, trying to clear his head.

"Enough," I replied, pretending that I too had only just recovered from the effects of the blast. "But I suggest we get clear of the mountains, just in case I've encouraged some of it to fall upon our heads."

I got to my feet and started marching towards Alice Springs, sure the rest of them would follow. They did.

"Terrible shame, really," said the professor, glancing

back over his shoulder. "It would have been fascinating to have studied their culture."

"Too dangerous," said Fairburne, "as much as I hate to admit it, we were lucky our new friend was there."

"It was nothing," I said. "I've been doing a little prospecting, so the dynamite was in my pack."

"And you weren't scared of 'em?" asked Gracie. "Most people would have been."

"Oh," I replied, "I have some small experience in these matters."

"So do we," said Nalangu. "It is our duty to protect the world from creatures like that."

"Well, there's a thing," I said, "I don't suppose you have a vacancy, do you? I'm at something of a loose end at the moment."

PECCAVI,
OR IF THY FATHER
MIMI MONDAL

THE SMALL EARTHEN bowl of turmeric crushed in milk sat insistently outside the bathroom. The sight of it made Anjali almost smile, then well into tears. The bowl had been placed there by Sabarmati dai, nursemaid, nanny, now elderly housekeeper; the only servant who still remained in the sprawling fort and palace of the Kishangarh Maharaja. It was tradition, the old woman grumbled. A Rajput princess, especially one in the prime of her youth and ready to be wooed by suitors, must under no circumstances neglect her beauty. That meant diligent coconut-oil massages to restore lustre to the hair, icy splashes of rosewater to the face every morning, turmeric paste to scrub off dead skin before bathing, until each part of her body glowed again like the rare jewel that she was. And would you look at that girl, dear God—come back from Vilait all skin and bone, chapped lips, hair like the head of a broomstick, looking every bit as scruffy as a beggar woman from the village. Was that any way for a princess to be?

Anjali grimaced as she absently picked up the bowl and started rubbing the coarse paste to her arms. The comforting fragrance of crushed turmeric overwhelmed her, as the shimmering winter sunshine filtered through the filigreed terrace of the Phool Mahal Palace, overlooking its lake—so golden, such a world away from the bleak, watery light that lay over Oxford University, half-buried this time of the year in snow.

This was how Anjali's ancestresses had lived, looking upon this view century after century. Rajput queens and princesses were famed in history for being valiant, but theirs was not the valour of war. While their men struck terror in the hearts of the enemy on the battlefield—repelling every invader from the Greek to the Muslim to, yes, even the British—Rajput women had held strong to their fortresses, never hesitating to fling themselves into the immolation pyres rather than enduring defilement at the hand of the enemy. The Rajput royal blood that flowed in Anjali's veins was an untainted stream of glory, its purity to be preserved at any cost.

Not that Anjali was going to present herself to suitors any time soon, a fact that was incomprehensible to her adamant old dai. Her current fate was closer to the immolation pyres of yore—with her two older brothers recently turned up dead; and her senile father, Maharaja Amarendra Singh Rathore of Kishangarh, counting his own last days within his shady bedchamber at the heart of the palace, the last male member of their line. But this was the twentieth century. Anjali was a scholar at the Oxford University, preparing to take the bar exam next year. All of the British Indian Empire was thrumming with nationalistic fervour, and so many other, unseen tensions roiling beneath the surface. In the midst of all that, Anjali had no intention of setting herself on fire.

Turmeric paste applied, she stepped out of her dressing gown onto the cool stone floor of the bathroom. There was no claw-footed bathtub, unlike her flat in Oxford, but the water drawn in buckets from the lake was cool and painstakingly filtered, all by that bent old woman who had once bathed Anjali and her brothers by her own hand. Anjali poured mugfuls of water over herself, willing it to wash away the horror of the past few months.

All it managed to remove was dead skin, something she barely cared about any more.

THE LARGE DINING room at the palace lay unused, for Anjali now took her meals at her father's bedside. The once valiant Maharaja Rathore—six feet tall and barrel-chested, renowned hunter, the terror of his subjects though his kingdom was nothing but a decorative title under the British Empire—now lay wasting away in his bed, with an illness the doctors called 'paralysis,' for the lack of any better explanation. The best doctors in the country, including the Viceroy's private physician from Delhi, had failed to determine what precisely was wrong with

Maharaja Rathore. Not that the family—or what remained of it—didn't know, but the thing they knew was not the sort that bore any relevance in the twentieth century.

The family did not discuss such things at mealtime. There were appropriate times for every conversation in the royal household of Kishangarh, and for some of them there was never an appropriate time. It was why Anjali was not informed immediately after her two older brothers—Ajay, twenty-five years old, and Abhay, twenty-two—were killed in "hunting accidents" months ago. She never saw their bodies, never attended their cremation nor observed the week of mourning afterwards, although leaving a message for her at St. Hilda's College in Oxford could surely not have been impossible. "The tragedy had happened; we had lost what we lost," said her father when she returned, resorting to the formal, royal plural she'd always despised. "They were not going to return to us. We did not find it necessary to disrupt your studies during the term."

Sabarmati dai served lunch on a tray—the thin khichdi, rich with ghee, that was the only thing the Maharaja could swallow any more. As the old maid receded, glancing uncertainly from father to daughter, Anjali proceeded to spoon the broth patiently into the Maharaja's mouth. Her father was the only parent Anjali had known. He had been generous and liberal—providing her with a Western education that few women in the country received—but never quite intimate; not in the way he had been with her brothers. A daughter was nevertheless a daughter, not to be taught hunting or drinking or womanizing as becomes of the princes of a Rajput royal estate. Instead, since her mother died when she was but a few months old, Anjali Singh Rathore was brought up under the close supervision of Sabarmati dai, going to school and studying as hard as she could, knowing that would be her only route out of centuries-old Rajput femininity.

She was also protected from family secrets. Ajay and Abhay had known exactly what came for them, and it wasn't some poor starved tiger barely managing to stay alive in the dwindling forests of Sariska. Anjali only had the foggiest idea, and her father refused to say more.

"Would you—would you recite to me some more of that—of that poet?" her father managed. "That Irish chap who's all into Hinduism and Tagore."

Anjali sighed. "W.B. Yeats?" The Maharaja was an incurable Anglophile, also a master of changing the subject. At another time, she would have shared his enthusiasm. It was what she had studied with the greatest passion all her life, after all.

"Please," her father said, smiling. "I feel like his words soothe my soul."

With another sigh, Anjali recited from the leather-bound chapbook she had picked up in London in summer that year.

"Some may have blamed you that you took away
   The verses that could move them on the day
   When, the ears being deafened, the sight of the
      eyes blind
   With lightning you went from me, and I could find

201

Nothing to make a song about but kings,
Helmets, and swords, and half-forgotten things
That were like memories of you—"

"Stop! Stop, that's enough," groaned the Maharaja, stilling her mid-recital. He made a pained expression. "So condemning, dear God! Is there no joy to be found in the world anymore?"

"Not in the poetry of Yeats, I'm afraid," Anjali sulked. "There is only so far you can run from the truth, Daddy. The world is on fire. Your sons were just—"

"Enough!" her father growled.

Anjali turned to see Sabarmati dai—that elderly, soft-footed maid—come to collect their empty dishes, along with a bowl of warm water and a rag to wipe the Maharaja's mouth. Her father leaned back on his pillows and allowed her to perform her service.

Why had this old woman stayed, Anjali found herself wondering? The other servants of the estate were only too happy to be relieved. Word of the curse had been spread. No official statement was ever made, but rumours were hard to keep suppressed in as superstitious a country as this. Even the driver who had taken the family Austin to the airport in Delhi to bring Anjali home had been hired for the day, and legged it as soon as he collected his fee. But Sabarmati dai had been there, waiting for her, taking care of her father, as she always had.

Did she not have any family of her own? Anjali clearly remembered her son Mahesh—a thin, dark-skinned child, nearly the same age as her—for he was the one she grew up playing with, while her brothers were away at boarding school in Dehra Dun. Mahesh was always loitering in the palace grounds, since he never went to school, and at that age Anjali did not understand why; merely assumed he wasn't diligent enough. With the years they had grown apart, as Anjali got busy with her schoolwork and friends, and Mahesh started being sent out for small chores for the estate. This time around, she hadn't seen Mahesh at all. She couldn't remember if he was there when she'd visited the year before.

"Daddy, where is Mahesh these days?" she absently asked.

"Eh, who?"

"Mahesh. You know, Sabarmati dai's son."

"Honestly, I have no idea. I thought he found a job in Calcutta or someplace." The Maharaja grimaced. "What a random question to ask."

A thought flashed through Anjali's head for the first time. The sheer certainty shocked her—but it made sense. It made other thoughts clearer, thoughts that had been prickling her for days. Ajay had been the first to go, and Abhay within a couple of weeks of him. Nothing had happened to her yet, but she did not believe she would be let off. Blood curses did not care for gender.

"Daddy, why did Sabarmati dai stay? Everyone else left. Even the vegetable seller and the woman who draws water from the wells don't cross our threshold anymore," she said. "Why didn't she go away to live with Mahesh? Where does her husband live, or her family? What's left here for her?"

"How would I know?" Her father's voice grew irritable. "Why are you asking me these questions?"

"Because I need to know, Daddy. My life may depend on it. How long will you hide the truth from me?"

"You will go back to Oxford next week," he grumbled. "You will be safe, far from all this."

If only that were true, Anjali thought with a bitter smile. Her father's vision of England was painfully idyllic—the heart of an invincible Empire as it had been in his own college days, at the turn of the century. Her father hadn't seen the ravaged buildings in the wake of the Great War, slowly rotting under the damp, grey skies; the rumours of unspeakable horrors that haunted the student halls at Oxford. Only weeks before she left for India, a hell-beast of unprecedented nature had attacked Dr. Archimedes De Quincey within the very premises of Queen's College, barely steps away from her private accommodations on High Street. Anjali wasn't acquainted with the man per se—and was attending her own classes at St. Hilda's at the time of the outbreak—but she had gone with her friends to listen to a seminar by him in her first year.

The next day Dr. De Quincey was nowhere to be seen, his classes assigned indefinitely to a junior lecturer. Rumours had spread like wildfire through the cloistered student community of Oxford. No student walked alone after sundown for the rest of the term. The churches saw a sudden influx of those who had formerly taken great relish in proclaiming themselves atheist. Anjali had been only too relieved to leave, find herself again under the bright skies of India, which blazed away all miasma of horror or gloom.

"Daddy," she insisted. She had to. An ugly distress had clawed its way into the room, amidst the crisp winter afternoon. "Sabarmati dai never had a husband, did she? It was never the three of us—it was *four*—Ajay, Abhay, Mahesh and me. And now it's Mahesh's turn to die. If he isn't dead already. But you wouldn't know if he was, I suppose?"

"Certain conversations are indecent," the Maharaja snarled. "Especially between father and daughter."

"Nobody told me the curse spared daughters!" Anjali snarled back, finally at the end of her tether. Funny how similar they looked in their rage. "It said each of your offspring—didn't it? Everyone of *your* blood! Nothing about your wife's blood, not just your sons—but I suppose women have never been a consideration in the glorious Rajput lineage! I suppose you don't care if I die next, just as you don't care for Mahesh! Neither of us will carry forth the royal lineage of the Rathores of Kishangarh. As far as you are concerned, the line is *dead*."

"The curse is poppycock, and you, Rajkumari Anjali, will address us with greater respect the next time," said the Maharaja through gritted teeth, turning his gaze to the far wall.

Anjali stormed out of the room, without making an apology, a part of her wondering how she got to be so brave.

SHE MADE A phone call. Her school friend Sujata had got married to a wealthy clothing merchant in Calcutta. It was not common for young women of families like theirs to travel alone, but everyone knew that Anjali's father was bedridden and her brothers recently deceased; and how could she do her necessary research for Oxford otherwise?

Once she had replaced the phone back on its hook, she found Sabarmati dai waiting in the room.

"You will go looking for Mahesh," said the old woman, plainly, fixing Anjali in her gaze.

"Yes," she had to admit.

"Calcutta is a big city, I hear. Almost as big as Delhi. How will you find one boy among it all?"

"I was hoping you would help me, dai," Anjali implored. If Sabarmati dai refused to talk, she had nothing to start with.

"Very well," Sabarmati dai said. "Mahesh has been working as a waiter at one Auckland Hotel. It is an establishment patronized only by sahibs, and aristocratic Indians like yourself. The pay is good. The work doesn't break his back. It is the best a boy like him can hope for in life."

"It is not!" Anjali flared up, blood rushing to her face. Mahesh should've had the same opportunities as her brothers in life.

"You do not understand, beti. What your father did those many years ago—other royal men have done worse. It is the way of the world. At least your father gave us shelter in his estate. There is no place for a soiled woman with no husband in our villages; I could never have returned to my family. Mahesh would've starved in the desert. Instead he grew up here, well-fed and safe, learning to read from the books your brothers and you outgrew every year. That is how he managed to get a job at the sahibs' hotel. As for me, I lived well too, better than any woman from my village. I got to love and raise three more children that I never gave birth to—especially you, who have been the joy of my wretched existence."

"You didn't *deserve* a wretched existence!" Anjali railed. "He should've married you, especially after—especially after our mother passed!"

"Oh, my sweet, innocent child, if only that were possible," Sabarmati dai gave a weak, bitter laugh. "The Maharaja of Kishangarh marry a lowly Bhil woman? This country couldn't bear the weight of the scandal! Why, that is exactly what that witch demanded. And you know what happened with her."

"I... *don't*, actually," Anjali bit her lip. "He refuses to tell me anything. Even—even after... all this."

"And so would I have, but I believe you have the right to know." The old woman sighed. "Beti, I have loved your father all my life, though he has never loved me back the same way. It does not please me to discuss his misdeeds, but he committed his share of them, especially in his youth. It is the prerogative of the royalty to take what they want, as it is the burden of the lowly like us to suffer their whim. Such is the will of the gods. I do not question it. But there was once a woman who did. It was perhaps thirty years ago, before any of you were born.

"She was not a maidservant like me. She was a priestess—a priestess of a tiger goddess, who came from the forests of the east, walking barefoot all the way to our land. But she was a low-caste anyway, a forest girl with skin as black as rocks, matted hair bleached auburn by the sun, thick calluses on her feet. A girl who could barely speak the language of civilized society, leave alone any English.

"It was a blighted time for Kishangarh. There had been a drought that summer, which drove the tigers from the forest of Sariska to hunt towards our villages. The forest was much larger then, with many more tigers than today. Every night there would be a child carried away by a tiger, or at least a goat or a cow. The people appealed to your father, who was a young Maharaja then, but already renowned as a hunter. The British government wasn't interested in the fates of us lowly villagers, so your father alone brought together hunting parties and went raiding the forests. He killed two or three tigers, but more kept coming.

"That was when this priestess appeared. She wasn't local to our land, but she claimed she could make the tigers retreat by appeasing her goddess, and overnight there was a shrine for her under the banyan tree in our village, with people from far in the desert bringing her offerings.

"This kind of thing very quickly tilts to insubordination, so the Maharaja had to investigate. When he arrived with his men, he found the young priestess surrounded by hundreds of devotees under her tree. There would be a rebellion if he ordered her to be driven from his land, especially since he had failed to cull the tigers himself. But there was something else. There was a strange aura to that young woman—rough, dishevelled, unlettered, but emanating power and wisdom far beyond her age or station in life. She was nothing like any other woman he knew, either high-caste or low, and even at that young age, your father had known many women already."

Sabarmati dai let out a distraught sigh.

"And, you must understand, touched by a goddess though she might have been, this priestess was a very young girl. Much younger than you are now." Anjali's skin crawled—she had turned eighteen barely a month ago. "A young girl newly arrived from the forest, where life is very different from the way it is in civilization. In the forest, among the lowest castes, they do not know shame. There any woman can choose any man and start a family; it is accepted. They make love on the forest floor and do not care for the dirt. He came to her in supplication and wonder—this young, charming king, so worldly in his ways—and the priestess of the tiger goddess fell violently in love.

"A few months later, she arrived at his palace demanding acknowledgement for the child in her belly. Obviously, the Maharaja laughed. He was at that time actively seeking a bride from another royal family—someone of equal stature to join him in lineage and estate. A scandal like this would ruin his prospects, so he ordered the forest priestess to be shown out of his premises as swiftly and ruthlessly as possible. Unfortunately, in those months the priestess had become wiser to the ways of the world, so she threatened to take up the matter with the British governor in Jaipur. This, then, endangered much more than your father's marital prospects. Our British overlords, as you know, have no understanding of our ancient caste system and consider it unequivocally evil. If it was proved that the woman's unborn child was his—and there would have been witnesses in plenty, for she had many followers still—the Maharaja would be compelled to marry her, and that would destroy the nobility of his lineage forever. If he refused, he might lose his estates altogether and go to jail.

"So your father did the only thing he could think of to placate her. He agreed to meet her at a secluded spot in the forest, far from prying eyes, hoping to appeal to the love that she still bore for him. He offered her unimaginable wealth, lifetime upkeep for her child, a magnificent temple built to her goddess in the middle of Kishangarh—any price she named!—but the priestess would not relent. She was not his servant, or even his subject; she would accept nothing but marriage. Their exchange grew angry, passionate. The Maharaja feared her raised voice would attract the attention of nearby forest dwellers, though it was late in the night. The threat of tigers in the area yet remained, so he had carried his rifle.

"What happened next is not entirely certain. He thought he heard a growl, or saw a movement in the dark, and he scrambled to his rifle and fired. The bullets caught her: not one but many. She dropped to the ground in front of him, bleeding, dying."

"He killed her," Anjali said, amazed at the flatness of her voice. "My father killed that innocent woman, and their unborn child. And then he destroyed her corpse, like a cold-blooded murderer."

"He didn't, if you can believe it." There was a glimmer

at the edge of Sabarmati dai's eyes. Anjali wasn't sure if it was tears, or for whom. "The Maharaja was stunned, terrified by what he had done. You must not forget he was a young man too, just like your brothers, and recently returned from Vilait with a college degree. He was a renowned hunter, but shooting game is not the same as shooting a woman, much less one who is carrying your child. Besides, there were probably still tigers skulking in the dark. He backed away slowly and fled, no longer caring what might happen if his crime was revealed.

"Fortunately, the body of the priestess wasn't discovered until some days later, by which time tigers had devoured it to the extent that there was no bullet wound to be found. No case was brought against the Maharaja to the British courts. The priestess' following exploded, for that was how she had always predicted she would go—devoured by the beasts she commanded. If you ever visit that part of the Sariska forest, you will still find a shrine in her honour. Villagers and forest people alike lay flowers on it to this day. In her death, the priestess became a goddess."

"And the curse…" Anjali said.

"The curse, yes," Sabarmati dai nodded, an infinite sorrow settling at the corners of her mouth. "No one knows for sure. In his frenzy after he fired at her, the Maharaja saw many things. He thought he saw the woman turn into a tiger herself, about to bite his hand off as he crouched beside her to stop the blood. He thought he saw tigers—thirty, forty of them—emerging from the trees, surrounding them, waiting to spring as soon as her breathing would still. And then he thought he heard her last words, promising she would return to kill each of his offspring, every one born of a 'purer' womb that he deemed worthy to live, unlike hers. That she would see to the end of the lineage that he held dearer than her love and her child. No one knows if she actually said those words or if he imagined them in his grief, as he imagined so many things. But those words became a fever in his brain. For years afterwards, he would wake up screaming in the middle of the night: 'She said she would kill my children! She would return to destroy my lineage!' That's how word of the curse got around, though few know what happened in the forest that night."

"But Ajay and Abhay died in the same forest, killed by tigers." Anjali held up a hand. "Don't bother to repeat the lies Daddy has fed me already. I get out of the palace. I've asked around."

"Very well," Sabarmati dai said. "Your brothers were never much of hunters, nothing in comparison to your father. God knows what got into Ajay that he took a holiday from his job and wife in Delhi and returned to the ancestral estate, eager to hunt for big game. Your father expressly forbade him from going, but you know your eldest brother had never been the obedient kind. As for Abhay, he was only investigating Ajay's death. A chunk of my heart went to the pyre with that boy, but he barely knew how to hold a gun the right side up. He couldn't run up a flight of stairs without doubling over and demanding a glass of sherbat. That fictional curse has turned into a self-fulfilling prophecy for this family of hardheaded fools. I am glad that you are at least headed to Calcutta, and not into the damned forest yourself. The tiger population in Sariska has dwindled over the years, but they exist still. And an inexpertly wounded tiger would kill you, vengeful dead witch or not."

Anjali wouldn't stand a chance against a tiger. Their father had never trained her to shoot. The only thing she knew to stab with was a fountain pen, though she always suspected she did a cleaner job of it than her brothers.

"Mahesh will be happy to see you," said Sabarmati dai. "He has always loved you as a brother, though he did not dare express it. When you meet him, tell him I think of him every day, remind him to phone more often. And return home safe."

"Yes, dai." Anjali bent down to touch the feet of the old woman, wiped the dust on her head for blessing.

"And, beti, try to forgive your father. He was no worse than any other king of his time. He has done his duty by you, and even by his other illegitimate child. He is dying now."

To that Anjali had nothing to say. She took the next morning's train to Delhi, then the train to Calcutta from there. She did not return to the Maharaja's bedchamber to say goodbye.

CALCUTTA PUT HER in mind of a brighter, noisier, more decrepit London. Sujata's husband picked her up from the train station. Clothing merchants did not move in the same circles as the British crown, but once Anjali was in the city, there were other connections to be found through her Oxford credentials. A few days' socialising found her draped demurely on the arm of a young captain, headed to the Auckland Hotel in the afternoon for tea and a discourse on modern poetry.

He was surprised at her preference for the old hotel on Chowringhee Road over one of the more exclusive clubs in Calcutta. The Auckland's star had fallen in recent months, following the gruesome murder of a young Englishwoman in the tea room that had provided local newspapers gossip fodder for weeks. The only people still frequenting the place were its sworn devotees. Anjali had to appeal for the value of privacy to make her companion agree.

Mahesh was the waiter who served at their table, bringing in tea pot, china and dainty cucumber sandwiches, but he gave no indication of recognizing her in front of the amorous Englishman. Afterwards, with the tip, Anjali slipped him a scrap of paper. They met up the next afternoon at the corner of Imperial Museum, after he took an early leave from his shift.

Anjali wanted to squeal and rush into Mahesh's arms, perhaps dissolve into tears, but of course that would be inappropriate for a grown man and woman at a busy street corner in Calcutta. She had dressed in the plainest cotton sari she could find at Sujata's house, oiled down and worn her hair in a long plait, turning herself into the closest imitation she could of a young working-class woman, who wouldn't seem incongruous with a man like Mahesh. Despite her alabaster skin and his deepest brown, they could almost pass as brother and sister.

"Shall we?" he grinned, as they joined the queue in front of the Museum. No conversation in English any further; they would blend in with the hundreds of tourists who turned up to gaze at one of the largest museums in the world, the shelter of its elegant Grecian colonnades providing the most unremarkable meeting place in the city.

They walked from gallery to gallery, conversing in Hindi as they had done back home, keeping their voices below the din of the crowd. Mahesh knew of the deaths of Ajay and Abhay—his mother had phoned, and besides, the official version of the news had made it to the newspapers in Calcutta. But their deaths happened right around the time of the shooting at the Auckland Hotel, followed by weeks of rumours and police investigation. It would've been impossible for him to get leave to go home.

"Not that anyone missed me at their funerals." He shrugged. "I would not have been required to light their pyres, or tonsure my head for their mourning. I am not a Rathore." Mahesh's hair was a thick brown mop, lending a roguish charm to his bony face.

They kept walking. "But the curse—whatever it is—will descend on you too," said Anjali.

"I'll remember to never make a trip to the Sundarbans, then! Some of the guys at the mess were planning to go." Mahesh chuckled. "But really, Anjali, will it? Do you think I am the only illegitimate child of your father who lived? Not all of them were born of unmarried maidservants or crazy forest priestesses, either. Some of them go by names just as reputable as yours; maybe even British names. Ma never told me the details, but tigers weren't the only thing your father was renowned for hunting in his youth. None of those other children would give a damn about the extinction of the Rathore line, even if they knew. There, would you look at that bear?"

They stood in front of a large mounted figure of a Himalayan black bear, labelled and encased in glass. Anjali had been to other museums in the world, but Mahesh was occasionally pausing in their walk to enjoy the exhibits. She did not begrudge him that. She had all evening; wished she had more, to make up for the years they had lost as siblings. They were surrounded by chattering families, children running among the exhibits, softly whispering lovers—all ordinary people out for a day in the city, with little actual care for the contents of a museum. She wondered what their lives were like, full of love, with no ominous secrets.

Glass shattered with a crash right behind them, echoed in the cries of scattering tourists, which then drowned in the unexpected roar that rang out through the narrow gallery. Before Anjali could turn, the Bengal tiger leapt between her and Mahesh, no longer a hide stuffed and mounted, but a prowling animal. It turned its face at her, eyes alive with feral menace. Then it roared again, and a warm, putrid breath hit Anjali's face. She screamed.

From the other side, Mahesh rushed at the beast, brandishing a dagger—she had no idea where he might have found it. The blade did not even make contact. With one massive paw the tiger swatted him away like a fly. Mahesh was flung to the floor a few feet away, three straight lines of blood blooming on his chest where his shirt had been slashed. The tiger turned to Anjali again.

She backed away as it advanced, and her cheap hawai slippers slid from her feet. Something sharp stabbed her underfoot—she looked down to find the checkered marble floor littered with splinters of glass. She picked up a jagged shard and held it in front of her, suspecting it would cut her before it could even graze the tiger's hide.

A few security guards arrived at the other end of the gallery. One of them yelled, "Ma'am, get down, get down!" and as Anjali covered and ducked, the rattle of bullets from their ancient rifles filled the room, the noise magnified by the high ceilings. A ricochet, some more glass shattering, the figure of a sambar deer tumbling from its mount. In a space so narrow the tiger should've at least been injured, but no bullet seemed to touch it. It turned to the guards and let out a mighty growl, and they fled, though it did not chase them. A panicked despair started coming over Anjali as she realized that the tiger did not care for anyone but her.

The same thought must have occurred to Mahesh, who had stood up, staggering, during the distraction with the guards. Now he yelled, "Anjali, catch!" as he threw his dagger across to her, its dark blade glinting as it caught the glow of the tube lights overhead. The tiger swept at the flying weapon, rearing to its full height, and it landed far across the gallery from Anjali. For a split second she was grateful, for she had ducked as the dagger arced towards her as well.

Then she made a desperate rush for the weapon, feet burning and streaking blood across the floor as more splinters dug into them, the tiger leaping at her as she turned. She had one useful skill at that moment—though she knew nothing of fighting or hunting, she had been a sprinter at school. As soon as she closed her fingers around the hilt of the dagger, marveling at the blade—as long as her forearm and almost completely weightless—the tiger was upon her, crushing her under its weight, its roar and its stench obliterating all other senses.

Pain exploded at Anjali's left shoulder as she struggled on the floor under the animal, its teeth barely missing her jugular. She would die, she would die in a world of pain, just as Ajay and Abhay must have; she was dead already. Blindly she stabbed, stabbed, stabbed at the face, the neck, the forelimbs of the tiger, everything erased from existence in the deafening roar and the warmth that rained on her face.

Some sense returned. She could hardly see through the bloodshed, but the weight of the tiger's grip on her had shifted, and she could sense Mahesh was near, could hear his screams. She knew he was on the back of the tiger, directly above her, stabbing away with another blade. Where did all these weapons come from? Had he swiped them from the other galleries at the museum while she wasn't looking? "Keep stabbing at it, Anjali!" she thought she heard him say. "Don't stop! Only you can kill it! I am only providing distraction!" Anjali tightened her grip on the dagger, plunging it again and again as if into a hardened slab of butter, almost mechanically, knowing this was what she would do to the last of her breath.

Finally, the tiger made a noise that sounded more like a long yowl—it went on and on, she felt, filling the air with the putrid vapours from its maw—and then its entire weight slammed into her, driving the breath from her lungs. She was finally dead, it occurred to her, and the thought almost filled her with relief. But then there were arms dragging at her—Mahesh's arms again, Mahesh's voice—pulling her out from under the animal, which no longer objected.

A few other people stepped forward tentatively— Anjali had no idea who—and soon there were more arms pulling at her, dragging the dead weight from over her body. Someone rubbed her face with a cloth and she saw more grey than red, though her vision was still swimming and her head felt like it was being repeatedly hit with a gong. Someone put a bottle to her lips and she drank, feeling grateful at the blessed coolness that spread down her gullet. Someone even fetched her hawai slippers and purse, and she accepted them, put the slippers to her feet— obedient, mumbling. People moved around and talked in inchoate words. Mahesh was holding her up; she leaned against his body through it all. When Mahesh told her to get up and walk, she walked.

"We need to get away from here before more people turn up," he whispered in her ear as he pushed her forward. Everything hurt. "You don't want to talk to the police right now. Let's scram while everyone is still confused."

There was much confusion even outside the zoological gallery, all over the museum premises. Other people had been hurt—if not as dramatically—by flying glass shards, falling debris, stampeding crowds as they spilled from the gallery before. Some had simply fainted. Everyone was busily narrating the version of events they thought they'd seen. Mahesh guided Anjali quickly through the shadows, outside the building, where thankfully the darkness of the winter evening had spread over the city. He hailed one of the horse-drawn boxcars waiting for passengers outside the museum. The driver demanded forty rupees to take them to his mess—an exorbitant sum. Mahesh was going to argue, but Anjali pressed her purse into his hands.

HER PURSE WAS further lightened at the mess—a residence for working-class men in a squalid part of the city—but finally Anjali managed to secure a room with a bed. Even a discreet local doctor was acquired—wounds were cleaned and dressed, tetanus injected, painkillers swallowed, away from the usual hospitals where the police might search.

After the doctor departed, Mahesh sat on a chair by her bed, polishing the daggers he'd produced out of nowhere in the museum. On closer inspection Anjali had no doubt they were fighting daggers—blades of a shiny black metal that she didn't recognize, intricate carvings all along their length. No cutlery or kitchen tool these; not after they had managed to kill a demonic tiger that no bullet or shard of glass could pierce. How had Mahesh come to possess such things?

"That sahib who shot the woman at the Auckland Hotel never checked out of his room, did he?" Mahesh flashed a grin when she asked. "I have always fancied having a blade of my own, just like Ajay saab and Abhay saab. You can keep the other. Seems like you may need it more than I do from now on."

The reality of his words took a minute to sink into Anjali's mind. "What will I do now, Mahesh?" Tears welled up in her eyes, the pain all over her body suddenly unbearable. If it ended right now—quietly fading to darkness on this bed—that would be the best. She could not bear to go through another of those horrors again. "Daddy thinks I'll be safe in England, but I don't think I'll be safe anywhere. Strange and terrible things are happening in the world—or maybe they have always happened, we just did not have the eyes to see. And now I'm thrust in the middle of it. I don't even know who to ask for help."

"Surprisingly enough, I seem to have an idea!" Mahesh said, leaving the daggers on the table and suddenly leaning over her bed, an urgent look in his eyes. "A man hears a lot of odd gossip if he waits tables at a sahibs' hotel, especially if the patrons don't suspect he follows their language too well. What you just said—strange and terrible things happening in the world—I have heard that sentiment echoed at many tables I have served, always hesitant, always hushed, but never quite dispelled. More than once I've caught the mention of something called the Strange Brigade—"

"What's that? Such an odd name for a military unit."

"Couldn't tell," Mahesh shrugged. "I doubt any of those sahibs could either. None of them were part of it. They spoke of it like a rumour, but one that has existed in their community for centuries. Rather long for a baseless rumour to last, don't you think? I also heard the mention of a name. Webster. A woman—they said 'she.' When you go back to England, maybe you can keep an eye out for these people?"

"A woman called Webster isn't much to find one person

in all of England," Anjali smiled, weakly. "About the Strange Regiment—"

"Brigade."

"—Brigade, well, I wouldn't even know where to start."

"I could only help you so far, I'm afraid," said Mahesh, despair creeping into his voice. "You see, Anjali, I too think it's best for you to go back to England. You have friends and professors there. I'll be fine—the curse doesn't care for me. I wish I could stay close to you, but I don't have the means. I can no longer go back to work at the Auckland Hotel—it's barely a mile from the Imperial Museum, sooner or later I'll get identified. I'm not sure I should continue to live in Calcutta at all."

"You should come back with me to Kishangarh."

"And do what? Live as a servant at my father's estate, clean his chamber pots every day?" Mahesh gave a bitter laugh.

"You're his only remaining son," Anjali protested. "Of the ones we know, anyway. You're next in line for his title and estate."

"I should be so lucky!" He laughed again. "Anjali, the next Maharaja of Kishangarh will be the man who marries you. That's how royal lineage works."

"I don't think I'll marry anyone. I won't even live long enough to marry."

"Sleep, Anjali," Mahesh said softly, placing a cool hand over her eyes, closing them. "You've had a devastating day, you aren't thinking straight. I will keep watch from this chair. In the morning, we'll switch. We can plan for the future after we've had a couple of days' rest."

Anjali slept fitfully, dreaming of tigers and a woman's voice threatening to return and kill her. The pain in her body congealed into fever; she woke up several times shaking, clutching the blanket, drifting back to sleep. When she finally awoke, it was noon. Mahesh was dozing in the chair next to her, dagger gripped close to his chest. She nudged him half-awake, directed him to the bed, and went downstairs to make a phone call home.

Sabarmati dai received the call at the palace in Kishangarh, and Anjali was immediately shaken awake by the volley of questions that were flung at her. "Anjali! Oh, God be thanked—where were you?! I kept calling Sujata's house all night! They said you did not return home! You did not leave a message! What happened to you—?!"

"Oh, dai, don't worry, I'm alive, I just woke up—let me catch my breath and I'll tell you." And then the suspicion hit. "Why did you call Sujata's house at night?"

Sabarmati dai told her.

Anjali finished the conversation, replaced the phone, returned to their room, and shook Mahesh awake.

"We must leave for Kishangarh on the first available train," she told him as he sat up, grumbling and rubbing his eyes. "You're coming with me. I'm in no state to travel alone."

"Anjali, I really don't—"

"There are no more chamber pots to clean."

He gaped at her, then slowly closed his mouth and said, "Oh."

* * *

THE MAHARAJA OF Kishangarh had died of a heart attack in his sleep the night before, after being tormented by the same nightmare that had chased him for decades. In the empty palace, whose only other inhabitant was an old maidservant who slept in the servants' quarters, the Maharaja had started screaming in the middle of the night, "She has returned! She has returned! She will kill Anjali too—she will end my line!"

The screams awoke the maidservant, but by the time she lit a lamp and dragged her aged body all the way to the Maharaja's bedchamber, he had fallen quiet again. She checked and did not find a pulse, then went downstairs and phoned the local hospital for a doctor. By daybreak, everyone in Kishangarh had heard the news.

Like clockwork, Anjali performed the last rites for her father. There were only the three of them in the large, sprawling estate. Even the cooks, the cleaners, the construction men who were hired for the shraddh did not want to linger beyond the needful in their premises; all the guests who visited to pay their regards left immediately after they had eaten, politely declining to spend the night in the Phool Mahal's many bedrooms.

When all was said and done, Anjali told Mahesh, "I will need an estate manager. My studies at Oxford are not yet complete, and you've told me yourself that I would be safer in England."

Mahesh stared at his feet, shuffled them.

"No one else will accept my employ, Mahesh. I am a cursed woman. Your mother is a fine housekeeper, but I need someone who can speak and read English, manage accounts, execute our relationship with the British government. You can charge any salary you want—I don't care for the inheritance anyway, I may not even live to enjoy it. Find yourself a wife, fill these dreary rooms with your family. Call yourself Mahesh Singh Rathore if you want. No one will be happier than me if you do. You're the only family I have left in the world."

Mahesh looked her straight in the eye—a gaze so hard that Anjali almost staggered. "Promise me you'll find this Strange Brigade, and that Webster woman," he said. "Promise me you'll move heaven and earth until you find them—you won't go down without a fight, won't sink into despair and let this curse kill you. You will teach yourself everything you need. Only then will I agree to be your servant again."

"Brother," she said.

"Whatever," he shrugged. "I'm not the one getting jumped by tigers out of random tapestries."

Anjali's face split into a grin. "I promise."

With those words in her head and her newly acquired dagger sheathed and tucked underneath her overcoat, Anjali Singh Rathore stepped out of the airport in London a week later. It was a new year, and the world was about to change.

THE ISLAND
OF NIGHTMARES
PATRICK LOFGREN

THE CAVE ENTRANCE yawned wide, like a mouth emerging from beneath the skin of the earth to swallow the hunting party. Above it was a slab-faced cliff as high as Mt. Fuji with none of the peak's grace, rising in stark answer to the jungle. Here the canopy ended: no more trees the size of battleships, spiders the size of tanks, endless violence invited by too much life living on top of itself. The cliff wall was clear and sterile.

Inside the cave the air sharpened. Water followed Lieutenant-Commander Hachirō Shimizu and his captors into the cave mouth, dropping through a cleft in the rock into some deeper trough where it guided them through the dark with its endless gurgling. Though there was no longer a sky above them, Hachirō felt his claustrophobia ease. The jungle canopy was a crueler mistress than any cave could be.

Though he was a prisoner, he was not bound. There was no need for it. Hachirō and his men had been disarmed, denied the opportunity to end their own lives honourably or to take the islanders with them into death. Escape offered only a slow and painful death at the hands of the jungle. A captor guided him on each side, propping him up with their shoulders, using their spears as crutches to make his weight easier to bear. One was black, the other white. Their teeth were filed to points, to better tear at raw flesh. Their eyes had a yellow, sickly, sheen. They were thin, though Hachirō knew they'd eaten recently.

There were twenty men in the hunting party, one beast of burden the size of a trolley car with bamboo gibbets woven into its shaggy, dirty fur, and a great lacertilian monster bound to a sledge. Hachirō's men hung in the gibbets. Some were dead, their bodies slumped against the bamboo cages like bratty children made to wait too long; others still lived, by turns catatonic and submissive or howling against their fate. All of them were Hachirō's men. All of them had looked to him, once, for guidance, for advice, for leadership. He was their commanding officer, had sailed with them for years. He'd dreamed of leading them to glory and instead he'd led them here, to die as food stock instead of samurai.

It was called the Island of Nightmares, and it was a land of myth. Many at High Command doubted the island even existed; and they were not fools for the belief. No ship had ever returned from the storm-wracked waters rumoured to conceal the island, between Vietnam and the Philippines. But if there *was* an island, and if that island could be occupied, then it would be a perfect staging ground for the invasion of Southeast Asia.

Hachirō had been a student of the Nanshinron all his life, and Japan had finally chosen that path, abandoning its foolish ambitions for the Siberian wastes. His great nation's fleets were unleashed upon the world to begin the work of building the Co-Prosperity Sphere, of wresting the Pacific from colonial hands. European occupation had turned Asia into a cesspool, and Japan would be the divine wind that scraped their cloying grasp away. Asia would be the jewel it was always meant to be, with an Emperor to guide it.

The island had never been mapped and no ship had ever returned, but no ship sent before was a Fubuki-class destroyer, the most advanced warship afloat, besides maybe the carriers sliding out of Japanese shipyards even now. The Admiralty believed Hachirō could accomplish his mission, could return to civilization with the information needed to build a base on the island. He had believed it too. Now, just a week after landing, thoughts of Japan and Asia and conquest and glory all felt distant and foolish. He knew he would never see his home again; he would join the men in gibbets soon enough.

THE HUNTING PARTY travelled deeper into the cave and Hachirō felt with each step like he was being swallowed by a creature too great to comprehend. The heavy, shaggy beast pounded the rocky floor, a steady metronomic rhythm guiding the party deeper and deeper into the belly of the island.

As they walked, the men of the hunting party spoke in a harsh, alien language like nothing Hachirō had heard. Their skin ran the spectrum from obsidian to porcelain, and though they all bore the marks of the island's cruelty, they clearly had no common origin. Their ancestors had no doubt shared Hachirō's ambitions; their nations had dreamed of conquering not just the known world but the unknown. They were the lost and forgotten sailors of a thousand nations, who had, in their time, nursed the hubris that let them believe they would master the nightmare. They lived in a world of endless consumption, of man eating man, eating beast, eating man, eating insect, eating man in a vicious chain where nothing could live or grow or blossom.

The fates of these men, of their ancestors, made him sick with shame and fear. All of them had at one time thought they would do this great thing. Maybe they believed themselves at the centre of history, or exempt from the suffering that afflicted others, or maybe they'd simply been following orders. Whatever the case, they had all come to this island and their crews had died here, eaten either by the island's titanic monsters or the descendants of their predecessors.

The party pushed deeper into the cave, leaving behind the sodden stench of the jungle and pressing into the cool, clean, sharp-scented air of the cave. Soon they lost the last daylight and lit torches. The fires painted ghosts on the cave ceiling, and as they travelled deeper into the chasm, the walls slowly fell away. The flickering light across the uneven stone grew more distant until, somewhere on the journey, the party became a star set adrift in the murky black.

They stopped at a sort of hovel and yoked the giant beast of burden on the edge of a subterranean lake where bioluminescent fish traced circles beneath the surface. The hunters bound Hachirō's legs and stuffed his mouth with a filthy gag. He was placed on his knees next to one of the logs set as benches around a fire pit. Dirt caked his body and grit shifted under his knees and bored against his bone. He was disgusting, and the feeling of being tethered to such a wretched vessel sickened and saddened him.

The hunters left him kneeling as they fed the beast, bled the great lizard to keep it weak, and started a fire in the center of the pit.

He closed his eyes, letting exhaustion wrap its arms around him for a moment. When he opened them, the men and the beast and the lizard were gone. He was clean, still kneeling before the fire. All around him, the Milky Way carved the sky and the Earth. He had no sense of proportion or space. He could only feel the sharp gravel on his knees, the warmth of fire on his face.

A man approached from the gloomy distance. He wore a naval uniform, with brown leather boots and wraps tightly binding his shins to keep jungle water from seeping in. He didn't carry his gun, but a sword hung in its scabbard from his waist. He approached and sat next to the lieutenant. In the light of the fire Hachirō could see it was Hara, a boy from Hamada barely old enough to enlist. He'd joined up, dreaming of sailing the open ocean, fighting serpents and ship-eating whales. He'd died first upon landing, of a snake bite that swelled his ankle into a soft, bloated mass. He'd died in sight of the beach and their ship.

The boy sat down next to Hachirō, looked him in the eye, wiped a tear from the lieutenant's cheek.

"What do you have to cry about?" he asked.

Hachirō wanted to answer, but the gag in his mouth kept him from anything besides a mumble. This boy had trusted him and he'd failed. They'd dreamed of Empire and Hara died not in battle for a grand cause, but of an animal bite. It was simple and sad and humiliating.

Hara drew his blade and for a while the two of them sat and watched while the fire painted its steel surface. Hachirō hoped the moment would never end. Then Hara stood and Hachirō thought the boy might kill him, but instead the younger man cut his bonds and held the sword out for Hachirō to take. Hachirō lifted it, his hands shaking, though he couldn't tell if it was from weakness or fear.

"Cut me down," Hara told him. "You killed me already. Finish your work."

"No," Hachirō said. "No, I tried. I tried to help build something great."

"You failed."

"No!" Hachirō cried, and slashed at Hara with his sword. The boy crumbled with the blow, turning to dust and dispersing into the wind. His blade followed him, evaporating in Hachirō's hands like a longing held too tightly.

"No, no, no!" Hachirō cried, and would have gone on crying; but he realized it wasn't he who was screaming the words but someone else. Though they used his mouth, they did not have his voice, and their fear was an immediate, bodily thing he did not feel.

Hachirō woke, suddenly back on his knees, bound and gagged. The Milky Way remained for a moment, like the afterimage of a gunshot burned on the inside of an eyelid.

The hunters were pulling a man down from one of the gibbets, loosening the hempen ropes that tangled it to the beast and unlocking the cage. Hachirō couldn't tell who the man was. Sickness and starvation and exhaustion rendered all his crew into husks of their former selves, robbed of individuality and spirit.

The islanders could have chosen someone else. They could have pulled down one of the sailors who had expired earlier in the day—they could have cooked one of the dead—but they didn't just want a meal. They wanted something fresh and afraid.

When they brought the man closer to the fire, Hachirō recognized Kimura, a conscript assigned to his ship just a month before it left Japan. The man didn't like the sea, threw up constantly and came to Hachirō every few days with a new transfer-request-form. Hachirō hadn't liked him.

Now, they were removing his fingers, and Hachirō wished he'd taken Kimura's requests seriously. Perhaps they could have left him at the last port. There might not have been time to replace him. The ship might have had one less man to lose.

The hunters sucked the fingers dry before placing them in a small metal basket over the fire. Then they slit the man's throat, collecting his blood in a bucket before tying him to a stake and rolling his corpse over the fire. One of the men brought over a bag of rice and packed the grains into bamboo shoots before filling them with water and setting them over the fire to cook. Hachirō began to retch, and one of the hunters undid his gag and removed him from the circle to empty the pathetic contents of his stomach away from their food.

The hunter didn't bother replacing the gag when he brought Hachirō back, and Hachirō showed his appreciation by keeping quiet. They spoke in their strange, violent language, laughing and growling and making finger puppets as they told each other stories while their food cooked. Hachirō followed none of it, though at times he thought they spoke a word or two of Japanese.

When the meat was cooked they cut it from the body in thin strips and shovelled rice into bowls along with blood from both the man and the lizard. When all the rest had been fed, one of the hunters offered a bowl to Hachirō. He shook his head and the man removed the slice of flesh. Cannibalism aside, the hunter hadn't polished the rice. It looked fat and soft and was a dirty flesh colour. He wouldn't have eaten it in the most civilized circumstances.

The man shrugged as though he didn't care whether Hachirō ate or starved, and gave the bowl to one of the others. The hunters brewed a thick broth and told stories around the fire deep into the night. Hachirō wondered what it was that allowed these men to take such pleasure in each other when they had just murdered and devoured a man. How was it their compassion for one another was not extended to his crew? Why had that line been drawn, between man and prey? What could he do to move where the line fell?

THEY WOKE HIM with water drawn from the lake, pouring it over him. The dirt that stuck to his face like a second skin softened, and he felt a momentary relief so strong he could almost weep. He felt like he'd been caged and was just now being allowed to stretch his limbs. The hunter poured clean water into his mouth, letting him drink slowly until the water skin was emptied. The party began to move on. Hachirō walked unaided for a while, until his bones softened and his muscles grew brittle again.

The lake they'd camped by narrowed back into a little stream, and the bioluminescent fish struggled against it, like bands of starlight caught in amber.

"Hachirō," someone whispered.

It was Chul Soon, a Korean draftee sent to the navy as punishment for participation in a riot nearly two years before. He would never be Japanese, but he was a convert to the idea of the Co-Prosperity Sphere. He worked hard, followed orders, understood his place in the great engine in much the same way Hachirō did.

Hachirō angled his weak shuffle towards the beast, where Chul Soon hung in a gibbet.

"There is still time," the man said. "Find a way to free us and we can still escape the island."

Hachirō was about to respond, but a hunter approached and stabbed the sailor in the stomach. He screamed and

Hachirō made to attack the hunter, but was so weak he collapsed at the man's first parry.

"Nobody speak to you," the hunter said in broken Japanese. "Anyone who speaks dies."

Those few sailors still living out their short time in the remaining gibbets sealed their mouths and stared intently ahead. Maybe they hoped Hachirō would save them, maybe they were formulating their own plans, maybe they'd already resigned themselves to their ghastly fate. Hachirō couldn't tell and the hunters would not allow him to ask. He tried to ignore Chul Soon's whimpers as the man bled out, losing his grip on his entrails.

A light not of their making appeared in the distance. It was like another star sent into the cavernous void to guide them. As they approached, it grew, expanding from a pinprick to an all-consuming blaze. It drowned out their torches, which the party doused, returning them to a sack at the beast's hip. The cave roof, hundreds of metres above them, softened from slick black to a soft orange, as though the sun were rising within the cave. Hachirō had to shield his eyes against the light as he drew closer. He wondered if he had truly died at some point and if his spirit was just now, finally, approaching its resting place.

He would have liked to lay down.

The wall of light was nothing: the cave's terminus, an opening on the far side of the mesa. As he grew accustomed to the brightness, the light gave way to a wide lake and a village rising up the slope beneath him.

Hachirō's lungs collapsed, and his legs followed suit. It was only the arms of his captors that kept him from falling onto the dirt path. If he'd been dead, at least the light might have heralded some end to this waking nightmare. He could have hoped for rest. Instead he was alive, and some of his men still lived, though none of them had any hope of escape. They would all be tortured and consumed by day's end, but there was still time to suffer.

The lake was wide and deep, judging by the royal colour of its water. Fresh water from the cave river emptied into it, and in the distance Hachirō could see waves breaking on a shallow sand bar. The village on the hillside was small but well-constructed, with bamboo, thatch, and mudbricks smoothed by plaster. They looked like the amalgamation of a dozen rural architectures. They were sturdy and close, built to weather the island's storms. They rose in a semi-circle up the hill, ranged around a tower or perhaps lighthouse. Between the buildings were paths of stone, though the widest roads were dirt. Above the village, rice terraces had been cut into the mountainside and Hachirō could see a tower granting access to the plateau.

In the lake, bamboo boats moved under the poles of their pilots, carrying baskets across the lake. Cormorants dived into the water to retrieve the blue glowing fish. It was not these little boats that caught Hachirō's attention though—that made him physically ill. Nor was it the buildings, the stone pathways or the strange tower at the centre of the village.

It was the ship.

In the middle of the lake rested a vast wooden ship, many times bigger than the *Yamato*, the flagship of the Japanese Empire. Such a construction should have been impossible. These people, hardy as they might be, were primitives, the lost tribes of ships centuries dead, driven to cannibalism and barbarism by a violent island. A ship large enough to host a city should have been far beyond their capacity. Hachirō could not imagine the generations it must have taken to complete the vessel.

They moved along the shoreline. Men and women came down out of the village to unclasp the gibbets from the hairy beast's side and drag the remainder of Hachirō's men up the stone paths and into the village. Hachirō fought, screamed and struggled against his captors, but he was too weak. The last of his men called to him, but he could do nothing for them. He was powerless, a failure to his country and his family and his crew.

When his men had been carried off, the hunting party continued around the lake and followed a wide dirt road to the ship. A massive dock rose to meet the vessel, strong enough to bear the weight of both the beast and its titanic cargo.

A short drawbridge was lowered onto the dock, emerging from the hull of the ship like a tongue newly extended from a dry, splintered mouth. They entered.

Within was a riotous cacophony. The deck they entered was filled with cages: some small, holding deadly-looking snakes or praying mantises the size of dogs, but most much larger. In one, a spider the size of a car spooled its thread around a goat. In another, a massive lizard sat lazily in its cage, a tongue the size of a man flicking in and out. In another a snake lay exhausted, its jaw unhinged and its body writhing with the effort of swallowing a horse whole.

Hachirō struggled even more to stand, even with the aid of his captors. His limbs were as weak as ever, but burned with adrenaline. His heart felt like it might jump up his throat, and he realized he was breathing heavily, as though having just finished some great exertion. The hunters seemed unimpressed.

When Hachirō was a child, his father moved the family from Kobe to Tokushima. It wasn't a long way, but their new home lay in the shadow of Mt. Tsurugi. Hachirō walked beneath the mountain, lived at its feet, was astonished by its beauty. He promised himself he would never forget the majesty of the thing, he would always remember what a special place he lived in.

He hadn't kept his promise, though. Hachirō couldn't even remember the last time he'd looked up at the mountain.

The hunters and the crewmen of the ship were like Hachirō beneath that mountain. They lived among predators from another geological age, they walked in the presence of god-like monsters, and they did so as casually as if they were tending cattle in a field.

The deck was a single vast space. Modern ships sectioned their hulls, so that if any one was breached it wouldn't sink the whole ship. As impressive as this vessel was, it was an old design. At the end of the deck was a wide staircase, and Hachirō had to be carried up the flights onto the top deck. On top of the ship was a small city, with store houses and dormitories and commissaries. In the centre was a fortified castle, made of wood like the rest of the ship, with high, thick, walls.

His captors took him to the gate at the front of the fortress and though the small gatehouse. Inside the castle was a maze of rice-paper-and-bamboo rooms. It was strange to be suddenly thrust into such a familiar space. Hachirō had been in buildings of the same style a thousand times, but for such a place to exist on such an alien island was disorienting, all the more so because of its familiarity.

At the centre of the castle was a wide throne room, with low tables on either side, and pillows for kneeling. At the back of the room, a narrow staircase led up to a red-stained carved wooden throne. On the throne sat a man Hachirō thought he might recognize. A few supplicants stood before their lord, speaking in their language with its clipped, short words. Upon entering, the guards bowed and knelt, leaving Hachirō to stand under his own power between them.

The king raised his hand, silencing the man who was talking and drawing the attention of the whole room to Hachirō. With all their eyes upon him, he felt more like prey than ever. The king said another phrase and the others left them.

He walked over to Hachirō, put a hand out and brushed the man's cheek.

"Come with me," he said in Japanese. "I have so much to explain."

THEY ASCENDED A narrow spiral staircase tucked away behind the throne room, ending at a crow's nest looking out upon the vastness of the ship and the village ringing the bay. It was all Hachirō could do to stand.

"What is this place?" he asked. For a moment he forgot his hatred and shame and misery. That a place like this could exist on this island defied explanation. He felt, too, immense pleasure from speaking the phrase. It felt like a lifetime since he'd last spoken to someone who wasn't begging him to find a way to save them.

"There is a rock formation," the king said, "you can see it if you look closely, that breaks the waves. It makes our little lake and the bay just beyond peaceful, even though the storms never cease."

He turned around, waved along the ridge.

"The cliffs rise sheer out of the island. The only way into the bay by land is through that cave, and it is well laid with traps and snares. Sometimes monsters try to scale the cliffs, but we patrol them. We are safe here."

"Who are you?"

"I am King Takeshi Mitsukawa. I was captain of the *Akatsuki*. At the turn of the century I was sent here to map the island and determine if it could be made into a staging ground."

It was strange that Mitsukawa used the term "king." Hachirō would never have expected it from a former captain of the Imperial Navy. Then he realized what the man had said.

"What?" he asked, frowning. "That was my purpose."

Mitsukawa shook his head; he looked disappointed, angry.

"I was not the first either. We are part of a long lineage, you and I. When I arrived here, this ark was a dream, barely the skeleton of the vessel it is today. The king of that age was a Javanese shipwright, sent by his prince, Diponegoro, to capture the mythical beasts of the sacred island and bring them back to unleash holy vengeance upon the Dutch occupiers. He never left. His crew was lost and consumed until he found his way here and rose to the throne. When Japan abandoned me and my crew, he took pity on us, brought us in as those before did to him."

"He brought in all of your crew?" Hachirō asked, confused and jealous and bitter.

"No," Mitsukawa said. "Not everyone. The people here have built something extraordinary, but it is fragile. Add too many to the village and it might collapse. Besides, eating human flesh has become our culture. When a ship arrives, they chose one or two of its crew to survive, preferably the command, and the rest we use as feedstock. We have children of our own. We don't need anyone else draining the stores."

An itch rolled through Hachirō and he longed to escape his skin. All his men, dead of infection or poison or feasted upon by monsters or butchered by the locals, all of them were chosen. He felt the opposite of special, or blessed; like all the world was a miserable joke and he was the only one who didn't know. He wanted a bed and warm tea. He wanted to be home, to do something as small as share just one meal with his mother.

"So, what is this?" he finally mustered the will to ask, pointing down at the titanic ship.

"It is an ark. It is big enough and strong enough to carry us through the storms shielding the island. It will carry our people away from this nightmare, and deliver our gift to the world."

"Your gift?"

"My mentor was sent to collect the beasts of the of the island so that he might set them upon the Dutch. The ark was designed to house the island's monsters for that purpose, but my focus is not so narrow. The world abandoned us here. I think it only right we deliver this place unto the world."

"Set the monsters free? On other islands?"

"Not just other islands; on the mainland. They'll feed and devour, breed and conquer the world."

"What will you do then?"

"We'll all be long dead by then, but at least the world will have joined us, rather than forgetting us."

THEY DESCENDED FROM the crow's nest, back to the throne room, where a servant waited with clean robes and Hachirō's guntō.

"Binh will take you to your new home. I'll send for you this evening and we'll feast together. We have much to discuss."

The servant led him out of the throne room, through the castle and down back onto the holding deck, where the monsters lurked in cages. Hachirō still felt the urge to flee, looking at all those beasts, any one of which could crush or swallow him without notice. The servant, Binh, didn't seem troubled even by the ear-splitting roars some of the bigger lizards issued. They walked down the ramp and back along the shoreline.

Once, when he was a boy, Hachirō had stood on the

beach outside Kobe with the other kids and watched as a typhoon barely missed Japan. Hachirō and the boys stood in the rain while the wind dug sand from the beaches and flung it at them, each grain biting at their skin, digging trench lines through their flesh for the rain to run along. The boys stood, eyes shut tight against the onslaught, skin biting, clothes waterlogged. One by one they left the beach, fled the typhoon's kiss and returned to their homes, to the scoldings of their mothers, chastised for their foolishness. Hachirō stood in the sand while a drift built up in front of each ankle, his hair heavy with water, his white clothes turning a sallow, capillary brown. Hachirō waited until the wind exhausted itself, until the clouds grew light and stopped shedding their weight, and when he opened his eyes he was alone on the beach.

His father beat him—he had been missing more than a day—but what punishments could a man give out when a typhoon could not break you?

Mitsukawa imagined Hachirō was broken. He was not unreasonable for doing so. Hachirō had watched while his ship danced on its anchor and cracked in half to sink in water not deep enough to hide its radio antenna. He'd seen his men die one by one of stupid, inglorious things; they'd been tortured in front of him, offered up to him as sustenance. Hachirō should have been broken. But instead of snapping Hachirō's final tether to the world, Mitsukawa had offered a lifeline. In hoping to turn Hachirō to his cause, the king had unveiled his plan. Hachirō could stop it, could prevent Mitsukawa's apocalyptic vision from playing out. He could recast all the deaths he'd witnessed as the sacrifices needed to stop this one, final cataclysm. If he could destroy the ark, his men would not have died in vain.

"Pleasant night," Binh said.

Storms came and went unpredictably on the island, but for now, for just this moment, the night was clear and warm and Hachirō could see all the stars above.

"Yes," Hachirō answered. "Yes, it is.

BINH TOOK HIM to a small house on the edge of the village, up the hill, close to the cliff face. They passed under the tower Hachirō had seen; it was indeed a sort of lighthouse, with a great fire at its crown. But it was something else too, half gallows, half butcher's post. From it hung the corpses of men, some recently dead, some dismembered and flayed, ready for butchery. At the base of the tower was a sort of amphitheatre; people gathered all around it, talking in small groups, sharing a meal. Children played by the tower's base.

Beyond the cave, in the jungle, when the islanders hunted his crew, he'd believed they were savages, cannibals who knew no other way than mindless consumption. This, the ark, the village, told a different story. They were something more terrifying than monsters; they were men, and men could do anything given the time to grow accustomed to it. Here, children played in the shadow of human beings butchered like livestock.

Hachirō had done rotations in Korea, putting in to port and spending days in the occupied cities, sometimes venturing into the countryside on leave. He'd seen Koreans tried and executed for crimes they'd only been incidentally involved with; some of his own crew were conscripts ripped from their lives to serve Japan's ambitions.

As Binh led him past the village square Hachirō suddenly saw himself, not as he hoped to be, but as he was. He was a soldier, a servant of a violent machine, a butcher who'd grown used to his trade. How many people had looked at him and seen the rabid animal he'd thought these islanders were? He felt sick. The village, the island, Mitsukawa's plan, the Hokushinron, the Nanshinron, occupation and national destiny—they all made him sick. He could barely stand. A coughing fit seized him; his body, having nothing to evacuate, settled on denying him breath.

"You must rest, lieutenant-commander. A long, wearying journey is ending. Rest now, and tonight you'll eat with the king. You'll feel better then."

HACHIRŌ WOULD NOT rest, would not eat with the king, would not play a part in the wretched culture that had consumed the island and its inhabitants. Mitsukawa may have been capable of forgetting the fate of his own crew, but Hachirō could not. Men he'd fought with would be a part of the night's feast. If Hachirō had been selected to survive, then so too had his men been selected to die; so many young, brilliant Japanese lives destroyed by the choices of long lost captains.

Hachirō understood the circumstances of the island, but he could not accept them. Had he been in Mitsukawa's position, he would have perished before turning on his men—and he would gladly starve before he butchered them. Horrors had been visited upon this small civilization since its inception, and it had grown to reflect those horrors.

If Mitsukawa's plan succeeded, the world would die. However broken it might be, Hachirō could not accept that all of it must burn. His country had sent him to die on a foolish mission, and others had done the same to all the people here; Hachirō's suffering was not unique, to this island or any other. Mankind suffered greatly, every day, across the globe. It only hurt so much this time because it was happening to him. To take that pain and burn the world for it would be an act of singular selfishness. There was no question Mitsukawa had been denied the life he deserved, but Hachirō would not allow the man to do the same to others.

Reunited with his sword and given clean clothes, Hachirō waited in his quarters until the moon ascended and the stars wakened to the night. Thunderous cries echoed from the island's outer reaches. Hachirō slid open the paper window to his room and dropped into the muddy alley behind his temporary home. Nobody stood in his way. There was no reason to guard him – he had nowhere to go. If he escaped back out into the island, a monster would surely find and eat him, and guards always watched the ark. If Hachirō decided to die in a foolish bid for freedom, that was his choice. He made it gladly.

The rest he'd taken, just a few hours in a soft, uncomfortable western-style bed, had done him good. He felt rejuvenated, though he'd still barely eaten anything in the last few days. Far up the hillside, past a reservoir dug into a ledge, the ground dried out and turned to scree. Further on, he had to climb on his hands as well as his feet, until eventually sheer rock confronted him. By then, only about ten metres lay between him and the plateau above.

Closer to the town, a staircase rose to the guard tower. It would be the easiest way up onto the plateau, but it would surely be watched. He shuffled along the cliff face until he found a route up the rock.

He reached the top and lay on his front, gasping. His hands and feet burned, pushed beyond their limits. He would have laid on the stone face all night if he'd been allowed to. The climb had sapped nearly everything he had. It was only the sound of footsteps, and the nearing voices of a patrol, that pushed him back onto his feet and across the mesa.

He followed the stars north, back towards the center of the island. The plateau was barren. Endless cycles of wind and rain had carved it into a maze of grottos and clefts. Hachirō stopped frequently, laying or sitting down to rest his legs. Inevitably a patrol would pass and he would move on, but each time he did he was a little slower. If he didn't find a way off the plateau soon, the patrols would discover him and return him to the village. He doubted he would receive as courteous a welcome the second time.

The sun rose, creeping over the horizon and gently cooking the island. Hachirō's mouth grew dry, his spittle as thick as wet cotton. Every step vibrated through his legs and up into his torso; his teeth chattered, loose in their housing. His robes clung to him, no longer clean, rubbing sweat-grimy dust into his arms and back. When the sun was high, he found he was lost, forgot which direction he was walking in. Hajime, his chief comms specialist, walked with him for a while, telling Hachirō about his daughter. She was three, born in a blizzard up in Iwate where they'd lived before he was stationed further south. He had a son too, on the way, maybe four months out.

"They won't have a father," he told Hachirō.

"Millions don't."

"I suppose that's the price."

"It is. It's too high."

"I wish you'd saved me."

"Me too."

Hachirō thought he saw his mother beckoning to him. She looked tired, weary, pale. She'd outlived her husband, and now she would outlive him. Soon she would stand on a train platform and wait for a masked man to hand her an empty box with his name on it. Lost at sea. His mother called to him, told him to quit playing and come inside from the rain.

It was raining, though the sun was still out and the air was still hot. Hachirō slipped, grimaced as stone rose to meet him. He lay in a growing puddle, waiting to die, content he at least had not doomed the world, though he'd failed to save it.

Waiting there, his mind conjured one last illusion. A great black orb descended from the thickening clouds, a great hum coming with it. Hachirō wondered if it was a giant beetle come to swallow him, but as it approached he saw it was a craft of some sort. A ramp opened and two women dropped down with it. One was white, young, dressed in overalls. The other was black, her clothes red and green, her hair dyed the colour of fire, white markings running along her arms. They gathered him up in a hurry, hefting him between them; it felt so real to Hachirō he thought perhaps they were not an illusion, and he was saved.

He woke some time later, on a cot, his soiled robes removed, a sheet covering his body. He was in a small infirmary. There was only one bed and if his body hadn't already been so broken by his time on the island, the pillowy cot would have done just as much damage to his back and neck. Medical equipment was stowed away with naval efficiency. Out of the port hole, uniform white clouds stretched forever. Finally, he had died. Now he could truly rest.

A woman opened the infirmary door: the black woman from his hallucination, still dressed in her strange clothes. She carried neither spear nor rifle, but there was a dagger at her waist.

"Ah, he awakens," she said. She spoke in English. Hachirō wouldn't call himself fluent in the overwrought tongue, but he could carry a conversation. The British government had long consulted with the Japanese until it became clear the two countries' views on the Pacific were incompatible. Hachirō had even fought alongside British troops at the Siege of Tsingtao, in the early, long distant days of his career.

"Where am I?" He sat up, the sheet falling from his chest. Her eyes skipped across him and her gaze made him feel inescapably weak. She was a warrior, strong and well-muscled, fit and ready for a forced march or days under siege. In contrast, his muscles had withered so that they were barely canvas stretched over bone. He could easily count his ribs, and his skin hung loose from his arms and his jaw.

"We're classified as DA-01. But those who know us prefer 'The Strange Brigade.' You're aboard our dirigible, above the Island of Nightmares."

The Strange Brigade. He'd never heard of such a thing.

"How did you find me?"

"By accident. You're very lucky. We wanted to land and do an initial survey of the plateau before descending into the jungle, but the storm swept in. A few minutes later and we'd have had to leave you there."

Hachirō felt a strange mix of relief and exhaustion. He very much wanted to sleep and never to wake. An eternity of bedrest could not offset the weariness in every strand of muscle, in every joint and ligament. He was in this woman's debt, but the idea of paying off that debt sent a shiver through his spine.

"I am in your debt," he forced himself to say nonetheless. The woman smiled kindly.

"I'll leave you to rest and bring you some food in a couple hours."

Hachirō's eyes widened. "You have food?"

"Um. Well. Yes," the woman said.

"Please, there will be time to rest later. Take me to food."

THE STRANGE BRIGADE was less a brigade and more a squad. Besides the woman who'd come to him at the infirmary, whose name he learned was Nalangu, there were four others: three British and one American. One of the men had clearly done time in the army, one was a professor, one some sort of cowboy or circus performer; and there was another woman too, who appeared to be something of a cross between a street urchin and a combat engineer. They'd been sent, like so many before, to explore the island. Unlike the others, their ship floated upon the air, and when the island's freak storms threatened to drown them they simply rose above the clouds.

Hachirō ate ravenously, tearing into the stale bread and dried meats stored on the vessel. Fairburne, a captain in the British Army, made him some tea, which Hachirō swallowed in a single gulp. It burned his throat and sat warm in his belly, and when Fairburne offered another he took it greedily, though he had the patience to sip the second cup. After his first plate, the professor advised they remove the food. Hachirō had gone a long time without it, and too much at once might do more damage than good. They'd let him have a snack later.

Hachirō tried to tell them the story of his ship and his crew, but to state the facts of what had occurred was unbearable. Each time he tried to utter the words, his lips quivered and his eyes stung. The women kindly focused on their own cups of tea, and the cowboy, who was apparently called 'Bash' Conaghan, took off his hat. Fairburne looked at Hachirō with a warrior's understanding. If he could not utter the fate of his men, Hachirō could at least tell them of King Mitsukawa and his plans.

"Okay," Fairburne said, when Hachirō had finished the insane tale.

"You believe me?"

"We've seen stranger things than a man with a grudge," said the engineer, Braithwaite.

"And you will help me stop him?"

"Shoot," said Conaghan, "it's what we do."

IT WAS AN easy thing. Surprisingly so.

Hachirō's proposal was that they descend onto the plateau at night, during a lull in the storms. From there they could approach via the guard tower and take the staircase down into the town. They could fight their way through onto the ark, then kill Mitsukawa. Hachirō was confident that even in his weakened state, the island warriors would be no match for him. Even if they had to kill the whole village, they'd succeed. He was sure of it. He did not have a plan for escape, and nor did it concern him: Japan had forsaken him, his crew was lost. He could do this one last thing and die with honour.

"Or, what if I rigged up a few crates of TNT and we shoved them off the cargo ramp? Just bomb the ship from up here," Braithwaite suggested.

"I like her plan better," added the professor.

So, they did. In the afternoon, the clouds cleared well enough to spot the ark from the air, and Fairburne brought them into position high above it. From the dirigible's great height, Hachirō realized the town was much smaller than it looked on the ground. The ark was still a wondrous vessel—an engineering masterwork made even more impressive by the village's limited resources—but the village itself was small and sparse. The buildings were narrow and short, crumbling and waterlogged. It was barely sufficient. In comparison, the castle atop the deck of the ark was nearly the same size, with well-made towers and decks spotting its imposing form. Hachirō wondered what the village might have looked like, had the small society focused their efforts on their homes, rather than the imperial dreams of their kings.

People were running in all directions. They could obviously see the dirigible, but it was far beyond their reach. They knew something was coming, but could not yet do anything in response, so they ran; it didn't seem to matter which way.

Good, Hachirō thought. *Feel, just for a moment, what I felt, when I landed on your shores.*

When they were in position, Hachirō and Braithwaite and Nalangu and a man named Bey all worked to shove the three crates of TNT out of the cargo hold. The boxes fell, taking much longer to hit the ship than he thought they would. They seemed to fall and fall without ever getting anywhere, the way solid land warps and rolls after you've stared at the sea for too long. Then they weren't falling anymore. Great orange flashes grew out of the ship, like brilliant, voluminous trees bursting forth. For a long time after the flash, there was no sound. The ship burst outward, great splinters the size of men peppering the whole of the town and up onto the hillside. Beasts roared from within the vessel, some set free, others maimed.

Hachirō had watched similar things before. He'd fired on enemy vessels, on shoreline fortifications. He'd watched his enemies die in the distance from his actions. This felt different. The people below him had no means of retaliation.

The mission was finished. The ark was destroyed and they could escape now. There was no need for the nightmare to continue. All he had to do was turn away and shut the bay door. But it wasn't right. It wasn't right that Mitsukawa and his people were down there, under attack, and Hachirō was up here, distant and safe, dispensing death without fear of consequence. Furthermore, he had no way to tell if Mitsukawa had been killed in the blast, and the king was the only one whose life Hachirō truly wanted.

He took a parachute from a hook at the back of the cargo bay, pulled it around his shoulders and tightened the straps till the canvas was gnawing at his bones. Then he took a step up to the edge of the ramp and jumped.

Bey screamed, and Hachirō was sure he heard Braithwaite cry, "Mercy!" but then the air flooded his ears and he could hear nothing but the scream of his descent. He pulled the cord on the parachute, opening its wings. The straps snapped against him and he felt weakened muscle pull tight against his bones. He was still falling fast, and had very little control over his descent; luckily the ship was a vast landing field. Braithwaite's makeshift bombs had torn holes in the hull easily big enough to render the vessel worthless, but they had not truly destroyed the ship. Three holes bored through the aft section, but most of the main deck and the castle atop it were okay.

Hachirō landed forward of the castle amidst a bedlam of running bodies, everyone in frantic motion, trying to save themselves or stop the calamity he'd set in motion. He'd seen scenes like it before, in his own men and his enemies. This was the chaos of defeat, of a force that had already routed but didn't yet realize it.

Few cared or took notice of the man who had just fallen from the sky. The great beasts within the ship were loose, and without cages and traps, the islanders were outmatched. They might have been able to kill one of the monsters if they organized, but the ship's hold contained enough monsters to storm the world.

Then a squad of the king's guard did notice Hachirō, and they began to fan out around him. Unlike the village hunters in their tattered rags, these men wore white robes and bamboo plate, and held short, obsidian swords and axes. Hachirō drew his blade.

Something fell to his right and he turned, raising his sword to cut it down.

It was Nalangu. The warrior had landed, rolled, and was out of her parachute before Hachirō had turned to face her. Braithwaite, Conaghan, and Fairburne joined them a moment later.

"You're a madman," Nalangu said, smiling.

Hachirō had not imagined they would follow him; surely they would leave him to die, float away from this hellish place, their mission accomplished? For some reason they'd jumped with him, followed him down into this pit. Hachirō would have done the same for a man of his crew. But what was he to these people?

The king's guard charged and the Strange Brigade were ready to meet them. Hachirō caught a blade with his sword, parried and re-directed the blow into the deck. The spear stuck, vibrating like a tuning fork, still in the hands of the stunned attacker. Hachirō plunged his sword through the man's gut, felt a hollow sort of pleasure when his blade met the bleak resistance of the man's spine. The guard cried and fell, and Hachirō moved on to the next man. The rhythm of battle fell in around them and Hachirō gave himself to it. War had a pattern—it was a tapestry to be read—and Hachirō was deeply familiar with its subtleties.

The Strange Brigade bore guns of varying types and calibres. Cutting a path through the castle's defenders was not difficult, but Hachirō felt no guilt. He would not pity these people. When they reached the castle, the others formed up outside the heavy double doors, ready to repel further attackers.

"Go!" said Fairburne. "Do what needs doing."

INSIDE THE CASTLE it was dark; the rice paper flickered with the forms of panicked crew and the vessel sang a sad song as it rocked with the force of the beasts rampaging below.

Hachirō moved carefully through the shadows, heel to toe, his guntō in a guard position in case of attack. None came.

King Mitsukawa sat motionless on his throne, in a daze, like a man who sees his death approaching and knows there is nothing to be done. He looked vacant, more than anything else. He'd lost all his life's work in a few moments. For now, he could only gaze inward. He barely noticed Hachirō's entrance.

"Mitsukawa!" Hachirō cried.

The king glanced down, looking through him. Hachirō wondered what distant past he had returned to: a father's beating, a mother's comfort, the day a bully bested him, or the day he stood up for himself? Where did this man go when he'd lost everything, twice over?

The king stood and slowly descended the staircase. Once he reached its base he removed his loose outer robes and drew his katana, placing the sheath on the ground.

"You could have been my heir," he said. "This could have been your home. The Emperor abandoned you. He threw your life away like it was nothing. He'll do it again, too. He'll keep doing it until he dies, and then the next ruler will do the same. The only way to stop the suffering of men like us is to end it all. And now you've shattered that possibility."

The king approached Hachirō, his blade ready.

"I had no choice," Hachirō said.

"Yes, you did."

The king attacked, raising his sword to bring it down on Hachirō's head. Hachirō brought his own sword to meet it, spun and slashed at Mitsukawa's ribs. The older man slid back and away from the attack, sword still high, and came back with a quick strike at Hachirō's head, followed by an undercut. Hachirō blocked them both, turned his own sword in a tight circle and brought it back up to slash across the king's chest. He connected, staining the white robes red.

Mitsukawa stumbled away, clutching at his wound. The cut was deep and long, but it would not kill him. Hachirō allowed him a moment to collect himself.

When the king was ready he extended his blade once more, the effort clear on his face. Hachirō extended his own until the blades rested against each other, each singing to the other. They stood still a moment, gazing into each other's eyes.

Hachirō made the first move, a quick cut to the king's wrist that he slapped aside. Mitsukawa lashed out with a riposte that would have slit Hachirō's throat, but the lieutenant-commander ducked back and away from the blow. He was off balance, and Mitsukawa pressed his advantage, swinging over his head again and again; Hachirō could barely keep up.

In the fury of the attack, Hachirō found his opening and dove forward, trusting his speed to save him from the king's next blow as he plunged his blade through the man's chest.

Where Hachirō expected shock in Mitsukawa's eyes there was only a deep, lonely sorrow. The king had known his fate when he stepped down from his throne. He pulled himself along Hachirō's blade until their faces were almost touching, and gripped Hachirō's hair.

"They do not deserve you."

He died, and Hachirō laid him gently on the floor.

A MAN CRIED out.

Hachirō turned a saw a dozen men and women had entered the room. They stood at its periphery, held back by their shock. They had surely come to the throne room to seek their king's counsel.

Now he was dead.

The man who had cried out charged. Hachirō ran; he might be able to cut three or four of them down, but eventually the mob would smother him. He made for the staircase behind the throne room. There, atop the crow's nest, he could defend himself.

He was barely ahead of them as he climbed, taking the steps two or three at a time, stopping from time to time to slash behind himself with his sword. When he reached the apex, he stabbed the closest man to him and slammed the trap door shut. From here he could better see the damage.

The town was a ruin, monsters the size of houses killing and feasting upon the people. The ship had been further ruined by the monsters' escaping. A snake as long as a Fubuki lay dead, and a lizard like the one that had been trapped with Hachirō was thrashing across the deck, spears jutting from its shoulders and ribs as it bit and stomped its way through the crew. The Strange Brigade was gone, finally giving in to sense and escaping.

Hachirō would wait here and defend himself until he was overcome or until the ship collapsed. He had fulfilled his mission. He could die here.

A shadow loomed over him, perhaps a great spider, and he readied himself, raising his sword and turning to face his foe.

A rope dangled in from of him.

"Grab on!" Fairburne called to him from the dirigible.

After everything, even now, the world would not allow him rest.

Hachirō took the rope and held tight while the others pulled him up into the cargo hold and away from the Island of Nightmares.

THEY ASCENDED INTO the clouds, and for the first time in a long time Hachirō did not mistake the moment of peace for the calm of death. Indeed, he was *full* of life, something he could not remember ever having felt before. The crew went about their duties, content to let him take in the moment by himself.

A few hours later, Fairburne joined him.

"We can take you as far as Okinawa. From there you can rejoin your Navy and go about your business. Off the record, a favour to a friend."

"That is a kind and generous offer, captain. But there is nothing for me in Japan. My Emperor threw away my life, and the lives of my crew. I was a student of the Nanshinron all my life, and where it should have brought me and my men glory, it only consumed us."

"Huh. Well, *we're* always hiring. We could use a man with your talents."

"It would be an honor to serve with the DA-01."

"That settles it, then. There's a few spare bunks. You're welcome to take your pick when you're ready."

Fairburne left him.

Hachirō Shimizu, lieutenant-commander in the Imperial Navy, was dead. He had died days ago, on an island that defied reason. Cast out and forgotten by his country, he'd perished with his ship and with his crew. A new road stretched out ahead for the newest recruit of the Strange Brigade.

TESSIE'S SONG
JOSEPH GUTHRIE

"I SWEAR... IN the whole world this is th' only place I came back to as regular as my house." The disdain in Tessie Caldwell's words as she stared at her glass of bourbon was painfully obvious to everyone within earshot.

The barkeep serving her—a tall, skinny, bronze-skinned young man wearing a white shirt with the sleeves rolled up, a black vest, and black trousers—stared transfixed at Tessie, drying the tumbler glass she'd handed back to him a few minutes before.

"But you know what really annoys me?"

The barkeep continued to stare at Tessie, his face carefully expressionless. "No," he replies. "No ma'am, I don't."

"Well let me go 'head and break it down for you, then.

I'm annoyed that I've done all of these things… things that most men couldn't even *dream* of doing, and these *same* men have the nerve to get in my way."

The bartender's expression gradually shifted from stoic to anxious, but he didn't interrupt Tessie's monologue. He continued to listen, while dutifully drying the tumbler.

"Don' get me wrong: I knew I'd have to work five times as hard as any man just to get a third of what I've already gotten; but if anyone told me all these men were trying to stop me because their yella-bellied asses were scared of what I'm even *potentially* capable of?" Tessie chuckled, swirling her bourbon around in her glass, then flashed a wry smile at the barkeep. "I would've laughed them out of whatever room we were sitting in."

The barkeep's anxiety was palpable now, further underscored by the fact that he was still wiping down the glass he'd been holding since Tessie began her soliloquy.

THE BARKEEP QUICKLY surveyed the room to see if anyone else was eavesdropping on the conversation. To his left, he saw three other pilots—all white men—who seemed to be preoccupied with whatever they were discussing. Just behind Tessie's position at the bar, the only other woman in the establishment sat, dressed like one of the engineers—overalls, plaid flannel work shirt, work boots, hair pulled back into a ponytail. Perhaps she *was* an engineer, but the weird necklace she was wearing threw him off. She hadn't touched her drink and simply sat near the window staring wistfully outside. The barhand couldn't be sure if she was in her own world or slyly intercepting Tessie's speech, though.

Finally, there was a gentleman seated alone in the furthest right-hand corner of the bar, wearing one of the finest suits he'd ever seen. He was nursing a neat gin and fully invested in the book that he was reading.

I sure hope none of 'em are listening to this, the barkeep thought as he looked back at Tessie—dressed in her aviator uniform complete with goggles resting slightly above her forehead—who seemed to take his look as a cue to continue her speech.

"I CAN'T WIN for losin', I swear. When I'm not doin' anything, I've got men tellin' me what *they* want me to do. When I'm doing what *I* want to do, I've got men tryin' to stop me from doin' it. It's ridiculous. Y'all men need to make up your goddamn minds 'cause I have all this work on me. I ain't come to play." Without even so much as a pause, Tessie knocked back the whiskey in her glass in one gulp and wiped her lips on her leather jacket.

"And you know what el—" Tessie finally noticed the fresh horror on the barkeep's face. "What? You ain't never seen a woman drink like me before?" she asked.

"M-ma'am, I—I—I think... I think it... it might be best we get you on yo' way."

Tessie Caldwell's hackles rose. *I know this man ain't tryin' to get me out of this bar just because I took a shot of bourbon*, she thought.

She was about to say something to that effect when the

barkeep's grip on the glass he was wiping loosened and it smashed on the hardwood floor. His quavering arm slowly rose.

Tessie slowly turned around to see three grotesque beings—barely human—staring back at her to her left, hulking over one of the tables.

The engineer woman and the well-dressed chap had gone, their respective drinks abandoned untouched. Tessie's look of shock transformed into one of her trademark wry smiles.

"So y'all must not have liked what I said," she boomed, managing to command the attention of all three of the terrifying entities.

One of them, head tilted to the side, began to let out a blood-curdling gurgling noise as the other two turned their heads toward Tessie. The barkeep bolted for the door to the kitchen.

Tessie laughed to herself, shaking her head. "He runs faster than he pours a drink. Typical." She addressed the monsters. "See what I mean about men? Can't live with 'em, can't kill 'em."

The three monsters only gurgled in response. They rose and started taking slow, deliberate steps toward Tessie.

"Nah, y'all *didn't* care for what I was sayin' earlier. Too bad, I ain't taking it back!"

A chilling hum flooded Tessie's ears just before a powerfully bright light flooded the entire bar. Figuring something was about to go down, Tessie jumped over the bar, putting a bit more space between her and the freakish ghouls. The creatures themselves didn't get a chance to move; all three of them suddenly burst into flames, their gurgling turning into deafening, perfectly inhuman screams.

The ghouls flailed about as they burned, destroying every table and chair they could reach. One of them flailed so chaotically it went through a window. The other two dropped to their knees, landing face down before taking their final form: an onyx-coloured pile of ashes.

The humming in Tessie's ears faded into nothingness, leaving only the sound of the wind blowing the ashes across the floor. Tessie slowly rose from behind the bar and saw a woman in an engineer's coverall sitting near the window in a booth directly behind her, furthest away from the bar.

No longer looking out of the window thoughtfully, she turned her head towards Tessie and said, "Terribly sorry about the commotion. It's quite hard to enjoy a quiet drink with dark magic and the undead about."

"How long were you sittin' behind me, lady?"

"Webster. Lady Webster. Pleasure to meet you, Miss Caldwell."

Tessie pondered her next question while she took stock of what was left of the bar and who was left within it. Except... there *was* no one else. Just her; this Lady Webster person; the evidence of the calamity that had just taken place, in the form of broken furniture and smashed glass; and the ashes of what could have been the undead.

"Your reputation precedes you, Miss Caldwell," Lady Webster continued, taking a sip of her drink. "I trust you still have a healthy appetite for adventure?"

Tessie said nothing, confusion stuck to her face like a painting on the wall of a gallery.

"I know what you've seen is unlike anything that you've ever seen before, so I don't begrudge you your feeling... suspicious of my being here," Lady Webster sipped her drink again. "Listen, Tessie... I'm not here for your autograph. A busy celebrity and pilot like you probably gets requests like that all the time, especially in a place like this."

"Nah, I can't say I've ever been asked for my John Hancock by some ghoul in some dive bar on an American airbase in the middle of Nowhere, Panama before. Webster, ain't it?"

"Lady Webster," she corrected.

"That's what I said. Webster," Tessie fired back, undeterred. "Guessin' you don't normally dress like this, then. You undercover or somethin'?"

"This is how I know I'm approaching the right person for this role," Lady Webster said with a grin. "You truly take no nonsense from anyone, Miss Caldwell. I admire that more than your incredible aviation skills. Yes, I thought it would serve me best to be incognito. I'll cut straight to the point: I administrate a... unique team of investigators, and we need a reconnaissance pilot. I've been monitoring your progress and achievements for years now, and I can think of no-one—"

"When do I start?" Tessie interjected.

Lady Webster's eyebrows rose.

Tessie's ironic smile spread across her face as she turned around to the top shelf and inspected what bottles of spirits hadn't been broken in the earlier commotion. "Look, Webster. You've done your homework on me and you obviously know I'm a woman of action. Now, I don' think it takes a genius to recognise that you still being here without a scratch on you after some gahtdamn... dead-looking things kinda shows you've got exactly the kind of action a woman like me wants and needs."

Tessie reached for an unlabelled bottle of a brown-coloured spirit, opened the bottle and took a brief whiff of the licquor. *Just what I was lookin' for*, she thought as the distinct aroma of cognac fills her nostrils. Conveniently, there was one unbroken glass within Tessie's reach.

"So, yeah. I'll fly for y'all. On one condition." Tessie poured the cognac in the glass, only filling it about a quarter of the way.

"What's that, then?" Lady Webster asked.

"I ain't callin' you 'Lady Webster,' miss ma'am. I work *with* y'all, not *for* y'all." Lady Webster reached for her glass and slowly raised it in salute.

"I think I can live with that," Lady Webster said, matching her smile.

TESSIE NEVER HESITATED to jump at adventure when it presented itself. It was part of who she was: adventure first, ask questions later. Anything that smacked of ponderousness or hesitation annoyed Tessie something fierce, and because she was always out chasing the next thrilling undertaking, she never really had the time to sit and wonder why she felt that way. She just never got around to thinking about doing things before doing them.

This wasn't to suggest that Tessie was a reckless person. She just knew what she wanted out of life and was increasingly defiant in her resolve to make sure she got every bit of it. Nothing more, nothing less.

Sitting under the wing of her plane, overlooking the expanse of the Galápagos from the cliff overlooking the Cerro Azul volcano on Isla Isabela, Tessie's mind should have been as free and clear as the air she breathed, but weirdly, it was anything but. One moment, she was taking in the breathtaking views of the archipelago; the next, she was flashing back to interviews she did for the national papers back in the States during her rise to superstardom. A shake of her own head, a pause, and a deep breath... Tessie was on a coach from Texas to Chicago for the first time, and the mix of emotions surging through her body all those years before were just as vivid and potent as the wind whipping against her frame and the plane at her back as she took in the spectacular visuals from Azul Peak's summit.

Tessie closed her eyes and removed her aviator cap and goggles, allowing her naturally curly hair to breathe. Usually, she would feel naked without her cap and goggles on, but every now and again, she found it liberating to remove her gear and just be Tessie rather than Tessie the Adventure Junkie. It was her way of presenting herself. It was her therapy; her meditation.

Tessie quickly checked the pocket watch that her grandfather gave her before she moved to Chicago. Lady

Webster had told Tessie to be ready to extract the team in a few hours, and the cool air was lulling Tessie into a sense of comfort. *A quick nap never hurt nobody,* Tessie thought, laying back on the warm rock. *I ain't but caught a couple winks in the last few days, so I should be all right to grab a couple more.* As Tessie's mind began to wander yet again, her eyelids became dense. *Just a couple of winks,* Tessie pondered. *Just a couple...*

"You gon' be a flyin' sensation one day, young one!" A warm booming voice flooded the darkness, reverberating off of the walls of Tessie's mind. *"That's right, young one! You gonna take to th' skies and win you a prize!"* The giggles of a young girl mingled with the stentorian voice of a patriarch; a voice that Tessie was all too familiar with.

"Gramps?" Tessie asked. The darkness offered nothing in the way of a response. It was as if Tessie's eager inquiry was cast out into an empty well. Frustration building, Tessie asserted herself a bit more, calling out again. "Gramps! Gramps! GRAMPS!"

Tessie's calls were met with a firm push to her left shoulder. Stumbling backward, terrified at what was going on, her eyes welled up, tears burning her corneas and blurring her vision. "Gramps, please! Please, Gramps! Talk to me! Please don't push me aw—" Another shove to the left shoulder caused Tessie to lose her footing and stumble backward.

The lightlessness was all-encompassing. Tessie could not see a single thing, she couldn't find the spectre of her grandfather. All she had were her wits and Gramps' voice. *"Don't forget t' do your pre-flight checks, young one! Proper preparation!"* Tessie couldn't hold it in any more, but she couldn't speak, she was overcome with grief.

A third firm shove to the same shoulder saw Tessie on her back; her head cracking against whatever the floor consists of. *"Ya heard what I said, young one? Proper preparation...!"*

"P—pre—preve—" Tessie couldn't finish the refrain. Her head swimming, her vision riddled with pockets of light; yet she still couldn't see anything, paradoxically. *"Prevents... poor... performance."*

Gramps chuckled. *"That's my Tessaleff! Aviator extraordinaire, I tell you what!"*

After one last push, Tessie came to, gasping loudly.

Breathe, Tessie, girl... breathe. She continued reciting this to herself, feeling the rough rock under her face, her sight not completely returned.

Just as Tessie managed to control her breathing, she realised there was something heavy on her back. Something heavy... and hard. Tessie bit down panic, kept her cool and carried on with her breathing exercise. *Breathe, Tessie, girl... just breathe.*

She couldn't look around but she could see the wing of the plane. She was back where she should be. *Azul Peak. Okay... What the heck is on my back?* Tessie fought off the urge to panic. Behind her, she could hear queer shuffling sounds, suggesting that something moving around behind her.

"Nothin' quite like not knowin' what you're up

against," she muttered, barely above a whisper so as to not aggravate... whatever was pinning her down.

A hissing, crackling noise came from the cockpit of the plane. Both unseen creatures responded with a sharp squawk and the shuffling sounds Tessie could hear behind her now circled anti-clockwise around her. *What... the hell... is that?*

Tessie froze as a huge clawed foot came down just yards away from her. The creature nearest the plane slinked down, spine bending like a ball python contorting, and she got the first view of one of the things she'd been spending time with since her impromptu nap. It had a cone-shaped head with an elongated beak, a gaunt body, skin like leather and massive wings complete with hooked talons at the top of each wing. *Looks like one of them dinosaurs with the funny name.* Tessie's lungs burned with every breath as the creature poked at the plane with its gigantic beak.

The radio static continued: "*...sssshHHHsssssHHH*essie? Tessie, come—*sssshhhhHHHHHHsss*—essie! Tessie, do you read?" Lady Webster's distressed pleas went unanswered: these creatures didn't strike Tessie that the sort to speak English (of course, Tessie certainly didn't know how to speak squawk, if there was such a language).

With Webster and the rest of the Strange Brigade seemingly in a bit of a bind, Tessie had to figure out how to get out from under whatever was holding her down and draw the creatures away from the plane. *That's it, No more naps on top of plateaus,* she solemnly vowed to herself as she tried to wriggle free.

Hm. Can't move.

The intermittent radio chatter continued: "Tessie, for God's sake! We need immediate extraction! We're low on ammo and we can't hold off these—*sssssHHHHH*!"

At that moment, whatever was pinning Tessie to the ground eased off enough for Tessie to make her move. In a flash, she'd slid out from underneath the creature and scrambled frantically away, before popping up to her feet and making a beeline for the plane.

Slaloming past the winged beast, she dived into the plane's cargo hold, harried by the urgent banging on the plane's fuselage.

Determined to at least answer Lady Webster's transmission, Tessie stumbled her way to the cockpit as the plane shook violently from the flying monsters' swipes against the plane. She looked out of the cockpit window briefly to catch a glimpse.

"You gotta be kiddin' me..." she said flatly as she scrambled for the radio mic. "This is Tessie, come in, Webster! Webster, I'm here. Where y'all at?"

"*SsssHHHHhhHHSHHSHHH*..."

Tessie had to get into the air. "Well, Tessie, girl... this is what they pay you fo'!" She sat in the pilot-side seat and began to buckle up, but jumped and screamed at a colossal *BANG* and the sound of smashing glass from the far side of the cockpit.

Tessie desperately began starting the plane, trying to put as much distance as she could between herself and the beast's probing beak, inching closer by the second. She primed the engines, but the ready light stayed dark; the dinosaur's frenzied snapping inched ever closer.

Tessie primed the engines one more time and shouted with relief as the ready light flickered into life; just as she hit the button to start the engines, she yelled, "I don't know what to call y'all but I know one thang: y'all should've stayed extinct!"

Tessie slammed the button and the plane's propellers roared into life. A gristly shredding noise suggested the blades had made contact with one of the beasts, and she squealed with delight and burst into laughter as the plane lurched forward toward the cliff edge.

She needed to turn around, and though the plateau was just wide enough to do that, she had to time it right, both to avoid running straight into either of the two winged monstrosities and to line up the plane properly for take-off.

Tessie pressed the radio transmission button on the console. "Hol' on, Webster! I'm on my way!"

"*sssssHHHHHHH*ESSIE! Miss Caldwell, thank God! We're really up against it down here!"

They're okay... for now, Tessie thought as she hooked the control yoke sharply to the right, the left front tyres just missing the edge of the cliff as Tessie prepared to line up for takeoff, finding herself face-to-face with one of the creatures. It flapped its wings maniacally, spraying crimson over the front of plane from where it was wounded. "Ah, heck!" Tessie shouted. She pushed the transmit button. "Webster, I'm not even in the air yet! I've been fighting off two... dinosaurs, I think! I can't believe I'm what I'm saying, to tell you th' truth! Whatchu call them dinosaurs that got wings and a long-ass beak? Start with a... p, you copy?"

"*SsssssHHH*ey're called pterodact*shhhhhHHHHH*I'll take you to the museum when we get back but right now, I need you to jolly well get us out of here!"

"I'm tryin', gahtdammit!" Tessie snapped back. "Damn! Ain't no need to get all stressy with me, Webster!"

"Just please get airborne and come get us, Miss Caldwell! Our coordinates are 0°48'27.7 south, 89°22'24.8 west, same as the drop-off. We're running out of time!"

"I'm coming, Webster, girl! Hol' on, okay?"

Tessie had to rely mostly on dead reckoning to get lined up right. "Okay... okay... that's the rock wall... still the rock wall..." The cockpit windows started glowing as the sun shone directly on them. Tessie could just about make out a flat line. "Horizon! Bye-bye, dino birdies!" She slammed the plane's accelerator forward and the plane responded dutifully with a sharp lurch forward, gathering speed as angry pterodactyl croaking filled the air behind her.

She sped towards the horizon. "Patience, Tessie girl... patience... aaand... NOW!" Tessie pulled up on the controls with all of her might. The plane started to lift but it didn't feel like she had completely cleared the ground. Pterodactyl blood started to peel away from the windscreen, marginally improving Tessie's visibility. "C'mon baby... c'mon! COME ON! GET UP!"

The plane rose steadily as Tessie hooked the controls again to the right, hugging the cliff wall over the volcano's caldera. The plane engines picked up an octave, letting out a supreme shriek as the revolutions per minute climbed exponentially. She grunted as she fought against the force feedback to hold her line and the plane responded majestically, allowing her just enough control to come away from the volcano wall and head towards the Pacific.

Lord almighty, how You gon' make a place so beautiful and so deadly? Tessie thought. *One minute, I'm gettin' a little shuteye and mindin' my business, then alla sudden, I'm being poked and prodded by hungry gotdamn flying dinosaurs! We coulda just kept on filing nails at White Sox, speakin' o' mindin' our damn business but nawl! You just had to be a pilot, huh?*

As Tessie began to level out, she hit the transmission button. "All right, Webster! I made it to the sky! Comin' to get y'all!"

THE SKIES NEVER felt so inviting as Tessie made her way to the coordinates Lady Webster gave her over the radio. The ambient sounds of explosions and gunfire, though dull from where Tessie was, high up in the air, sounded a lot more real now than they did as background noise to Lady Webster's transmissions.

"Webster, I'm making my approach! How're y'all holdin' up?"

"*sssssSHHH*ot good, Miss Caldwell! These things are closing in fast! How far out are you, over?"

"I'm right above you!"

"Right! We're heading for the clearing where you dropped us off, over!"

"Copy that, over! I'm just circling around now! Y'all make your way to the meeting point!"

"Copy, Miss Caldwell. Over and out!"

Tessie increased the plane's speed as she flew out over Isla de San Cristobal and into a wide circle. "Okay... time to go get 'em, Tessie girl."

Talking to herself had never seemed very odd to Tessie. The way she saw it, she felt compelled to be her biggest coach, critic, and cheerleader; especially when no one else is around to fill that role.

Especially when Gramps wasn't around...

The plane puttered along smoothly back toward Isla de San Cristobal and Tessie's eyes started flying around the console, making adjustments to the controls where necessary.

Her concentration was broken by a shrill cry from the left. *Damn*, she thought. *The other one*. Indeed, the second pterodactyl was coming in, the loud flap of its gigantic wings interspersed with its vengeful screeching. It was the second aberration and not the first: this one didn't have a wounded wing. Which also meant it was technically at full strength, and wouldn't be so easy to evade.

Lady Webster and the team would be no use to her until they made it to the meeting point; Tessie was on her own to stave off the threat. Her eyes cut to the radio on the console and then back towards Isla de San Cristobal. *Why tell 'em what's happenin' when they can see it for themselves? Might even be able to kill two birds with...*

Tessie, girl. Now ain't the time for puns.

Nevertheless, Tessie's trademark overconfidence kicked in. She went full throttle and turned the plane toward the spitting mad creature.

"Okay, you freak wit' wings... let's see if you can keep up!" Tessie growled defiantly. She was about to play Chicken with a prehistoric creature; and if she worked it right, she'd even buy her team on the ground more time. Doubtless in her ability, Tessie readjusted her instruments while she cannonballed along at the surging pterodactyl.

The radio crackled to life again. "sssssHHHSHH-SHHessie, come in! Miss Caldwell, do you read?"

"I hear ya, Webster! You at the spot, over?"

"Affirmative! We arSSSSHHHhhhsssHHH..."

Tessie pushed the transmission button repeatedly to try and reengage the lost signal, to no avail. *Gotdammit.* The plane pelted along relentlessly in its head-on collision with the avian atrocity. Radio static hiss warred with the engine's thundering around the plane.

Seconds away from a collision, the pterodactyl unleashed an earthshattering skreigh, trying to back Tessie down. Tessie stayed the course, mentally crossing her fingers. The plane's speedometer needle was buried as far right it could go. The pterodactyl's wings were completely unfurled, screeching like a flaming banshee bursting free from the bowels of hell.

Tessie's eyes narrowed, and she gritted her teeth. Neither party backed down... and just before the moment of impact, Tessie rolled the pilot's wheel, lowering the left wing. The pterodactyl, suddenly faced with the plane's propeller blades, countered by diving straight down; but not without taking a hell of a slash to its lower back. Tessie grunted hard as the plane shuddered savagely, released from her aerial dogfight into a struggle with her own flying machine. She wrestled with the controls as the plane continued into a slow barrel roll. *Come the hell on, Tessie, girl! Who's the boss: you or this damn plane?!*

Her efforts at first seemed ineffective, as the plane started to yaw down towards the cerulean waters of the Pacific Ocean. *You ain't goin' out like this, Tessie Caldwell! Get it together! COME ON!* She inhaled deeply, holding the breath as she loosened up her arms and shoulders, closed her eyes and let go of the yoke.

And then she heard him, chuckling faintly as if he were right in the co-pilot seat. *You know what to do, young one. I ain't gotta tell you a thang.* With Gramps' warm voice ringing in her ears, Tessie's eyes snapped open; bringing the stir-crazy pilot instruments back into full view. The wheel thrashed loosely from right to left, and she timed herself carefully, grabbing it just as it nipped back to the left.

She regained that familiar feedback feeling of the plane's weight and pulled back slowly, tilting the wheel back to the right as she carefully throttled down. The plane evened out and began to rise, kicking off the start of a massive loop. *There you go, Tessie, baby! There you go!* And she cheered herself on to pulling off the unthinkable as the plane continued its loop.

DOWN ON THE island, Lady Webster was running at breakneck speed through the trees, alongside three of her compatriots; one dressed in a fine suit, another completely decked out in Maasai warrior garb but barefooted, and the third wearing an outfit like Lady Webster's, sans overalls—flannel shirt and dusty khaki trousers, with a bandana holding back her hair.

"Does Tessie know where to meet us?!" Gracie asked as they ran from the ghouls, Nalangu and De Quincey providing cover fire.

Lady Webster didn't answer but instead slowed down to look towards the coast.

"Our Tessie seems indisposed at the minute, Gracie." She kept her eyes on the plane as it finished its loop, its attacker limping off over the waves. "Nalangu! Archimedes! Can you buy us some more time until Tessie gets here?"

A disgruntled De Quincey, head and shoulder pressed firmly against the crevasse wall interspersed his reply with rifle fire. "If we… must, Lady Webster! Frankly… Tessie has taken more… time than we can afford, but what's… another few minutes? Not like we're… running for our lives or anything!"

Nalangu snorted at De Quincey's tone as she lay blind fire from the opposite wall. "Professor, you really must choose a better time to make these observations! More shooting and less sarcasm!"

De Quincey answered by taking aim at one of the undead and popping it right between the eyes with a single shot. "That to your liking, Nalangu?" He released the empty bullet magazine, patting around frantically for his next one. "Blast… I think I'm out."

Nalangu tossed over one of her spares. "That is my second to last one, professor! And to answer your question, what I would like is for you to make it *count!*"

The horde's numbers seemed only to rise as the crevasse filled with more and more of the undead, leaping over the lifeless bodies of their fallen fellows. Lady Webster was still looking around the sky to see if Tessie had managed to make it back towards the clearing. She wiped the sweat beading on her brow, glancing back to Nalangu and De Quincey holding the ghouls back before turning to see Gracie aiming a flare into the air. "This is why I usually stay back at headquarters," Lady Webster murmured to herself.

No sooner had Lady Webster spoke than the familiar sound of an airplane reached her ears. Tessie rocketed past them over the threes, turning immediately to land the plane and touching down just a few hundred meters away from the Brigade in the clearing ahead.

Lady Webster expected Tessie to stop, but the penny dropped as she realised the plane was still rolling. "Right, you lot!" she shouted. "We've got to make a run for it!"

De Quincey's rifle clicked as he shot his last bullet, sending another undead into a crumpled heap. "Fine by me!" He threw his rifle to the floor and bolted after Lady Webster and Gracie; Nalangu quickly discharged her remaining ammunition into the mob and made a break for the clearing herself.

All four of them ran out to the clearing as Tessie's plane began to roll up. The sound of the Brigade's feet pounding the earth of Isla de San Cristobal was all but lost in the stampede of the monstrous horde; they had to board the plane while it was still moving to have even a hope of getting away.

Gracie, huffing and puffing alongside Lady Webster, nodded toward the side of the plane. The side door was open, confirming Lady Webster's instincts: Tessie was evidently on the same page. The Brigade steered themselves towards the door.

Gracie, Lady Webster, Nalangu, and De Quincey never stopped running, but neither did the ghouls. De Quincey felt lightheaded and winded but carried on as hard as he could. Despite having a headstart on Nalangu, he was now trailing her slightly, and reflecting that he could probably be a bit fitter.

"Gracie!" Lady Webster cried. "You first. Get in!" Gracie threw herself through the door before falling to the cargo hold floor and extending her hand to Lady Webster. Nalangu made an enormous leap over the younger woman, and Lady Webster—still only half-on herself—reached out to her. De Quincey had no choice: either leap or be left behind. Without breaking stride, the professor launched himself into the air and toward Nalangu's outstretched arm and hand. The air was driven out of him as his chest slammed into the doorway, but his grip tightened around Nalangu's forearm.

Gracie's foot was hooked around a supporting bar, but she couldn't hold all three of them for long. If her strength didn't give out, her foot would slip; and both outcomes were odds-on to happen at the same time. Gracie pulled Lady Webster in as hard as she could just as Tessie's voice rang from the cockpit: "I gotta speed up, y'all! We're running out of ground! Y'all got to get in here NOW!"

Gracie kept pulling Lady Webster in. Seemingly

miraculously, Webster was able to get a knee underneath her and heave herself forward onto Gracie, who stumbled back, wrapping her hands around her waist. Nalangu's grip slipped from Lady Webster's arm, but she managed to ram her fingers in the gap at the edge of the door; she and De Quincey bounced around on the edge of the door.

"DO NOT LET GO, PROFESSOR!"

"I WASN'T PLANNING ON IT, NALANGU!"

Gracie shoved Lady Webster aside, diving toward Nalangu and grabbing her wrist. Webster winced in discomfort and rolled over, clutching her ribs.

"Y'all!" bellowed Tessie. "Get in this damn plane! If I don't speed up now, we're done for."

"HOL' ON T'SOMETHIN', Y'ALL!" Tessie shouted over the melancholy squawk of her prehistoric nemeses. Dive-bombing towards them like rain from the cloud, Tessie knew any wiggle room they had was spent. She hammered the throttle and the plane lurched forward sharply, causing the Brigade to slide further inside the hold and the pterodactyl to miss the plane and plummet straight into the mass of sprinting undead.

"Took y'all long enough!" she called back gleefully. "Get that gotdamn door closed and let's get the hell outta here!"

Lady Webster returned to nursing her ribs as Gracie, Nalangu, and De Quincey pulled the door shut, the charging undead already scrabbling against the metal frame to their quarry.

"Sorry, you ugly scallywags!" De Quincey called as he closed the cargo door and Nalangu helped Lady Webster into a seat. "This flight is full!"

"Webster, you ain't tell me anything about no damn flying dinos back in Panama before you offered me this gig!" Tessie said as she pulled back on the controls, finally getting the plane's wheels off the ground.

Lady Webster grimaced in pain as Nalangu strapped her in. "I'm many things, Tess. One thing I'm not is clairvoyant."

Tessie pulled further back on the stick as the airplane climbed away from the Galápagos and laughed. "Ain't that the truth, Webster. Ain't that the truth."

The plane glided above the Pacific Ocean and into the horizon. Tessie thought back over everything that had transpired, looked over at the empty co-pilot seat, and cracked a faint smile before turning her attention back to whatever awaited them on the horizon. One thing was for certain: after this waltz with dinosaurs, undead peculiarities and death, a warm drink, a hot plate of food, and a hot bath wouldn't go amiss. Tessie lifted her goggles from her face and rubbed the bridge of her nose, sighing with relief.

"Let's get y'all home before we meet the rest of the pterodactyl family."

DAYBREAK.

Tessie's body was flooded with the familiar waking sensation of each of her limbs activating one by one, alerting her brain to the fact that they were all still present, functioning, and accounted for. Tessie's hearing fizzed in, the sound of a bustling marketplace sidewinding its way through a nearby open window. She tested her motor skills, moving each of her legs and arms underneath the blankets before blinking her eyes and nuzzling against the pillow. Gradually rolling onto her back, she stared at the wooden beams holding up the ceiling, then eased her neck forward, so she could get a healthier look at her surroundings.

She didn't appear to be in a hospital. No medicinal instruments or doctor's clipboards to be found. The open window brought in the sounds of the street below, calling Tessie to come and take a look outside the building.

She moved her legs over to the edge of the bed, sitting upright and extending her arms into a luxurious stretch. *Whoever's apartment this is sure mus' be payin' a pretty penny fo' it,* Tessie speculated, looking around at the wood-panelled walls and expensive furniture as she reached for her socks. She slid them on and made her way to the window and stuck her head out.

"La Libertad," she mumbled, reading the massive sign to her left; the town's name, she guessed. Tessie closed her eyes again when the seaside winds began caressing her head, neck and face. It reminded her of the serenity of Azul Peak, before she sank into her now-infamous nap. The scenery was obviously less untamed, though... and thank God for that, Tessie mused as she watched the street below.

In the middle of a humming marketplace were

schoolboys playing a ball game of some description, and various vendors canvassing potential patrons passing by their respective stalls. La Libertad was colourful today, in the colours of the fabric roofs of the stalls, the flowerbeds dotting the windowsills as far as the eye could see, the pageantry of the senoritas dancing along to the musicians busking outside of a local bar.

"Oh, good. You're awake." De Quincey's dry tone was unmistakable.

Tessie sighed heavily before turning around to face the professor. "This part's always so... so damn dull, y'know?"

De Quincey's brow scrunched up with confusion. "What do you mean?"

"I mean compared to fleein' a jungle island, fightin' for your life in th' process, standing in an apartment in a place you only stoppin' in for a night or two," Tessie replied. She reached for her trousers and the rest of her clothes, moving them over to the bed to straighten them out one by one. "This just ain't as excitin'. It sure is peaceful, tho', I'll give you that." She moved to the door across from the bed and out to the bathroom. "I'spose it wouldn't be much of an adventure if it didn't have the borin' bits too."

The frown faded from De Quincey's face, along with the rest of the tension in his body. He stared out of the window. The sound of running water could be heard coming from the bathroom. "I suppose you're right, Tessie. But one is grateful for these moments of clarity."

Tessie let that sentiment go unanswered as she tested the heat of the water in the bottom of the bathtub.

"So what happens now, professor? Is that clear to see?" she asked.

De Quincey walked across to the window and stared down. "Well, that's what we're about to discuss over a spot of breakfast. Lady Webster's starting to feel a bit better and is getting ready, as it goes."

Tessie poked her head through the door way. "Well, I'll see you down there."

Back still turned, De Quincey took a breath. "Tessie, I... I have never seen an airplane do that kind of manoeuvring before. Truly, we should've died back on that rock."

Tessie straightened a bit more and slowly emerged from behind the door back into the bedroom.

"I daresay if it weren't for you, we very well *would* have died back there," he continued. "Because of your unorthodox methods, and... frankly immense skill, we're all still here, if a bit battered and bruised." A brief silence creeped in like a rolling fog.

Tessie continued to stare at the back of De Quincey's head. "Shoot, professor... I was just doing what I'm supposed to be doing. Y'all brought me in to get y'all in and out of dangerous places."

De Quincey laughed as he watched the ball game in the town square. "No need to be modest, Miss Caldwell."

"So, what am I meant to be, professor?" Tessie asked as she turned back into the bathroom, cutting the water off, testing the temperature once more.

De Quincey looked over his should, noticing Tessie was no longer standing behind him. He turned and made his exit from Tessie's room, but stopped at the doorway.

"Proud, presumably."

"Oh, honey, I am. I'm very proud. But I also know that I'm not finished takin' y'all places."

De Quincey bowed his head and smiled. "No, dear Tessie. No, you aren't."

"You gon' tell me where I'm taking y'all next or what, professor? You know I don't like guessin' games or beatin' around the bush."

De Quincy stepped back towards the bathroom door, looking at Tessie's reflection in the mirror where she was inspecting her face and brushing her teeth.

"Have you ever been to Egypt, Miss Caldwell?"

ABOUT THE AUTHORS

Guy Adams is the author of the *Heaven's Gate* trilogy—*The Good, the Bad and the Infernal*, *Once Upon a Time in Hell*, and *For a Few Souls More*—as well as many audio adventures for Big Finish's *Doctor Who* range.

Joseph Guthrie is a self-professed jack-of-all-trades based in the capital of the United Kingdom (London, for the uninitiated). Joseph is a writer, photographer, musician (singer-songwriter, drummer, pianist, and produces on the very odd occasion) and IT professional, and a mature student at the University of Westminster computer games development (BSc Hons). When he's not taking photos, you can safely assume he's working on something as part of one of the aforementioned roles.

Jonathan L. Howard has worked as a scriptwriter and video game writer, including writing credits on the highly successful *Broken Sword* series of video games. His first novel, *Johannes Cabal the Necromancer*, was published in 2009.

Cassandra Khaw writes many things. Mostly these days, she writes horror and video games and occasional flirtations with chick-lit. Her work can be found in venues *Clarkesworld*, *Fireside Fiction*, *Uncanny*, *Lightspeed*, *Nightmare*, and more. *A Song for Quiet* was her latest novella from Tor, a piece of Lovecraftian Southern Gothic that she worries will confuse those who purchased *Bearly a Lady*, her frothy paranormal romantic comedy.

Patrick Lofgren holds an MFA from Sarah Lawrence College and is an enthusiastic graduate of Clarion West 2017. He lives and writes in New York with his partner, two ferrets, a hedgehog, and an axolotl.

Mimi Mondal is a Dalit woman who writes about politics and history, occasionally camouflaged as fiction. Her first anthology, *Luminescent Threads: Connections to Octavia E. Butler*, co-edited with Alexandra Pierce, was nominated for a Hugo Award, a Locus Award and a William Atheling Jr. Award, making Mimi the first Hugo Award nominee from India. Mimi holds three masters' degrees for no reason but pure joy. She lives in New York, tweets from @Miminality, doesn't very often update mimimondal.com, and always enjoys the company of monsters.

Tauriq Moosa is a contributor to the *Guardian*, *Daily Beast* and other publications. He focuses on ethics, justice, technology and pop culture. His work has been referred to by *The New York Times*, the *Washington Post*, *Forbes* and other places. He once debated Desmond Tutu about God.

Gaie Sebold has written several novels, a number of short stories, and a slightly disturbing amount of poetry. Her novel include *Babylon Steel*, the sequel *Dangerous Gifts*, and *Shanghai Sparrow* and its sequel *Sparrow Falling*. She lives in leafy suburbia with writer David Gullen and a paranoid cat, runs writing workshops, grows vegetables, and cooks a pretty good borscht.

FIND US ONLINE!

www.rebellionpublishing.com

/rebellionpub   /rebellionpublishing   /rebellionpub

SIGN UP TO OUR NEWSLETTER!

rebellionpublishing.com/sign-up

YOUR REVIEWS MATTER!

Enjoy this book? Got something to say?

Leave a review on Amazon, GoodReads or with your
favourite bookseller and let the world know!